"Hannah, maybe you should accept that I'm here to stay?"

She frowned. "I will accept that, Tate, around the same time I accept the bad recommendations you've made for Snowy Sky."

"Hannah—"

Interrupting with her hands, palms up in a conciliatory gesture, she said, "Okay, shoot, I'm sorry. I wasn't going to get into this again. I want to apologize for the snowball. I don't lose my temper very often and I—"

"Good, because I don't want to fight with you, either."

Something hitched in her chest because his voice was low and smooth and his eyes were pinned on hers.

"Quite the opposite, in fact."

Hannah's face felt hot and her pulse began to pound because the opposite of fighting was...

Dear Reader,

I was fortunate to be born into a family of optimists. I'm talking about the kind of people who, if a car breaks down in the middle of nowhere on a dark night with no cell phone service, will say something like, "I only had to walk five miles." Or "At least it wasn't raining."

Hannah James comes from this kind of family, too. She is just this type of person, dealing with every devastating blow life hands her with a steadfast and cheerful grace because, in keeping with her eternal optimism, she truly believes that things will improve. But even the most positive among us have our breaking point. For Hannah that point is rapidly approaching. The dream she's worked so hard to achieve is in danger of being snatched from her grasp. And to complicate matters, she's falling for the would-be dream-snatcher, Tate Addison.

Tate wants to make a home in Rankins, Alaska, for the nephew he's gained custody of. To Tate, a home requires a family. But how can someone who's never had a family make a home? Especially with such a broken and dysfunctional background as his? And even if he could, how could he ever expect to make a family like Hannah's?

Thanks so much for spending some time with me in Rankins. Check out my website, carolrossauthor.com, for social media links, the latest book news and other titles in the Seasons of Alaska series.

All my best,

Carol

HEARTWARMING

A Family Like Hannah's

Carol Ross

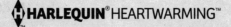

Recycling programs
for this product may
not exist in your area.

ISBN-13: 978-0-373-36775-7

A Family Like Hannah's

Copyright © 2016 by Carol Ross

Printed in U.S.A.

Carol Ross lives in the Pacific Northwest with her husband and two dogs. She is a graduate of Washington State University. When not writing, or thinking about writing, she enjoys reading, running, hiking, skiing, traveling and making plans for the next adventure to subject her sometimes reluctant but always fun-loving family to.

Books by Carol Ross

Harlequin Heartwarming

Mountains Apart
A Case for Forgiveness
If Not for a Bee

For Aaramie, my niece, friend, fellow adventurer,
food enthusiast, joke sharer,
amusement parker and travel buddy.
You are my "Hannah" inspiration.

CHAPTER ONE

Tate Addison stared down at the single piece of luggage on the dingy, threadbare carpet and felt the knot of tension cinch even tighter in his chest. How could that tiny suitcase hold everything Lucas owned in the entire world?

Tate frowned at the woman standing nearby, the woman who had given birth to him. He refused to call her mom. She'd never earned the title.

"Penny, where are the rest of Lucas's things?"

She blinked as if surprised by the question. "Well, Tate, this is it. This is all of it. You'd be surprised how much you can pack in one of these soft-sided suitcases."

"This isn't even the suitcase I sent him, and I've sent him enough to fill twenty suitcases. Where is his skateboard, his tablet, the movies and games, the game system…? His baseball glove?"

Penny swiped a casual hand through the air.

"You know how kids are. They break things, grow out of things, lose things…"

It dawned on him then. A hot flash of anger bolted through him. "You sold his stuff?"

"Just what was I supposed to do? He couldn't eat that baseball glove. Kids are expensive, not that you'd know anything about that while you've been living the high life and I've been stuck here taking care of him. Do you have any idea how hard that has been on me?"

Now she sounded like the selfish, defensive, passive-aggressive, alcohol- and drug-dependent mother he knew and despised, yet continued to care about. Out of some twisted sense of obligation or responsibility or…something.

"What did you spend the money on I sent you every month to take care of you both? Why did you fight me for custody?"

"He's my grandson."

Tate narrowed his eyes menacingly, waiting for her to answer the first question even though he knew she wouldn't. They both knew very well what she'd spent it on.

"You mean your meal ticket?"

"Lexie left him with me, remember?"

Shards of grief and guilt and anger took turns jabbing at him. But not because of anything Penny said, but because he hadn't been able to save Lexie from their mother's poison. He had survived, and even though he hadn't been able to save his little sister, he was determined to save her son. His nephew.

His jaw flexed so tightly he could barely speak. "Don't talk to me about Lexie."

Penny crossed her bony arms over her chest, her face twisted into an ugly scowl. "I know you blame me, Tate. Just like you've always blamed me for every bad thing in your life and Lexie's. But it's not my fault she died, you know? I didn't pour those drugs down her throat. She never did know when enough was enough. Nobody's perfect, not even you. You don't know how hard it is, but you'll see and then you'll be begging me to take that kid back—"

He had learned long ago not to engage with his mother. You can't reason with irrational and he couldn't fix her addictions, although he kept trying.

He interrupted sharply, "Where is he?"

She pinched her lips together as she lifted a finger and pointed down the hall.

He took a few steps before turning to face her again. "Viktor is waiting right outside the door to take you to the rehab center. After you get out this time you'll have two months of expenses paid. That's it. Do you understand? I can't—I won't—enable you anymore. I don't want to see you, hear from you, or even hear about you ever again."

She pitched her voice high and dramatic as she tried to squeeze out some tears, "But you're my son and you can't keep Lucas from me. He's my only grandchild—"

"It's official now. I have legal custody. Lucas is my responsibility. He is no longer your free ride. Do you understand? When you get out, do not call or contact us in any way."

"Where are you going?" she cried.

Tate ignored her and went to find his nephew. There were only two doors positioned along the dim hallway of the sparsely furnished apartment. The first contained a small filthy bathroom so he continued on. He found Lucas in the next room sitting on a dirty, rumpled sleeping bag atop a bare mattress lying on the floor. The room smelled faintly of mold and urine. Shockingly few items were scattered around—a brown paper bag, a clothes hanger and a bright orange plastic bucket with a large crack in the side.

Lucas held a book clutched to his chest. He looked up when Tate walked in and he hoped he wasn't imagining the spark that lit amidst the weariness in the child's arresting blue eyes. A mix of love and relief and anger swirled within him as he studied the pale, forlorn face of his nephew, the only thing left of his sister, Lexie.

He knelt in front of the tiny boy with coal-black hair that so closely matched his own and wondered if, at six years of age, he should be so small.

"Hey, buddy."

"Hi, Uncle Tate."

"You ready to hit the road?"

He nodded. "Do I need my sleeping bag? I can't zip it up anymore because the zipper's broken."

"Nope, you'll be sleeping in a real bed with sheets from now on."

Lucas's bland expression told Tate he'd heard similar promises before. Empty promises, broken promises, nights without a warm bed and days without food; memories he recalled all too well from his own childhood with Penny, before Viktor had taken him away.

"Uncle Tate, you won't leave me in the dark, will you?"

The fear in his voice seemed to pierce Tate's very soul. "No, Lucas, I won't."

Placing a hand on each of the boy's thin

shoulders, he caught his gaze. "Lucas, I know other people have told you things before that weren't true. Made promises they didn't keep. But I've never done that, have I? Made you a promise I didn't keep?"

He shook his head and whispered, "No."

"Well, I'm making you another one right now. I will never leave you. From here on out—it's me and you and Viktor, okay? We're a family. No matter what." Tate silently vowed to do whatever was necessary to make a family for Lucas, even though he wasn't sure what one was exactly.

Lucas nodded and climbed to his feet and Tate thought that a child of six-years shouldn't look so tired and…broken. Tate reached for him and Lucas threw his hands around his neck and squeezed. The rush of love he felt was so intense he almost couldn't contain his sob.

HANNAH JAMES STEERED her SUV up her friend Edith Milner's long driveway. As she neared the massive architectural masterpiece of a home, she immediately spotted the tire tracks in the fresh dusting of snow. She was happy to see the renters had finally arrived.

She parked her car, climbed out and headed around the side of the house along the covered sidewalk. Edith had informed the management company that Hannah would be caring for the atrium in her year-long absence, absolving the renters of having to worry about the exotic plants or the koi that lived in the atrium's indoor pond.

Unlocking the door to the breezeway, she planned to slip in unnoticed and check on the plants and feed the koi without bothering anyone. The hallway to the right connected the atrium to the house. She turned left and pushed the button to open the pneumatic door. A blast of warm, humid air greeted her. She'd been coming here for nearly two years now, but she still couldn't get over the magic that Edith had managed to create in this remote Alaskan setting.

Edith and her husband had built their five-thousand square foot home nearly two decades ago, but Edith had only added the atrium after her husband of forty-two years had passed away.

Hannah took a moment to admire the atrium's inviting niches. The bluish-green light glowing through the fat panes of tinted glass. The mosaic tile floor sparkled in muted pastel colors, a perfect setting for the wrought iron garden furniture. The space was a work of art inside and out, and it soothed her soul to spend time there.

She stopped in front of a recessed control panel, checking to make sure the temperature and humidity readings were correct.

The storage room contained an electronic lock with a keypad. She tapped in the combination and went inside. After scooping out pellets for the koi she crossed to the far side of the room, smiling as she approached the large pond taking up roughly half the space. The pond's surface was smooth and peaceful, broken only by the gurgle from the fountain in the center. But as she walked closer, the swirl and soft splash of water let her know the koi were aware of her presence.

Enjoying the flashes of orange, white, silver, black and red gliding through the water, she began tossing in the pellets one handful at a time. She called the fish by name, commenting on the beauty of their markings or how gracefully they could swim.

As she silently practiced the spiel she planned to pitch later that day at her meeting, she looked up to notice a gorgeous tropical flower blooming. One she'd never seen before. That's when movement from the other side of the pond gave her a start. A flash of black hair followed by a pair of dark eyes peeking out from behind a ficus tree told her a child was hiding there. Relaxing, she realized Edith's renters must have a child.

"Hello, there," she called out.

No answer.

"Would you like to come over here and meet these guys?"

She heard a rustling sound before a small black-haired child sprinted toward the house. The door made a swooshing sound as it opened and then closed again. *Poor kid,* she thought, *must be shy.*

She looked at the time on her phone. Too bad she couldn't stick around and introduce herself. She needed to get to work. As project manager of Snowy Sky Resort, it would probably be bad form for her to be late for her first meeting with the ski-area consultant the board of directors had hired.

TATE STUDIED THE figures in front of him, satisfied with the projections for the profits from the latest snowboard bindings he'd designed and patented. The Zee Tap had been on the market for only two years, but it was already fast approaching status as the year's top-selling binding in the world. Even though Tate knew he was doing well, something compelled him to keep continual tabs on his finances. He knew that "something" was undoubtedly his own poverty-ridden childhood.

Since retiring from his professional snowboarding career, he was aware that he only had a limited amount of time to capitalize on his past success. That's why he'd diversified and taken on consulting jobs like this one at Snowy Sky Resort. Although accepting this particular job happened to be motivated by much more than business.

"Uncle Tate!" Lucas ran up to him nearly out of breath, his eyes wide with excitement.

"Slow down, buddy. What's the matter?"

"There's a fairy woman in the fish room."

"A fairy…what?"

"A fairy woman. She's in the fish room."

Tate smiled. Lucas had taken to calling the atrium the fish room. He loved to hang out in there. At first Tate had been concerned because of the water feature, but after a few days he felt certain that Lucas wasn't going to get in the pond with the fish and if he did somehow fall in, Tate was confident he could climb out.

Even so, he had been thrilled to learn Rankins had a community center with a pool. He'd already enrolled Lucas in swim lessons.

He wondered if it was normal to worry and fret about most everything where a child was concerned.

"Come and look at her."

Tate stood and moved from behind the desk in the spacious room the owner of the house had graciously cleared for his use as an office. She'd left the antique books in the floor-to-ceiling shelves that took up one entire wall and he was glad. It lent the room a cozy feel.

"Okay, but what makes her a fairy exactly? Does she have wings?" Tate assumed Lucas was referring to the woman caring for the atrium in the homeowner's absence. He'd been relieved when he had learned that he wouldn't have to look after it. There were plants in there he was certain his brown thumb could wilt without ever touching, not to mention the goldfish.

Lucas explained patiently as he led the way. "No, Uncle Tate, fairies don't let humans see their wings. Only other fairies can see their wings."

"I see. So…is she wearing a certain dress or playing the flute or something? Is that how you know she's a fairy?"

"She talks to the fish."

"Fairies talk to fish? Do they talk back?"

Lucas had picked up his pace and kept glancing back as if he wasn't moving quite fast enough. Tate walked faster.

"No, *this* fairy talks to the fish. I'm not sure if they talk back because I don't speak fish."

Tate felt a mixture of affection and amused confusion.

But when they entered the atrium they found it empty of both humans and fairies.

"Oh, no..." Lucas's face fell as his eyes darted around the warm, bright space. His voice was filled with such abject disappointment it tugged at Tate's heartstrings. "She's gone."

CHAPTER TWO

HANNAH SLIPPED ON her snow boots and wrapped the soft, teal-colored mohair scarf around her neck. She arranged the matching hat on her head and silently thanked her cousin Janie who had knitted the set.

Lift number two had become fully operational today and she was going to check it out before her meeting. She wanted everything to be perfect for Tate Addison. As not only project manager of Snowy Sky but founder and shareholder as well, she was used to doing things her way. She relished the freedom she'd had thus far in seeing her vision becoming a reality.

Hannah was fine with getting a "second opinion," and yet, having the resort—her hard work, her dream, her baby, her second chance at achieving success—evaluated in this manner? Well, it was bound to be a little nerve-racking for anyone.

Hoisting a hip onto one of the many railings

gracing the lodge's massive front steps, she slid down to the frozen ground and then headed for her snow machine. She couldn't help the welling of pride as she took in the tall T-shaped metal poles marching up the hillside. Snowy Sky wouldn't be officially opening until next year, but enough had been accomplished that it was already looking like a real ski resort.

Tate Addison had recently retired from the sport of snowboarding with one of the longest and most successful careers of all time, and although he was several years older than her, she had seen him compete when she'd been on the professional skiing circuit.

She squelched a ping of jealousy; thinking of her own career cut short so cruelly still filled her with a painful longing, a yearning for the medals and accolades she'd been so close to achieving.

Jeez, Hannah, she told herself, *bitter much?* Mourning the past was most definitely not a part of the "postaccident healing plan" she and her sports therapist, Dr. Voss, had developed and that she had executed over the past few years.

Hers and Tate's different backgrounds and experiences shouldn't matter, though. When he looked at the big picture, as he'd been hired to do, everything would be fine. All she really needed to do was collect his stamp of approval. She would answer every one of his questions thoroughly and eloquently. Then, at the board meeting next week, he would inform them of what a great job she was doing, collect his fee and be gone.

Simple.

Hannah headed toward lift two and found Freddie there waiting for her in the control booth as she'd asked. Freddie was a hometown boy, an avid skier and one of the first employees she had hired.

"Freddie, I'm going to ride around one time to check things out and then on the second go-around I'll radio you when to stop the lift, okay?"

"Awesome. Have fun. Um, I hate to bring this up right now because I know you've got this important meeting and all. But Park was in the rental shop this morning snooping around and telling me how to arrange everything. What's up with that?"

She felt a surge of annoyance. Park Lowell was a shareholder, board member, snowboarder and all-around pain in Hannah's neck. He also coveted her job and everyone knew it.

"Trying to impress Tate Addison, no doubt.

I'll talk to him." *And remind him who the project manager is*, she added silently.

"I didn't listen to him anyway. Just thought you'd want to know."

"Definitely. I'm always interested in what Park is up to, especially where Snowy Sky is concerned."

Freddie nodded. "Amen to that."

TATE ARRIVED NEARLY two hours early for his meeting, wanting to inspect the resort's progress thus far without any biased commentary from the project manager. He'd been using a snow machine Park Lowell had set him up with to scout things out when he noticed that one of the chairlifts was operating. He watched the lift smoothly glide along for a few minutes, admiring the triple-fixed grip chair units before he realized someone was riding on one of them.

Hmm, good timing, workers must be performing some maintenance or running a test. Nice to see construction appeared to be right on schedule or perhaps even a bit ahead of projections, an incredible feat for a project of this magnitude.

Suddenly the lift slowed and then halted completely. Movement caught his eye as the rider then slipped from the chair and sailed downward through the air. He felt his stomach fall right along with the rider, followed quickly by a genuine burst of fear when the person hit the ground and disappeared beneath the deep snow, a puff of powder drifting up to form a white cloud.

Tate hurriedly throttled up the snow machine and sped in that direction. A fall like that could be disastrous—deadly even. His heart hammered loudly in his head as possibilities surfaced, each one more gruesome than the last. He forced himself to focus on what he needed to do. Stopping the machine as he neared the location, he hopped off and moved quickly toward the spot. When he got close he dropped to the ground and crawled toward the indentation.

Calmly, but loudly he called out, "Hey, buddy, are you okay? Can you hear me? Say something if you can hear me?"

HANNAH'S BLISSFUL MOMENT was abruptly interrupted by a deep voice shouting at her. Was she okay? Of course she was okay. She had assumed the sound of the snow machine was Freddie coming to fetch her even though she'd asked him to wait for her call. But this wasn't Freddie's voice.

She opened her eyes and found herself face-to-face with a handsome and concerned-looking Tate Addison. She groaned. What terrible timing.

"Where does it hurt?"

Why was he shouting? "Nothing hurts," she said flatly. He was going to think she was crazy. This was also a tad embarrassing. How could she explain?

She tried to distract him instead. "I'm fine. How are you?"

"Miss, are you okay?" Voice even louder now as he enunciated very slowly, "Did you hit your head?"

Sitting up, she dusted snow from the front of her coat. "Yes, of course. Why wouldn't I be okay?"

"I saw you fall." He pointed up.

"I didn't fall. I jumped."

"What? Why?"

"Because it's fun?" Hannah posed the question-answer with a sheepish grin.

It was true that she didn't want the guy anywhere near her resort, but it was also true, she admitted, that it was cute how his mouth dipped down at the corners along with his brows.

She knew he was nice looking, but she hadn't expected him to be so…

Stern, she finished the thought as he went on in a very serious tenor, "It's *fun* to fall twenty feet into a pile of snow? That's dangerous. Are you aware of what could happen if you got stuck or how about landing on something—a rock or a branch? Did you think of that? And what if you landed wrong and broke your neck, or worse?"

Hannah wasn't sure what to make of his anxious tone. She supposed witnessing the "fall" had made him nervous, but she certainly wouldn't have done it if she'd known he was here. Besides, he wasn't supposed to be here for at least another hour or two, and why was he nosing around on his own?

In an attempt to reassure him, she said, "Twenty feet is a bit of an overstatement. And I wouldn't do it any old time. I'm aware of the conditions. There are no rocks here, there's a deep enough base, plenty of fresh powder. And you fall backwards—like this, so that when you land…" Leaning her body back to demonstrate, she caught a glimpse of his disapproving expression. Suddenly she felt like a teenager defending herself to a stodgy grown-up.

He shook his head, a look of incredulity

stamped on his face. "I don't understand why you would knowingly take such a risk. I mean, what are you…?"

She kind of wanted to tell him to lighten up, but knew it would behoove her to make a good impression on him. The more he liked her and Snowy Sky, the less change he would recommend and the sooner she could get back to normal.

Untying her hood, she pushed it back from her face, turned on a bright smile and stuck out a snow-covered glove. "Mr. Addison, it's nice to meet you—even in this rather, um, unconventional manner. But how's this for some great snow?"

What looked like a mix of skepticism and disbelief furrowed his brow. "What? Who… are you?"

"I'm Hannah James, project manager here at Snowy Sky."

TATE STARED INTO the pretty golden-brown eyes of the woman in front of him and felt a stir of something—no, a mix of so many things.

She was project manager? He knew the project manager was a woman named Hannah James and that she was a former professional skier. But he didn't know her. He'd thought the name sounded vaguely familiar, but he'd been expecting someone older. And much less… attractive.

She tucked a thick brown braid into the back of her jacket. Smooth, honey-toned skin made it impossible to tell her age.

He found himself blurting, "How old are you?" And immediately wished he could take the question back.

"Excuse me?"

Why had he asked that? Back in his early snowboarding days he'd hated when people had asked him that very question, which they'd done a lot because he had been young and talented and often competing against guys much older and twice or three times his size. He had never thought his age was relevant and now here he was asking the question of someone else.

"Sorry. So, uh, you're the project manager? Hannah James?"

"Yes. I am. Hannah James."

He noticed the tightness in her jaw and thought, *uh-oh*. He hadn't meant to offend her, and he knew very well this process would go a lot smoother if he could make friends with her, convince her the resort would benefit from his recommendations.

Attempting to reduce the tense moment with honesty and a touch of remorse, he winced. "Oh, man… Ms. James, I'm so sorry. I may not have had the most traditional upbringing, but I do know better than to ask a woman her age."

He added his own sheepish grin. "You, however, look very young and I was surprised. I am taken aback and embarrassed by my behavior. Can we start over?"

SURELY HE WASN'T implying she was too young for this job? *And why in the world would he think that, Hannah? After he just witnessed you jumping off the chairlift like some kind of reckless teenager?*

But she couldn't help it.

Since the accident she found herself constantly looking for ways to remind herself she was alive, that there were still thrills to be had even if she could no longer race. Dr. Voss said it was harmless, therapeutic even, as long as her forays didn't get too dangerous. Thus, she was only into "safe" danger. Although that might be difficult to convince Tate Addison of given the current circumstances.

Flashing her best carefree grin, she said, "Of course, Mr. Addison, you're forgiven. Call me Hannah. And please, forgive me, too. This probably looks really strange, but we all need a little fun sometimes, right? And I can assure you I am both old enough for this job and qualified for the position."

He looked relieved to be let off the hook.

"Great. Okay, I'm Tate." He placed a hand on his chest. "And clearly you are both of those things."

She brushed off his words with a wave of her hand. "It's fine. Don't worry about it. Let's get your tour started, shall we?"

She pulled off her gloves and removed her hat from inside of her jacket where she'd stashed it before she jumped from the lift. She arranged the hat on her head, tucking some stray strands beneath its softness. Finally she replaced her gloves and glanced up in time to catch his assessing stare; she didn't even want to imagine what he was thinking.

She needed to put this little setback behind her and do some damage control.

"After you." She gestured toward the groomed portion of the hill.

They hiked back to where he had left his snow machine. There was plenty of room for two, so when he suggested she climb on, she did. He took off slowly and putted along until she directed him to stop a few hundred feet up the hill where she began to give him the status report she'd practiced.

"We're almost directly in the middle of the ski terrain right here…"

Hannah went on to explain how the runs taking off from each of the four lifts would be arranged to accommodate every type of alpine skier—beginner, intermediate and advanced.

"Chair four—the last chair—will be a nice mix of beginner and intermediate runs along the front here, and has a dual purpose of allowing Nordic skiers access to the eastern terrain. It's full of trails where they can cross-country ski for miles. We have plans for a small lodge in that area eventually. Alaska has a substantial amount of cross-country skiers and I believe we should really capitalize on this…"

Feeling confident and cruising through her practiced spiel, she believed their awkward meeting was well behind them when he interrupted.

"What about snowboarding?"

"What about it?"

"Does the resort offer anything for snowboarders?"

She thought for a second. The man had been a professional snowboarder for many years; of course snowboarding would be the first thing on his mind.

"Yes, of course. They will be allowed to transport their boards up on the lifts for an extra fifty dollars a day. And we're only charging them ten percent more on rentals, food and lodging."

His dark brows dipped down, midnight-blue eyes full of consternation. The man really was serious. Much more so than she had expected. And definitely more than seemed called for. Every snowboarder she'd ever known was pretty much the opposite of serious.

"I'm kidding," she finally said.

"Oh… That's funny." He let out a laugh. The sound was deep and rich, and it surprised her. He should laugh more often, she thought, because it made him seem much less uptight.

Inexplicably proud of herself for the grin still on his face she went on. "Seriously, though, we will offer snowboarders the same things we offer skiers—top-of-the-line equipment rentals, meticulously groomed slopes and plenty of beautiful dry powder. As you can see, we have the most delicious snow here."

"No terrain park? Or a half-pipe? Quarter-pipe at least?"

Disappointed to find his intensity already

back, she recovered quickly. "Not at this time. Too expensive. We're a family-friendly ski resort catering to the recreational skiers of beginner to intermediate levels. Our focus is—"

"Ski and snowboard resort," he interrupted again.

"What?"

"It's a ski *and* snowboard resort, right?"

She felt a furrow of frustration bending her own brow and made a conscious effort to ease it away. "Doesn't that go without saying?"

A thoughtful expression evolved on his face. "Not really, no—not from a marketing standpoint. Snowy Sky Ski and Snowboard Resort sounds better, don't you think? I do," he confidently answered his own question and then went on, "Snowboarders like to feel welcome. For so long we were looked down on, even banned in some places."

Was he serious with this? That had been, like, twenty years ago. He wanted her to change the name of the resort to that tongue twister so that snowboarders would feel *welcome*? Not happening.

But how best to state it diplomatically? "Um…"

"So, you expect the more advanced athletes to do what?"

She felt her brows shoot upward in surprise along with a spike of impatience. "Whatever they like. We have some advanced runs. And there's always JB Heli-Ski for you adrenaline junkies."

She was referring to the heli-ski operation she'd opened the winter before with her friend Cricket Blackburn. The business wasn't a part of Snowy Sky, but she knew Tate was aware of it because Cricket had told her that he had visited Rankins a few times in the past year. Cricket had even given him a ride in the helicopter earlier in the fall, before the onset of the ski season.

"I'm not an adrenaline junkie," he replied with a steady tone.

She had the feeling he was going to add something else, but he didn't. He just stared with that same sober expression. She tried not to fidget, but it was so disconcerting.

"I've seen you compete. You're telling me those tricks you do—the tricks you invented— that doesn't give you a rush?"

"It was my job. I was good at it." He shrugged like he was still thinking about the question. "Winning gave me a rush I guess. I like to win."

"Okay," she said slowly, trying not to let

her consternation show. "You should try heli-skiing sometime. It's fun."

"I snowboard. I don't ski."

Thank you for clarifying, Mr. Literal, Hannah thought, just barely managing to suppress the urge to roll her eyes. Instead she offered up a smile. "You can take a board into the back-country, too, you know? People do it all the time. I'm sure it's not as fun as skiing but…" she trailed off with an easy shrug.

"Yeah, no, I mean—I know. I've been boarding in backcountry before. That's not what I was referring to."

She had no idea how to respond. He really was a tough crowd.

Luckily, he changed the subject. He pointed in the vicinity of lift four and asked a technical question that got them back on track and into safer territory.

Hannah knew the answer, and after they'd toured a portion of each of the four lift areas, more of the runs and prospective runs, they headed to the main lodge. The building had been framed and roughed in before winter hit so the interior could be completed during the darker, colder months.

They ventured inside as she explained the

plans for the lodge, including the layout and its features, and even some of the design aspects.

Throughout the tour Tate took notes and asked numerous questions, none of which stumped her and all of which she felt she'd answered thoroughly and with ease. He seemed satisfied with her responses and as the time flew by, he seemed to relax.

She even made him laugh a couple more times. And something told her that might be just as much of an accomplishment as the meeting's success.

CHAPTER THREE

TATE HANDED A set of Christmas lights to his longtime coach, mentor and friend Viktor Kovalenko. He began unwrapping another string from its exasperatingly tight packaging, barely resisting the urge to use his teeth.

"I'm telling you, Viktor, she hasn't made one move to accommodate snowboarders. At all. Other than the resort will be offering board rentals in the shop. Park told me she has plans to order maybe a third of the equipment she has slated for skiing."

"Really?" Viktor started up the stairs, looping the string of lights around the banister. Tate had purchased the lights in town as well as a wreath for the door and some other decorations with the intent of spreading some Christmas cheer around the house for Lucas.

"She knows about skiing. I'll give her that. And she's doing a fine job there. She's working on an awesome cross-country set up. And the heli-skiing venture she started with Cricket is amazing. It's already becoming super popular with backcountry enthusiasts. I went up with Cricket when I was here in the fall. I got a glimpse of the incredible terrain they have access to. And now with this snowpack I'm anxious to get out there and try it out myself."

Tate had met Cricket Blackburn on his first scouting trip to Rankins. They'd become friendly over the course of three successive visits. Cricket had introduced him to Park Lowell, who had turned him on to the investment opportunity that Snowy Sky offered. Snowy Sky had tipped him over the edge when making the difficult decision of trying to decide where to make a permanent home for himself and his makeshift family.

"This resort could be really special, but she's limiting its potential. Plus, she seems awfully blasé about her position as resort manager."

Viktor paused. "Blasé?"

"Yes, she's young and she's…" He searched for a description but all he could think of was cheerful. "She's not unconcerned, but…"

Flippant? No, that wasn't exactly the right word either. *Lighthearted?* Yes, but there was really nothing wrong with that, was there? And he didn't add that she was funny and that he'd also had a good time with her. None of that mattered because he needed to think about the resort's future success. And Lucas. Especially Lucas.

"I don't know exactly. She's mostly professional, though maybe not quite *serious* enough or…" That wasn't right either. He gave up with a dismissive head shake.

"What are you going to do?" Viktor asked, plugging one end of the string into an extension cord. The multicolored strands flickered and then glowed with cheerful color. He surveyed their work and grinned with satisfaction. "Lukie will like this."

Tate agreed. "I asked him what kind of tree he'd like for Christmas and he told me he doesn't remember ever having a Christmas tree."

Viktor nodded sadly. It didn't need to be said that money had specifically been sent each and every year to give Lucas a proper Christmas because they both knew. There had been a tree the last time Tate had spent Christmas with Lucas and Lexie, but Lucas had only been three years old.

"This year we change that," Viktor stated confidently.

Like always, Tate appreciated Viktor's optimism. Tate knew he needed to make a lot of changes for Lucas's sake. It was difficult to even know where to start.

"Yes, we will." Tate adjusted the lights, making sure they hung evenly. He knew Lucas was asleep in his room upstairs but still he lowered his voice as he asked, "Was I as troubled as Lucas when you took me in?"

Viktor halted his ministrations, his hands twinkling with color, and thought for a long minute. "I am not sure how to answer. It is difficult to know the mind of a child—the damage that is done. It comes out over time. I believe as part of healing process. You were unsettled also, like Lukie, tentative and even quieter. But your dedication to snowboarding saved you as much as I did."

Tate smiled at the man who had managed to wrest him away from Penny at the age of seven—purchased him essentially after dating her during a brief stint of sobriety. She'd been waitressing at the ski resort where Viktor worked. He'd been kind to Tate, introducing him to snowboarding. Tate had been a progeny and Viktor, seeing his potential, had offered to coach him, eventually striking a deal with Penny that allowed him to raise Tate as long as she kept receiving financial help.

Viktor always downplayed the role he'd assumed in Tate's life, but they both knew very well that he wouldn't be where he was if it wasn't for Viktor—not anywhere even close.

"Let's hope that works for Lucas, too."

"Yes, we will hope. And if not, we will find what does."

But Tate wanted this to work. It had to because he didn't know anything besides snowboarding. He was counting on using the sport to forge a bond with his nephew. Just as it had between him and Viktor.

Viktor added, "He is two nights now without nightmare."

"Yes, he is," Tate said with a relieved sigh. "He loves that crocodile night-light you got him. Told me it keeps the darkness away. The actual darkness *and* the scary kind he has bad dreams about."

Viktor's lips curved up into a grin. "You had night-light, too. It was tooth. You remember this one? You get from dentist."

He did remember. He still had it, tucked in a box in his condo back in Colorado.

"I wonder if Lucas has ever been to the dentist?"

"We will check on that. Before toothache comes."

"Good idea," Tate replied. "As far as Snowy

Sky goes, I don't have any choice. I'll have to take my recommendations to the board. Now that we're investors we need to think about the bottom line, as well."

"Does Ms. James know how much of resort you own?"

He grimaced. "Not exactly." He joined another string of lights to Viktor's.

"Does she know you own any shares of Snowy Sky?" Viktor asked, adjusting the strings as he slowly descended the stairs.

"Uh…no."

"How do you think that will go over when she finds out?"

He shrugged helplessly and tried to squelch a surprising, annoying niggle of guilt as the tiny bulbs flashed on, as bright as Hannah's smile. He couldn't think about her smile or those amber-colored eyes that seemed to dance with a kind of mischief.

Cricket had mentioned the James family of course. He had even met a few people he now realized would be Hannah's brothers or cousins. Park had also filled him in about the status and reputation her family enjoyed in Rankins. Undoubtedly she'd had a storybook upbringing as a member of the esteemed James family. It was certainly easy to deduce from her demeanor that the woman hadn't known much hardship in her life.

But Tate had, and so had Lucas—which was why he needed to stay focused on the end-game.

"I didn't want that knowledge to influence anything she told me. I wanted her to think she was talking with an objective observer. And, I didn't want her to think she had to impress me."

Viktor slowly descended the last few stairs, admiring their handiwork as he went. When he reached the bottom, he turned a hesitant look on Tate.

"Hmm," he finally said.

"Hmm, what?"

"How are you objective?"

"In my capacity as a consultant I'm objective."

"But what about your capacity as snowboarder? How does that make you any more objective than Ms. James with her background in skiing?"

Tate conceded that Viktor had a point. But he didn't harbor any prejudice against skiing like she so obviously did against snowboarding. If only she would make a few simple—okay, maybe not-quite-so-simple—

adjustments, equality could be achieved. Then harmony between the two sports would naturally follow at Snowy Sky.

CLOSING HER EYES, Hannah forced herself to do one more set. The doctors and her physical therapist had told her that the better shape she remained in, the less the trauma her body had suffered would prevent her from doing what she wanted to do in life.

Which made perfect sense, but this was heavy; she'd added more weight to her routine this morning. She focused on pushing the bar up as her muscles began to quiver.

Uh-oh, she realized, *barbell now definitely heading in the wrong direction.* She was going to have to roll out from under it somehow.

Her eyes snapped open as the bar was suddenly snatched out of her hands. The clinking sound it made as it was dropped on the rack seemed to echo through the empty weight room of the community center.

Cricket scowled down at her. "Are you *trying* to kill yourself?"

Hannah grinned up at him, wiping her brow with the sleeve of her shirt. "No, but I admit I may have pushed it a little too far. Thank you."

He leaned over so his upside-down face was

only inches above hers. "You should know better than to lift this much weight without a spotter. It's weight lifting 101."

She shifted her gaze one way and then the other. She tried to sound casual even as the danger of her actions began to sink in. "Well, there's no one else here."

"That's because no one else in their right mind gets up at four in the morning to work out."

"You do," she spouted with a laugh.

"Yeah, so next time wait for me, okay?"

She sat up and mumbled a "fine" as she did so, because she knew he was right. That had kind of scared her.

He took a seat on the bench beside her. "How are you feeling anyway?" He motioned in the general direction of her left leg.

She nodded, but didn't make eye contact. "Good."

He kept staring. He always watched her close and for some reason she didn't mind. She had known Cricket forever, but the last year and a half since becoming her business partner he'd also become like a brother to her. Closer actually than her own two brothers, who were both wonderful yet...

Her family was close, but Hannah had always felt odd having been born the middle child among her siblings—five years after her sister Shay who had come just two years after their oldest brother Tag. Those two were tight. Then Hannah had come along, and five years later the triplets had been born; Hazel, Iris and Seth. Those three were their own special kind of unit. Which had left Hannah kind of floundering in the middle, and then she'd been away so much of her childhood, skiing.

She knew it would be pointless to lie to him. "Still having some pain. It's probably nothing, but I'm going to call the doctor."

"When?"

"Soon," she promised. "Right after the holidays."

"Hannah—"

"That's only a few weeks. It's not getting worse. It's just there. And I doubt it will make any difference."

He eyed her skeptically. "How in the world could you possibly know that?"

She chuckled. "I don't, but I was hoping you would buy it."

HANNAH HADN'T SEEN the little boy during the next couple visits that followed their first encounter in the atrium, so this morning she was

pleased to find him waiting for her. Technically, he was hiding again, but she felt confident he was doing so in anticipation of her
arrival.

She pretended as if she didn't see him as
she ducked into the storage room to collect the
fish food. She strolled over to the pond where
the koi began to swim at a faster clip as they
spotted her. Keeping one eye on the little boy,
she threw a handful of food into the pond and
then another.

"Ouch! My wrist hurts," she called out
and then shook her hand as if the motion had
caused her pain. She looked toward the pond.
"How will I feed you guys? I could really use
some help."

A soft voice floated over to her. "You should
use your other hand."

She stifled a grin. "Oh, I guess I could try
that." She reached into the bucket left-handed
and then made a show of sloppily throwing
the food on the floor. A few pieces dribbled
into the water where the koi quickly gobbled
them up.

A little breath huffed out its disappointment.
"That wasn't very good."

She smiled. "I know. Cut me a break, will
you? I'm not ambidextrous."

A giggle followed and Hannah knew she was making progress.

He added, "I already know you're not a frog."

She thought, *Ambidextrous? Oh, amphibian.* She laughed. "Are *you* a frog?"

More giggling and then, "No."

"Are you sure? I don't trust frogs. They're really jumpy. Have you noticed that?"

"Well, they hop."

"Yeah, what's that all about? It's suspicious. I think they should walk like normal people."

"But they're not people. They're frogs."

"Like you?"

"Nooo…" He erupted with a fit of laughter and the sound warmed her heart.

"Maybe you should come over here and let me see for myself?"

Still grinning, he stepped tentatively out from behind the tree. Hannah asked, "Do you want to help me feed the koi?"

He shuffled sideways a few steps. "The what?"

She pointed. "The koi. These fish, they're called koi."

"I thought they were goldfish."

"Nope, they're different. Come a little closer and I'll show you how and tell you their names."

"They have names?"

"They do." Hannah peered into the pond and then pointed. "That one—with the black and white, and the big spot of orange on its back? That is my koi and her name is Bridget. That spotted bright red and white one there is Jasmine."

He cautiously skirted around the edge of the pond until he stood by her side. "What about that one?"

She followed his finger with her eyes. "The one that's almost all orange? That's Carmen."

"Are they all girls?" Hannah thought he sounded disappointed by the notion.

"No. That's Henry and that's Emmett." Pointing to a large white fish with black spots, she informed him, "The biggest one there. That's Silvio."

An interested expression lit his face and she felt certain he was committing this all to memory. She looked forward to quizzing him next time.

"What's your name?"

"Lucas."

"Okay, Lucas." She handed him the bucket. "Go ahead and toss in some more breakfast. Remember we can only give them certain kinds of food or they might get sick, but after you've helped me feed them a few times, they'll start to recognize you when you get close to the pond…"

HANNAH BAILED OFF the magic carpet—the conveyor system she'd chosen for the resort's beginner slopes. The conveyor worked like a flat escalator allowing riders to easily step on and step off the belt. She pulled her tube across the hillside, stopping to assess their progress.

"Hey, Gareth, Reagan," she called to her cousin Janie's sixteen- and fourteen-year-old sons. "Let's go over to…" She traipsed about forty feet and stopped well before the giant metal chairlift pole. "Right about here. That way we won't have to worry about the little ones hitting anything."

She wanted everything to be perfect before Janie's four-year-old twins and the rest of their preschool class arrived for the sledding party.

Gareth and Reagan were going to assist kids on the magic carpet and with transporting sleds up the hill, while Freddie helped with unloading.

Hannah saw Janie's Suburban pulling in. Janie's husband, Aidan, had purchased it the day after they'd found out she was pregnant with her fifth child. The baby girl she was carrying would be Aidan's first, but Janie had already had four boys with her late husband when she and Aidan had met. Gareth and Reagan were the oldest of these.

Hannah waved. The boys whizzed down the hill past her on their tubes.

"It's awesome," Gareth called out to her.

Hannah loved kids and regularly volunteered to arrange special seasonal events like nature hikes, fishing trips, bicycling or rock climbing. Today's snow tubing would last two to three hours and they'd have hot chocolate, juice boxes and snacks served in the lodge afterward. "Hey, Gareth, I'm going to sled down to make sure Mindy has everything ready for later. I should be back by the time the crowd of ruffians arrives."

He gave her a gloved thumbs-up.

She nodded and carried her tube to the slope that led toward the lodge and prepared to take off in that direction. Freddie had just groomed this hill, and as she stared at the vast expanse of bare white snow, she couldn't resist the opportunity beckoning to her.

TATE HAD BEEN all over the mountain on a snow machine, but wanted to get a feel for the slopes firsthand. So that morning he'd loaded his board and rode as far up the mountain as he could. He'd arranged for one of the employees to bring him back up later to fetch the snow machine.

He hadn't been on his board in weeks and it felt great. Snowboarding was the one activity where he could really lose himself. It was second nature, especially since he'd quit competing and could now ride solely for fun. He thought about Hannah's adrenaline-junkie comment as he flew down the hill and wondered if his riding would change now that he didn't have to worry about getting injured.

Although now he had Lucas to think about; he immediately slowed and then stopped. From there he decided to switch his course and head toward the lodge in order to view the area where he thought the first half-pipe should be constructed.

After halting again about halfway down, he bent over to fiddle with the binding on his boot. He was trying out a new design and didn't have it adjusted quite right. Removing one boot from the board with the intention of making a further adjustment, he turned to assess the uphill landscape, and that's when he saw someone flying toward him on a tube—backwards.

HANNAH FELT THE impact before she saw what she'd hit.

Her tube flipped and she somersaulted through the air, eventually landing hard on one shoulder before flopping onto her left side. A pain shot through her leg and she was immediately grateful she hadn't landed on it with all of the force her shoulder had taken.

"What the…? Hannah? Is that you?"

Hannah couldn't contain a groan as she rolled onto her back. Tate?

He muttered something unintelligible and then asked, "Are you hurt?"

She winced up at him. "Are you?"

"No."

She bent her right leg at the knee and then slowly mimicked the motion with the left. A wave of relief followed.

"My shoulder is going to be sore, but I think my leg is fine. What are you doing here?"

"What is it with you and this reckless behavior?" He shot out the question in that stern, lecture-y tone she remembered from their initial encounter.

Why did she find it kind of funny? Her lips curved up into a grin. "Reckless? I'm tubing. What's reckless about tubing?"

"Backwards? You weren't watching where you were going."

"I was spinning. My sisters and brothers and cousins—we used to do this thing when we were kids where we'd spin our tubes while swerving across the hill."

Now he was scowling down at her so she quit explaining and asked, "What's the matter?"

"It's no wonder you look so young."

Hannah looked up at him in confusion. "What?"

"Obviously there's still a child dwelling behind that pretty face. Can you get up?" He extended a hand.

She felt her face grow warm at the weird compliment-insult. "Of course I can get up." Except that she realized she sort of couldn't, not without embarrassing herself.

He waited. She smiled up at him, wishing he would leave.

"Do you want me to help you up?"

"Nope," she said, pushing herself up to rest on her elbows. "I got it. I'm good."

"Okay." Placing his hands on his hips, he continued watching her, waiting obviously.

"Hannah?"

"Hmm?"

"Why aren't you getting up?"

"Well, Tate, it's complicated."

"Complicated? Are you hurt?" His voice went up several decibels and she realized he was worried about her.

Kind of sweet, she thought and added a smile before confessing. "My pants must have caught on your board because they are ripped on my south side."

A gloved hand went up to cover his grin, which Hannah thought was pointless because of the laughter now accompanying it. "Seriously?"

"Do you think I'm lying here in the snow because it's fun?"

He tipped his head as if considering the question. "I don't know. I've seen you do it before."

She opened her mouth, and then snapped it shut. She let out a laugh before asking, "Did you just make a joke?"

"Yes," he said, still grinning. "I guess I did."

"It was funny. You should do it more often." Keeping her tone nonchalant she asked, "Maybe you could go fetch my tube?" Which she'd noticed was now flat. She was probably lucky she wasn't hurt. Other than the jolt of pain in her leg, but it seemed fine now. Well, as fine as it had been lately.

"I can carry it behind me strategically."

She couldn't make out the words he muttered as he stepped toward her, bent and scooped her up—one arm beneath her shoulders one under the knees, and carried her toward the lodge.

She tried to look dignified, but she could tell Tate was trying not to laugh because she could feel the rumble of a chuckle deep in his chest. She gave up, buried her face in his jacket, and let her own laughter roll.

Mindy looked a bit startled when they came through the door both still grinning.

"Hannah?" she asked. "Are you okay?"

"Hey, Mindy. Yes, I'm fine." She added a wave, still cradled in Tate's arms. "Have you met Tate Addison yet? Tate, this is Mindy Reese. She works at Little Cubs Preschool and is in charge of the after-sledding snacks for the troops today. Mindy, this is Tate. He's working here as a consultant for Snowy Sky."

"Nice to meet you," Mindy said. If she thought it strange that Tate was holding her, she refrained from mentioning it. Hannah appreciated that.

He said, "You, too, Mindy."

Hannah pointed across the large expanse of mostly empty room. "You can take me down there. I have a room I use as an office."

He headed there where he finally lowered her to her feet. She could tell he was being careful to keep her backside away from the door, and she liked the gentlemanly approach.

He was gesturing backward toward the door with his thumb. "I'm just going to… Unless, is there anything else I can do for you before I go?"

She held up a finger as her phone buzzed in her pocket. She removed it and read the text from Janie. She cast a thoughtful look at him and wondered if it would be too much to ask. Although, he *had* offered.

"Yes, actually there is."

CHAPTER FOUR

TATE DIDN'T HAVE much experience with kids, but how difficult could a sledding party with a group of four- and five-year-olds be? He'd been spending nearly every minute of the past few weeks with Lucas and aside from the near-constant worrying, he felt as though he was doing okay.

Roughly a half hour later he held a firm belief that the preschool teacher Elaine deserved a raise—a huge raise, and probably a very long all-expenses-paid vacation. A little boy named Bryce kept licking his inner tube, another boy refused to get on the magic carpet facing forward, and a blonde pixie of a girl had removed her coat and refused to put it back on. Tate was afraid she was going to end up with hypothermia.

"Would you *please* put your coat on, Bea?" At least he'd learned her name.

She gave her head a hard shake, blond

locks peeking out from beneath a bright pink fleece hat.

He tried being firm. "Bea, put your coat on. It's too cold to go without a coat."

More head shaking.

"It's dangerous," he tried, which didn't seem to faze her in the least.

He attempted a gentle threat, "Do you want me to get your teacher? She might make you go to the lodge." Although he had no idea how to summon the teacher at this point, or even if she would do that. Elaine was currently on top of the hill with the rest of the tiny phenomenally energetic sledders.

She gave him another careless shrug.

He resorted to negotiation. "I'll give you twenty dollars if you put your jacket back on?"

She smiled, lolling her head back and forth in a figure-eight pattern while he held the jacket aloft like some kind of frantic matador.

"Fifty dollars?" Was bribery the same as negotiation?

He was ready to double the amount when he sensed a presence behind him—or maybe he heard the snickering. He turned to find Hannah watching him, humor dancing in her eyes.

"Thank goodness, you're here. She won't wear her jacket. I'm not sure what to do. The teacher is up there And she's..." Tate heard the desperation in his tone as he pointed at the top of the slope. "It's like ten degrees out here."

She took the jacket from him. "Bea, why aren't you wearing your jacket, girlfriend?"

"Because Shane said it's the same color as slime."

"Slime?"

The little girl nodded her head.

"Ah, I see. But he means that in a good way. Shane loves slime. I think the danger here is that Shane might love you, too."

Bea let out a gasp, her arms shooting out straight at her sides, allowing Hannah to slip the jacket on. Hannah zipped it up, tucked her scarf around her neck and made sure her hat was secure.

"Thanks, Hannah. How do my curls look?"

"Perfect—just like you, little one." Hannah flipped her head toward the magic carpet. "Now go get 'em."

Bea trotted off to join the others.

"Ask Shane if he likes slime," she called after Bea, who kept going as she gave her an over-the-shoulder thumbs-up.

"How did you do that?"

"Well, I have some inside knowledge."

Tate gave her a look that said he knew it was more than that.

"I will give you a tip, though, so you don't go broke. Five bucks, fifty bucks—kids this age don't really get the concept of the amount. In fact, hold out a handful of change in one hand and a couple bills—any denomination—in the other and see what they go for. To them, more is more—literally. Except when it comes to candy. You'd be amazed at what they'll do for one single piece of candy."

"I was desperate. I would have paid a lot more. I thought she was going to freeze to death."

Hannah laughed. "Not gonna happen—they'll seek shelter before they dip to the freezing level."

She pointed at her pink snow pants, her mouth forming a playful grin. "Thank you for holding down the fort for me so I could get these."

He felt his pulse jump at the thought of recent circumstances. "You're welcome. No problem. That was fast. You must live pretty close to here?"

"I do, you know that log cabin just up the road from the Faraway Inn? It belongs to my sister Shay. She owns the inn, and I rent the house from her. Have you taken a turn on a tube yet?"

"Um, no. Elaine suggested that I help the kids get back to the magic carpet after they arrive here at the bottom. It seems like a simple job, right? But they are a slippery bunch, not at all like my…"

He was going to mention Lucas when a pair of young boys with reddish-brown hair peeking from beneath their hats ran toward Hannah and enveloped her in a huge hug.

"Hannah!" They shouted in unison.

"Hey, my favorite twins! Wow, Finn I saw how fast you were on that last run. I'm thinking competitive luge is in your future, buddy. Gabe, guess what we're having in the lodge after sledding?"

"Don't tease me, Hannah-Banana, you better be talking hot chocolate."

She laid a hand on his stocking-capped head. "You know I wouldn't tease about hot chocolate. Hey, guys, this is Tate. He's a friend of mine. These little cuties are my cousin Janie's twins. As are the two teenage helpers there, Gareth and Reagan."

A tandem greeting followed, then one of them commented, "Except Gareth and Reagan aren't twins like us."

"This is true. Thank you for clarifying that for Tate, Twin-Finn."

The little boys nodded happily and galloped off…

"Later, twin-gators," Hannah called after them.

"After a while, Banana-crocodile," one of them shouted back.

Tate studied her. She seemed relaxed, amused and thrilled to be here. How did she do that?

"You're so good with them. Do you have kids?"

"Nope. Big family. Lots of experience. Plus, I know these kids. I volunteer at the preschool one morning a week. And do some fun things with them—like this." She gestured at the hill.

Hannah clearly had a gift—that kid-thing that some people were just born with, which served to remind him of how little of it he had himself.

"THAT WAS REALLY nice of the fairy to let you help her feed the goldfish. Next time be sure to come and get me when she's here." Tate smiled at Lucas who'd just finished relaying the details of his latest encounter with the fairy in the fish room.

"She hurt her hand so she needed my help. She thanked me and she told me the names of some of the kois. That's what they're called, not goldfish, Uncle Tate." He heard the pride in Lucas's voice and felt grateful to this lady for taking the time to make Lucas feel special.

He thought about Hannah and how natural her interaction had been with the kids on the sledding hill. He'd been reading books on childcare and child psychology, but he wondered if there was some kind of class he could take. Would it be weird to ask her for advice? What he needed was to get Lucas up on the snowboarding hill.

"That's so cool, little man. I'll try to remember that. Do you want to pick out a book for us to read together?"

Lucas examined the large selection on the bookshelf he and Viktor had stocked.

He chose a brand-new picture book, running his fingers over the cover. "The lady might not actually be a fairy. I think she might just look like a fairy. She has fairy—" he paused to think and then pointed at his own face "—eyes."

Tate stifled a laugh. Fairy eyes? He had no idea what that meant. "I see. Well, she sounds like a very nice young lady whether she is actually a fairy or not."

"She's really nice," Lucas assured him authoritatively as he moved toward his bed and peeled back the comforter. He liked to look at his sheets before he climbed in. This set was covered with tiny monkeys in goofy poses. Funnily enough, Tate remembered being fascinated by sheets, too. It was too much of a chore, or used too many quarters, for Penny to wash bedding so he'd always used a sleeping bag. Tate still hated sleeping bags.

"We're friends. You should see if she wants to babysit me sometime."

That was a good idea. Since Lucas had come into his life full-time, he hadn't wanted Tate to leave him at all. He'd finally reached the point where he'd stay with Viktor, but for Lucas himself to suggest spending time with someone else felt like a huge leap of progress. Tate thought since the girl was fish-sitting for the homeowner, maybe she'd be willing to babysit for him.

"That's a great plan. Maybe we'll do that."

He had intended to meet her and thank her for her kindness to Lucas, but so far she'd slipped in and out of the atrium without him even knowing she was there.

Tate knew he'd choose a book about animals. Lucas was enthralled with animals and

Tate was both happy and surprised by how much he knew about them. He picked up the book about a hippopotamus who thought he wanted to be a rhinoceros and began to read.

FRIGID AIR TICKLED Hannah's lungs. It was a gorgeous winter day. The sun might not have a lot of hours to shine in an Alaskan December, but today it had decided to make the most of the time it did have. Shards of light beamed through the grayish-blue clouds and spotlighted the snow-covered peaks in the distance. Pieces of heaven shining through, as her late grandfather Gus used to say.

She entered the beautiful wood-and-stone-constructed lobby of the Faraway Inn, removed and stowed her outer layers, and headed toward the restaurant. Delicious aromas assaulted her senses as she walked into the vast expanse of dining room. Her stomach responded with a hungry rumble as she thought about Chef Javier's cooking.

Waving to some of the other committee members already seated at a long rectangular table, she headed toward the drink station to fetch herself a cup of coffee. Her cousin Adele who was the Faraway Restaurant's manager appeared at her side.

Hannah and the rest of the James family hadn't even known of Adele's existence until a couple years ago, after Shay had hired her inadvertently as a waitress.

At that time Adele had only recently learned of her heritage. She had come to Rankins hoping to find a place in the James family while thinking she might be entitled to a share of the inn. She'd earned the former even though she'd been mistaken about the latter. She and Hannah had become close friends during the ensuing ordeal.

"How's it going?" Adele asked.

"Good. How about you? The dining room looks super busy."

Adele smiled, light brown eyes so similar to her own dancing merrily.

"Thanks to you. We've got another group of heli-skiers staying here. From what I can gather, if they're not skiing they are eating."

Hannah chuckled as she poured her coffee. "The sport definitely requires fuel. And Cricket does a great job of promoting the restaurant."

Adele's jaw tightened as she repeated his name.

Something had recently transpired between Adele and Cricket, but Adele wasn't talking— yet.

Cricket had once been considered Rankins's most sought-after bachelor, but his reluctance to date meant his status had gradually evolved from eligible to confirmed. Hannah secretly believed he and her brother Tag had turned their single statuses into some kind of competition.

"What about him?" Hannah asked.

"He's here right now. Over by the windows, close to the fireplace, he's having lunch with your snowboarder."

For some reason the mention of Tate made her heart skip a beat. "My snowboarder? Very funny, Adele. Tate is here? Where?" What was with her hopeful tone of voice?

"Yep, right here." She flinched as a deep, now-familiar voice sounded behind her.

She cast a wide-eyed look of horror at Adele.

Adele grinned and then whispered loudly, "Sneaky, isn't he? For a big guy?"

"I'll say," Hannah said and turned around.

Tate's eyes latched on to hers, an amused grin playing on his handsome face along with something else. Something that looked like interest and sent her pulse officially racing.

As embarrassed as she was, at least she managed to eke a bit of satisfaction out of the fact that she'd finally made him smile without even trying.

Laughter laced his tone. "Can I help you with something, Hannah?"

"Um, no…I was just… Hello, Tate." She gestured at Adele. "This is my cousin and—"

Tate smiled in Adele's direction. "I know. Hi, Adele."

"You do?"

"Cricket introduced us," Adele explained.

"Oh, that's good," she muttered.

He asked, "Hannah, do you have a minute? I'd like to ask you something."

Adele pointed toward the group of people seated at the long table. "Looks like the meeting is about to start, so I'll go join them, and fill you in on anything you miss."

"Thanks, Adele."

Tate motioned for Hannah to follow as he strode toward the lobby. Along the way they dodged Faraway Inn employees who were busy hauling decorated Christmas trees down the hall toward the restaurant.

"There is some serious Christmas spirit in this place. That's a lot of trees." He stopped in front of one covered with ski-related ornaments and sparkly snowflakes. "This one is really cool."

"Thank you. I did it. Well, mostly Janie and Adele did it with my moral support. I'm not very crafty. But, it was donated by Snowy Sky."

"There are no snowboards on it, though." He rubbed his chin thoughtfully and craned his neck around the tree as if searching for some.

She grinned, finding herself taken in by his teasing good humor. "Huh, that is weird," she answered, pretending to look puzzled. "I was sure that we put a whole bunch of snowboards *all* over it."

"Mmm..." He faked his own perplexed scowl and she was utterly captivated, and a little grateful that he didn't act like this all the time. Who would have guessed the man could be so charming? The last thing she needed was a crush on the ski-resort consultant.

"It's for a fund-raising event."

"Oh, right." He eyed the trees speculatively. "The Tree something or other."

Hannah was a little surprised that he knew about it, although there was advertising for it all over town. "Festival of Trees, and yes, actually that's what my meeting is about right now. I'm on the committee."

Slipping his hands into his back pockets, he

exhaled loudly. "Okay. You probably need to get to that. So, what I wanted to ask you is... I was just talking to Cricket Blackburn? About your heli-skiing operation?"

"Mmm-hmm, I know Cricket," Hannah said with her own teasing grin.

He let out a chuckle. "Of course you do... And you've been out heli-skiing with him, right?"

"Yes, of course, many times. We're partners, remember?"

He brushed a hand through his hair. "Of course you have... Um..."

Why was he acting so weird? It was almost as if he was nervous.

"I think we covered this already. It's an absolute blast," she added, trying to move the conversation along.

"I figured I'd take my board and go with him to check it out. And I wanted to see if you—"

Uh-oh. She could see where this was going. She interrupted, "No, thank you, Tate. I appreciate the offer, but that won't be necessary."

He looked confused. "What's not necessary?"

"JB Heli-Ski is a separate entity from Snowy Sky. We haven't requested your input or recommendations where it's concerned. Your consulting fee doesn't cover anything related to it."

A surprised laugh burst from his lips as he said, "Oh, I know that. I was just… Okay." He added a nod.

She smiled, glad that he was taking this so well. "Good, because I realize you're just doing the job you were hired to do here and I respect that. I am cooperating and assisting in every way I can. But I'm going to be honest with you. I didn't hire you. The board of directors voted on it because Park Lowell insisted…" She trailed off with a shake of her head. He didn't need to hear how she felt about Park.

"But that doesn't matter. You're here and I'm fine with that. Let's just stick to your original mission at Snowy Sky, though, okay? And leave JB as it is?"

He nodded. "Sure, okay. But I was actually going to…"

His eyes seemed to search her face and she felt a fresh wave of attraction. There was a vulnerability beneath his tough exterior that she found incredibly appealing.

She said, "You were going to…? I'm sorry

to hurry you along, but I do need to get to my meeting."

"Sure thing. I'll let you get going." He grinned. "You're a tough one—you know that?"

She was relieved that he didn't seem offended. It wasn't personal. He genuinely seemed like a good guy and under different circumstances she could see herself really liking him. She did like him, actually, and she could imagine... But these were not those different circumstances and it was pointless to spend time "imagining" anything at all.

"Thank you, I think. Because although I'm not sure what you're referring to specifically, I certainly don't mind being called tough." She smiled and added a wink before hurrying back into the dining room.

TATE WATCHED HER walk away, his head spinning from that parting look. She'd graced him with that gorgeous smile, which was bad enough, but when she'd winked he'd felt this sensation somewhere deep in his chest.

He'd never met anyone like her. He didn't think he'd ever met anyone who was so full of life. At first he'd had his doubts, wondered what kind of person jumped off a ski lift into the snow because it was fun. Then there was the sledding incident. She could have injured herself then, too. But her only concern had been whether he was okay. That, and her torn pants. Which she'd also handled with a perfect mix of humor and grace.

And watching her with those preschoolers had done something to him. He wanted to spend some time with her, wanted to talk to her about Lucas. He'd like to introduce her to Lucas.

Lucas.

It was probably for the best, he told himself, that she had shut him down without her even realizing he was about to ask her out.

Heli-skiing had seemed like a good bet for a first date. Regret surfaced even as he reminded himself that he didn't have time to get involved with someone. His focus needed to be on Lucas and creating the best home and family environment that he possibly could, which included his plans for Snowy Sky. Something told him that spending time with Hannah would definitely lead to involvement.

Cricket walked up to join him. "How did that go?"

Tate shrugged. "Condensed version?"

"Sure."

"She didn't get it that I was trying to ask

her out and then I very smoothly told her she was, uh…tough."

"Swept her right off her feet, huh?"

"Something like that." Tate chuckled wryly and shook his head in defeat.

"What did she say?"

"She thought I was trying to offer my consulting services to JB Heli-Ski. And then she very nicely told me to mind my own business."

"That's our Hannah." Cricket laughed for a few long seconds. He wrapped an arm around Tate's shoulder. "You know what? I like you, Addison. And because of that I'm going to let you in on a fact that is well-known here in Rankins. Save you some trouble, or at the very least some precious time figuring it out on your own."

"By all means."

"These James girls *are* tough, and Hannah in particular is incredibly tough and competent and brave. It's something you might not want to forget."

Tate liked that sentiment—a woman who was strong and courageous and confident in herself, although in light of what he would be bringing to the board in a few days, he wondered if those traits should also make him nervous.

CHAPTER FIVE

BOARD MEETINGS WERE usually held in the conference room at the Faraway Inn and this one was no exception. Hannah's sister Shay, who owned the inn, always saw to it that the necessary equipment was carefully and meticulously arranged; monitors, cameras and audio so even members participating long-distance were able to converse. The result was a modern, professional, yet comfortable atmosphere and usually she enjoyed the gatherings.

But not today, because now Hannah stared at Tate and listened to his comments and suggestions—and to his recommendations to completely and thoroughly unravel her ski resort.

He wanted to change everything.

He proposed turning nearly all of the runs under chairlift two—her prime intermediate ski runs—into snowboard terrain.

"I feel strongly that the construction of a half-pipe right here—" he stopped to point and she felt it like a jab in the chest "—would be the perfect location. Eventually the addition of a second half-pipe here…"

Was he joking? Two half-pipes? One would cost a lot—way more than they could afford at this point. Not to mention the continual maintenance. She looked down at the estimates he'd passed out before he started speaking. Two would be excessive to the nth degree.

"A snowboard-cross course or some slope-style components would also help to draw competitive boarders." He met her eyes for a few seconds before adding, "And skiers. Snowy Sky could hold competitions and I guarantee you would get some professionals coming here to train. I've already talked to…"

Rattling off names she guessed were supposed to impress them all, he went on to add credence to his economic points with more numbers and statistics. Then he mentioned that while the lodge's overall theme was "quaint and charming," the design should be "upgraded" and the layout "altered" for a more modern feel, and it should also include high-end penthouse suites.

According to Tate, even the restaurant should serve different food.

She glanced around the room, and at the

faces peering back from the monitors, and was struck with the feeling that she was the only one who hadn't been hypnotized by this magician. The one possible exception was her friend Edith Milner whose expression Hannah thought held some skepticism.

As one of Snowy Sky's largest investors, Edith had been instrumental in helping Hannah throughout this whole process—from permits to securing funding. Hannah had received a large settlement after the accident but not nearly enough to open the resort on her own. Edith had made it all possible, investing heavily and bringing others on board through her vast business connections, including her friend and fellow koi enthusiast Tiger Takagi.

But the other board members seemed riveted by Tate's commentary and suggestions.

Hannah felt like screaming.

She'd been ready for the subject of snowboarding to be addressed, had even thought about the places where she might defer—or at the very least compromise. But never once had he said he intended to recommend an overhaul of the entire resort.

He had ambushed her plain and simple.

She forced herself to remain calm, though, because in spite of his failure to disclose his intentions, she felt confident she had the votes to reject any proposals based on Tate's recommendations. Between her, Edith and Mr. Takagi, their block was strong enough.

Upon his closing remarks, Hannah sought permission from the chairman to speak.

"Thank you, Tate, for that informative report and those interesting facts. However, I believe I have explained to you that Snowy Sky's focus will be a family-oriented, vacation-destination type of ski resort. Skiing is not a cheap endeavor for most families and a huge part of our draw is the large amount of beginner and intermediate ski runs, affordable rentals, lodging and food. We're not interested in attracting professional snowboarders and competitions, or replacing our prime ski runs with snowboard terrain. One half-pipe is at best cost prohibitive. Two half-pipes feels disproportionate. How would we pay for one? And where would this influx of snowboarders come from that we could possibly justify two?"

"Skiers use half-pipes now, too," he returned.

"Not the average skier."

"The practice is growing in popularity." He sounded completely confident and a little dismissive as he shifted his focus back to the screen. "If you look at these numbers I've compiled, you'll see…"

After he finished his rebuttal, the board began discussing his various recommendations and asking questions. The level of excitement in the air reminded Hannah of a high school pep rally.

Over the din, Tate flashed another smile at her. But this was a smile she hadn't seen before. One of satisfaction? She should have known he wasn't taking her seriously. She'd thought they were becoming friends, had even found herself pondering whether they could be more than that. Something she hadn't considered about anyone in nearly three years—not since the accident. Not since Spencer.

Park was beaming. He tried to catch her eye; she ignored him. But she couldn't ignore the enthusiastic sounds of the board members discussing the additional revenue competitions could bring. Yes, it would bring in revenue, she wanted to shout above the noise, but it would also add untold, unsound expense.

Tamping down her frustration, she reasonably pointed out, "Please keep in mind that accommodating competitions and snowboarders in this manner would be expensive and also result in keeping families and recreational skiers away."

"I don't agree," Park countered. "The expense would be offset by the revenue. It's pretty clear that we need these half-pipes." He referenced some of Tate's statistics and then went on in his annoyingly superior tone, "As board members, it should be our job to focus on ensuring the economic success of Snowy Sky in any way possible."

Edith chimed in from one of the monitors, "That does not include reckless spending, Mr. Lowell. In my opinion, Hannah and the board's existing and more conservative approach has a much better cost-to-benefit ratio."

Tate diplomatically added that implementing his recommendations would still leave more than adequate space for the "run-of-the-mill skier."

Run-of-the-mill? Hannah felt a spike of annoyance. "These run-of-the-mill skiers you're disparaging are going to be our bread and butter," she countered smoothly.

He lifted his hands, palms up. "That's fine. That's great. I'm not trying to insult anyone here. All I'm asking is why not aspire to more than just bread and butter?"

"I know I would," Park chimed in. "I'd like

some steak and lobster every now and then."
An overly loud guffaw made him sound like
the jerk she knew him to be.

More discussion ensued until Terry, the
board's chairman, suggested a special meeting be held in the near future to address Tate's
report. This would give everyone time to read
and fully digest the material. Any proposals
to take Snowy Sky in a "different direction"
could be presented at that time. They voted to
hold it the week after Christmas.

As the meeting progressed to other items,
she barely heard them because those words,
different direction, spliced together with his
commentary replayed in her head, each time
blurring her vision for Snowy Sky—her dream,
her goals, her life—a little bit more.

She felt light-headed.

Then the chairman spoke again, "Before we
adjourn, Park has requested time to bring up
a new issue."

All eyes turned toward Park who made a
show of clearing his throat. He seemed to have
a special smirk on his already smirk-filled
face. Hannah felt a fresh swirl of dread as he
began to speak.

"As we all know, during the finance and
construction Snowy Sky Ski Resort Incorpo-

rated has sold two blocks of shares to investment firms, each block being twelve percent of the total shares. The purchasers were Pop Bottle Inc. and L-DOG Investments. L-DOG has just purchased the shares owned by Pop Bottle, giving L-DOG twenty-four percent ownership. L-DOG is ultimately one hundred percent owned by Tate Addison who according to our bylaws is now entitled to a seat on the board."

He made a motion for Tate's tenure to begin immediately. It was seconded.

Hannah sat in stunned silence, even as she reeled internally. She suddenly felt invisible within her own company—the company she had created. The resort she was building. These events seemed absolutely surreal. Tate owned a quarter of Snowy Sky? How could this have happened? Why in the world would Tate want a share of Snowy Sky?

None of this made any sense.

Before Terry could proceed with the vote, a voice of reason called out from her monitor again.

"Point of order, Mr. Chairman?"

Fixing her eyes on the screen, focusing on the face of her dear friend Edith Milner, currently vacationing in the south of France,

Hannah prayed she could somehow stop this nightmare.

"Yes, Mrs. Milner?"

"According to our bylaws there is protocol to be followed as to the addition of new board members."

"But this is an exceptional case," Park returned confidently. "Surely we can forgo the normal vetting process here. As Tate is already involved in Snowy Sky, we can assume his motives are pure."

"Surely you're not suggesting we make an exception to a legally binding procedure based on personal recommendations, are you, Mr. Lowell? One of our many responsibilities as board members is to keep the threat of litigation to an absolute minimum."

Park looked flustered, and irritated.

Tate jumped in. "Not only do I think Mrs. Milner's point is valid, I look forward to working with someone as astute as she clearly is. I suggest the vote for my tenure be tabled until the next earliest convenience."

Edith's voice boomed from the monitor again. "That's a wonderful idea. I emailed you the section and paragraph number, Terry, pertaining to the procedure for adopting a new member. Please forward it to the other members, so that everyone may easily locate and review the information."

Hannah wondered how Edith had found it so quickly, but knowing her friend the way she did, she wouldn't be surprised to learn Edith had the bylaws memorized. She couldn't wait for their next Skype session.

The motion was made and passed. As the meeting concluded, Hannah looked at her watch, pretending that she had some place to be. Gathering up her belongings, she left quickly with brief comments to a couple people and waves of goodbye to a few more. Snow started to fall as she strode out the door and across the parking lot to her SUV. She climbed in, started the engine to defrost the windows and tried to decide what to do.

Instead of driving the short distance to her house, she turned down the hill toward town. She needed to think.

An idea formed in her mind and she pulled into the parking lot of the grocery store. By the time she left with two packages of comfort cookies and a sack of oranges, flakes were falling in earnest, but she didn't even consider aborting her plan. At this point her only real comfort seemed to be the thought that at least there was one thing Tate Addison couldn't take from her.

TATE PULLED HIS pickup into the heated garage of his rented home. Home. He took a moment to relish that thought; funny how the big house was already feeling exactly that way. When he'd signed the lease, he'd only viewed photos online.

The custom-built structure had turned out to be even more incredible than he'd imagined and yet somehow managed to maintain a cozy feel. He thought the log-cabin design and the amount of warm Alaskan cedarwood accents probably played a big part in accomplishing this atmosphere. Every time he walked through the door he counted his blessings that the house had become available.

Viktor was in the spacious kitchen preparing lunch. He enjoyed cooking and the skill was one of many domestic tasks that he'd insisted Tate learn so that he'd know how to take care of himself. Luckily for him, Viktor liked to cook more than he did, so often he did the shopping while Viktor prepared the meals.

He looked up as Tate walked in; his pale blue eyes alight with curiosity. "How did it go?"

"Good, I think." He set a box of doughnuts on the counter and handed over the brown paper bag. "Look what I found at the bakery in town. You're going to love that place if you haven't been there already."

Viktor peeked inside and then dipped his nose into the bag for a sniff. He reached in a hand and brought out a small chunk which he popped into his mouth.

"*This* is rye bread," he stated and then mumbled happily in his native Ukrainian. "Thank you, Tate. We will have some with our lunch."

Tate took a seat at one of the stools behind the bar directly across the black granite countertop from Viktor.

"Great reception from the board." He thought about Hannah and amended the statement, "Most of the board."

Viktor grinned. "Let me guess—your skier— she was not so pleased?"

My skier? He thought about how Adele had called him Hannah's snowboarder. He'd liked that. Now he realized that he'd likely annihilated any chance of that. The thought depressed him to a surprising degree.

Despite her brave face at the meeting, he could see that she'd been upset. How upset? He wasn't sure. She'd left too soon after the meeting for him to find out.

He snagged a piece of roast beef from the platter Viktor was assembling.

"No, she was not so pleased." He repeated Viktor's words with a grin of his own.

Viktor began slicing the deliciously pungent rye bread. After slathering a chunk with butter, he took a healthy bite, reminding Tate of Hannah's comment at the board meeting about skiers being the "bread and butter" of Snowy Sky. A niggle of guilt poked him. He reminded himself that guilt had no place in this scenario. He was doing this for Lucas.

"What will you do?" Viktor asked between mouthfuls.

Tate shrugged. "There's nothing I can do. She will eventually see that my recommendations make sense. She can't just ignore snowboarders. Well, maybe she can, but the board won't—not now. And if she doesn't like that, then I'll have to make her understand how much this venture means to me—to us. This is more than a business deal. This is my life. Lucas's life. Your life."

Tate could tell Viktor wanted to comment further, so he brought up a hand in a scooping motion, gesturing for his friend to say what was on his mind.

"I am thinking…wondering is it possible it means much to her, as well?"

He considered the question. "I haven't seen

any evidence of that, nor has she mentioned as much or even alluded to it. She's dedicated, for sure, but not *connected* to Snowy Sky in the way that I am now."

Hannah might not take life quite as seriously as Tate did, but he thought she'd make an excellent resort manager, if she could see reason where the snowboarding accommodations were concerned. If not, then maybe Snowy Sky wasn't the place for her. It wouldn't be the first time the project manager of a company was outvoted by her or his own board. For some reason that thought bothered him, too. He comforted himself again with the notion that she would come around in time.

Lucas strolled in from the next room with a remote control in his hands. A flash of red and silver zoomed past them and into the kitchen where a radio-controlled car spun a fast circle and skidded to a stop.

"Hi, Uncle Tate." Lucas skipped over and held his arms up so Tate could lift him for a hug. As he did, he felt that now-familiar burst of love unfurl in his chest.

"Hey, buddy."

Soon, Tate set him back on the floor.

Lucas stayed put. "Can you come to the fish room with me?"

"Sure, do you think the fairy woman might be there?"

His face brightened at the idea and then just as quickly dimmed. "She usually comes pretty early in the mornings, so I don't think so, but I want to tell you the names of all the kois."

"Sounds fun. I should probably know their names since we live with them, right?" He turned to Viktor. "How long till lunch?"

Viktor was chopping fruit for a salad and informed them they had a half hour. Tate checked the time on his watch and he and Lucas headed for the atrium.

CHAPTER SIX

HANNAH INHALED THE tangy scent of citrus as she quartered an orange, tossed it into the pond, and watched the happy koi pounce on the treat. A growl from her stomach reminded her that she hadn't eaten since her very early breakfast that morning. There had been doughnuts at the board meeting, but she'd been too edgy to eat. Turned out, her anxiety had been well placed.

Her spirits sank further as she realized how much Tate's ownership share and accompanying seat on the board would weaken her own position.

But why would he invest in Snowy Sky? Why would he want to be on the board of directors? He had tons of other business interests and plenty of money of his own.

Tossing in another wedge of fruit, she forced herself to take a deep breath. Leaning back on the bench, she began peeling an orange for herself and tried to think about something else. The ficus tree across the pond caught her eye and she thought of Lucas.

An absolutely adorable child, although there was something about him. Something not quite right. He seemed anxious and too serious for a six-year-old. Hearing the swoosh of the door, she turned, hoping to see Lucas's eager grin, which she did along with…

Tate?

Thoughts and questions tumbled through her brain; Lucas was Tate's son? She realized now how the resemblance had been skirting around in her brain—those eyes, the dark hair and the shape of their faces. Why hadn't she seen it sooner? Lucas had said his mom was dead, but that would make Tate a widower? She was sure she would have remembered if he'd ever been married.

Wait. Tate had leased Edith's home? This atrium, this house? Her sanctuary and refuge temporarily belonged to Tate? Did this also mean he intended to remain in Rankins for an entire year? No, that couldn't be. Hadn't he disrupted her plans—her life, enough already?

Lucas released Tate's hand and continued forward; Tate appeared to be frozen in place. Lucas galloped toward her and that seemed to snap him out of his shock, but he looked about as pleased as she felt.

"Careful, little man, I don't want you to slip and fall."

She was unhappily surprised, too, to put it mildly, but she pasted on a smile for Lucas's sake.

"Lucas, hey! How's my assistant koi keeper today?"

He replied, "I'm good. This is my uncle Tate. We were wondering if you could baby-sit me?" He gestured at Tate and then dipped his chin toward the oranges. "What are you doing with those?"

"Hello, Uncle Tate." Hannah quirked a brow at him. "Babysit?"

"I didn't realize who…that you were…Lucas said…"

She hoped her stare served to further stir his obvious discomfort. She adopted a bright, more genuine smile for Lucas. "I'm feeding the koi a nice healthy snack. These guys love oranges and other fruit, too."

He grinned, clearly not sure whether to believe her. "No way."

"Yes way, do you want to do me a favor and feed them some?"

"Sure," he answered. He picked up an orange. She quartered another, and handed it over. He tossed a portion into the pond and let out a giggle of delight as several fish glided through the water and set about nibbling on it. He slowly skirted around the pond, keeping an eye on the fish as he went. He slipped the whole orange he was carrying into a pocket.

Tate's voice held a note of wonder. "I had no idea you were the fish fairy."

"The what?"

He ran a hand through his trim black hair, shifting his weight from one foot to the other. Pre–board meeting the embarrassment would have been cute, but now it was just grating.

"The first time Lucas saw you he thought you were a fairy of some sort." His mouth formed a tentative smile. "So we've been calling you the fish fairy."

"That's sweet. He's a doll. Your nephew, huh?"

"Yes, he also, somehow, led me to believe, or I guess I assumed that you were a teenager, which is how the babysitting thing came to be." He added a tentative smile.

"I'd be happy to babysit Lucas anytime."

He looked surprised. "Oh, well, I don't really…"

A cynical chuckle slipped from her, but she

kept her voice low and even when she spoke. "You don't really what? It's not enough of an insult that you don't think I can run a ski resort, but now you're saying that you don't trust me with a six-year-old either?"

He narrowed his eyes, undoubtedly trying to gauge her level of sincerity. "No, I didn't say that."

She shot him a dry, questioning look.

"Okay, I can see you're upset about the board meeting. But, you need to understand something. First, all I am trying to do—"

"I understand perfectly," she interrupted, maintaining an overly cheerful pitch for Lucas's sake. "You're trying to steal my resort. The part I don't understand is why? And why didn't you tell me you were staying in Rankins? You've moved here?"

"Wait a minute. I'm not trying to *steal* Snowy Sky and I thought you knew I'd moved here. It's not like it's a secret."

Hannah didn't like talking about this in front of Lucas in spite of their civility.

"This isn't the time or place to discuss your attempted theft. We need to have this conversation later or I don't know—maybe we don't. I think I have a pretty good idea of what has transpired between you and Park."

"Hannah…"

She turned toward Lucas. "Lucas, thanks for helping me out with these guys."

He nodded. "It's neat how they like oranges."

"It is."

"Can I keep this one?" He pointed at the pocket of the hoodie he was wearing where he'd stuffed an orange.

"Sure. They're yummy. I just ate one. You can eat as many as you want."

"Thanks." His face evolved into a relieved grin.

"You're welcome. It was fun to hang out with you, kiddo. I need to get going, but maybe I'll see you tomorrow."

His shoulders slumped. "Do you have to leave already? Uncle Tate said I could show you my room." The mix of hope and disappointment got to her. There was something about this kid. How could she resist?

Her anger at Tate didn't extend to his nephew, she reminded herself. "I suppose I can stay a little longer. And I'd love to see your room."

His little leap of happiness strengthened her resolve.

In her periphery she saw Tate expel a breath

as if he, too, was relieved she'd acquiesced, which seemed kind of odd considering the current state of tension between them.

As she followed Lucas through the house, she took note of the not-so-subtle masculine reminders that Edith did not currently reside there; a toy car, a worn football, boots and tennis shoes in the foyer. A man's down ski jacket on the doorknob of a closet where Edith often hung her bag.

They ascended the wide, wooden staircase and traveled down the hall until Lucas stopped before a door to a room Edith had always kept ready for guests. He led the way inside. Hannah followed and could immediately see why he wanted to show it off.

"Awesome," she exclaimed in a way that she knew a six-year-old boy would appreciate, and that the effort clearly deserved.

Finding herself in the middle of a jungle, she slowly turned a circle. Scenes had been painted on each of the walls—a towering green canopy of trees complete with monkeys peeking from the branches and a sloth clinging to one mossy trunk. A river teeming with caimans and hippos stretched along one wall as a tapir grazed along the banks. Monkeys, bats, elephants, orangutans...

She spotted a jaguar peering out from a grassy tuft while a troop of baboons perched on an outcropping of rock.

"Wow."

"Viktor did it. He's the best artist ever. He did it so I wouldn't ever be alone in my room again. I like animals and I don't like being by myself for a really long time."

Tate placed a gentle hand on top of Lucas's head. "Neither one of us will be lonely anymore. Will we, buddy?"

She watched Lucas wrap an arm around Tate's leg. She wondered who this clever Viktor might be and noted she felt a raging curiosity regarding Tate and his nephew, too. What was the situation here? She pointed at a large, coiled and uncomfortably realistic, for her tastes anyway, rendition of a snake.

"Is that a green anaconda?"

"Yes! How did you know?"

"My cousin Janie is married to a scientist and he used to live in the jungle. He has a photo of one of these bad boys that would stretch clear across this room."

Lucas peered at her, curiosity stamped upon his face. She could tell he was trying to decide if she was teasing him. "Honest?"

"Honest," she assured him. "He lives in

Rankins now, but he still visits the jungle sometimes."

The look of longing on his face had her adding, "Maybe when I babysit you I can take you to his house and you can meet him? They have four boys you might like to meet, too."

She watched the light of yearning flick on in his eyes. Then just as quickly the excitement faded and he executed a light shrug as if to convey that it didn't really matter one way or the other. But Hannah knew it did. Because something about his demeanor reminded her of herself; it was the look of dashed hopes and broken dreams she'd been battling ever since her accident.

But precious Lucas was far too young to have experienced that kind of despair, which only made her more curious about what was going on here with this beautiful sad child and his beautiful sad uncle? Why was Lucas living with his uncle? And what could the wealthy and talented Tate Addison and his adorable nephew possibly have to feel sad and lonely about?

She opened her mouth to reassure Lucas that her word was good when a tall, pale man with sharp edges for cheekbones and dancing sky-blue eyes entered the room. A trim, muscled physique and close-cropped, thick blond hair belied his age, but she guessed him to be at least a decade older than Tate.

"She loves it, Viktor," Lucas informed him proudly.

"Ah, the incredibly talented Viktor. This room is a masterpiece. It's nice to meet you."

She reached out a hand and he shook it. He seemed humble and a bit embarrassed as many artists did when you admired their work. She asked about his accent and the inspiration for the scene, and as he explained, she found herself utterly charmed by his crooked smile and amiable demeanor. Was he related to Tate and Lucas? she wondered.

"Ukraine," he supplied when she asked about his origins. "I am from Ukraine. I was born in tiny village in Carpathian Mountains. Have you heard of these?"

"The Carpathian Mountains? Yes, there is a beautiful little ski resort there—Bukovel?"

His face broke into a huge grin. "I was born there—near Bukovel. Is where I learn to snowboard."

"No! Really? That place is gorgeous. I skied there years ago with a friend of mine. I remember this little town nearby—Dobshky, Doshke, or something like that? Anyway, there's a café there where they make pierogis that melt in your mouth. I still think about them sometimes."

He laughed and repeated the name properly, making it sound as pretty as the town she remembered. "I know this place," he said and added the name of the café that she knew. Then he went on to tell a funny story about how as a child he and a friend had stolen a cake from the woman who owned the café.

She would place the pastries near an open window to cool and it seemed like torture for him and his friend who would walk by and be assaulted by the rich, buttery, fruit-laden smells day after day. Finally, after much preparation, they formulated an elaborate plan and snitched one.

"What happened?" she asked, thoroughly entertained by the tale.

"Obviously, we get caught and then have to clean her shop for two weeks to pay for cake. But it turned out to be wonderful experience. She feeds us so much goodies and as bonus, I learn how to cook and make the pierogis."

"No way," she said.

He nodded proudly. "Yes, I make for you sometime. Lukie, he love pierogi, too. You come next week for dinner?"

Lucas gaped in happy wonder at Viktor as though he'd just had the best idea in the entire world. Then he looked eagerly toward Hannah, awaiting her answer.

She shot Tate her best wide-eyed, "how can we get out this?" expression but he answered with a shrug and a decidedly unhelpful, "Sounds fun. Make sure you show up hungry because I would pull my own tooth for one of Viktor's pierogis."

"Sure," she said cheerfully, feeling honored and itchy and trapped all at the same time. "Dinner would be lovely."

CHAPTER SEVEN

THE COZY CARIBOU made the best waffles in the world. Especially when smothered in peanut butter, sliced bananas and chopped pecans. Hannah crumbled two strips of bacon on top and added a drizzle of birch breakfast syrup to the pile as she thought about canceling dinner. She picked up her phone and stared at the screen, trying to compose a suitable text excuse when Park Lowell slunk onto the seat beside her.

"That's an awful lot of carbs for a fitness freak like you. Comfort carbs? That board meeting upset you, huh? Need a tissue?"

She slowly lowered her phone to give Park a glare. She'd heard him called "cute" by some of the women in town, but she absolutely could not see it. With those close-set piercing eyes, small sharp nose and thin lips, he reminded her of a rodent.

She refused to let him get to her now when he clearly had the means to. "Park, you do realize the fastest route to getting your butt kicked by a woman is to make assumptions about how she'll react in a given situation, right?"

"She is right about that, Park," Adele said, sliding onto the stool on the other side of Hannah. Adele had ordered the fisherman's special—two eggs, bacon and a giant flaky buttermilk biscuit smothered in country gravy. The waitress set the plate in front of her along with a large orange juice. She and Adele were going snowshoeing after breakfast. They needed the calories.

She glanced at Park and stabbed a huge piece of waffle. "Did you need something? Or did you just stop by to try to ruin my morning? Because it won't work. You are nothing more than an annoying little gnat in the vast and beautiful wilderness that is my life." She shoved the entire bite into her mouth and chewed ungracefully.

He looked momentarily disgusted before placing a hand on his chest and saying with mock sincerity, "That is the most poetic insult anyone has ever paid me, Hannah." His tone shifted into smug seriousness, "I'm meeting Tate Addison for breakfast. We're going to work on our proposal."

He puffed out his chest like a cartoon pigeon, which had her desperately wanting to be the woman to implement that much-needed butt kicking.

Instead she scoffed and added, "That's great. I'm so glad you found yourself a tutor. Don't stay out past curfew, though, or your mommy might get upset."

Laughter erupted around them and the postman, Ralph Simpke, who was enjoying a pile of scrambled eggs and ham at the counter said, "She's got you there, Park."

Rumor had it that Park had come to Alaska to stay with his mom because he'd gotten himself into some financial trouble down in the lower forty-eight. The buzz from Hannah's gossip-loving friend Piper Davidson who worked at the town's newspaper was that Park's investment in Snowy Sky had been bankrolled by Mama Lowell. To whom Park now owed his soul. A fact she purportedly did not let him forget.

Hannah felt a tiny bit sorry for Park in this regard because Dixie Lowell was an overbearing, controlling woman who was difficult for most anyone to get along with on the best of days.

"Okay, that's funny. I'll give you that one."

Park tried to sound easygoing about the comment, but his body language assured her that he thought it anything but.

She mimicked his earlier gesture and placed a hand over her heart. "Thank you, Park, it means the world to me that you *get* me."

He stood and tugged on the waistband of his already unflatteringly high-waisted khakis. "Enjoy your breakfast, ladies. And, Hannah, you might want to prepare yourself for total humiliation in front of the board." He added a pompous cackle.

"Thanks for the warning. Hey, Park, maybe you could give me some tips on how to do that? Because you know what that's like, don't you? Total humiliation?"

He stalked off, muttering what she assumed was an insult of some kind, but which she hadn't quite heard due to the volume of laughter that had arisen around them.

"Wow, he is such a…" Adele fought for a word as Park disappeared into the dining area.

"Weasel?" Hannah happily supplied.

Adele laughed. "That's perfect. What is his problem with you anyway? It seems over the top. Like an elementary school kid with a crush."

"That's definitely not it."

She sipped her hot chocolate. "Aside from the fact that he's threatened by me because I'm frankly smarter and more athletic than he is?" she paused for dramatic effect.

"That might be enough," Adele answered flatly, before filling her own mouth with biscuit and gravy.

Hannah poured another dollop of syrup over her plate. "It could be, but it gets worse. To answer your question—he once made a bet with me—right here in the Cozy Caribou. He lost his pride and five hundred dollars in front of all his friends. He's never gotten over it."

"Five hundred dollars? Hannah…" Adele stopped talking and quirked a brow in her direction.

"What?"

"You better be careful."

She chuckled. "What do you mean?"

"I mean, my dear cousin—hell hath no fury like a man such as that being made a fool of in front of his friends." She waited a beat, then added, "And especially when the man is clearly threatened by *you*, woman."

They both looked up as Tate came through the doorway on the opposite side of the restaurant. He waved. Adele waved back.

Hannah lifted a hand, too. "Now, he's the one who should feel threatened right now, Adele—by me."

TATE SWUNG BY the hardware–sporting goods–computer repair shop, which also contained a nice selection of home goods for such a small town.

"Hey, Tate! How's it going, man?"

He extended a hand to the teenage clerk he'd befriended on previous visits. "Pretty good, Ian. How are you?"

Tate enjoyed how he was already getting acquainted with the people in Rankins. He was beginning to feel like a real member of the community.

Gloves were on sale, so he picked out another pair for Lucas, knowing from his own experience that boys could never have too many gloves.

"Getting some gear there, I see."

"Yep, gonna get Lucas up on a board pretty soon."

"Cool. Little dude will most assuredly have your skills. He looks just like you."

Tate appreciated how no one in Rankins seemed to care about his past beyond chatting like Ian did. No one treated him any differently, and that was what he'd been hoping for.

Not that he was all that famous outside the world of snow sports, but he had done some endorsements. It wasn't unusual for people to recognize him or ask for an occasional autograph.

"Let's hope so. I'd also like to take home a few more Christmas decorations if you've got any left. The Milner house is a lot bigger than it seems."

"We've got 'em. I just moved them over to this side of the store to make room for the New Year's stuff. Are you going to the Cozy Caribou on New Year's? Awesome band playing. Rushing Tide, have you heard of them? They're from here."

"I have," he answered. Tate loved music and they discussed the party-concert the restaurant would be hosting that night. Ian helped him choose a stuffed snowman and a plush reindeer to add to Lucas's Christmas collection, as well as three more strings of lights and some sparkly snowflakes that Viktor had requested.

They chatted about fishing while Ian rang him up.

"I almost forgot I need fishing line. Viktor

said he'd use it to hang the plastic snowflakes from the ceiling. Where do you keep that?"

Ian directed him to the back of the store, where he quickly retrieved a spool of line. He'd never ventured this deeply into the store before and on the back wall he noticed a sign that read Rankins Wall of Greats. Floor to ceiling, the entire space was devoted to the successes of local athletes—photos, articles, awards. A trophy-covered shelf ran the entire length of the wall.

His eye was soon drawn to the largest framed photograph; Hannah standing on the top spot of a podium, gold medal hanging around her neck. He couldn't help noticing that her smile was dazzling even in photos.

Thinking he recognized the resort in the background, he stepped closer and read the year and the event. Only three years ago? Hmm.

He had assumed she'd quit skiing because she'd burned out or had realized that she wasn't quite good enough to compete at the elite level. Obviously that wasn't the case if she'd won this particular competition where he knew the best of the best competed. Why in the world had she quit skiing?

He spotted several photos of a young, winning Hannah. Other members of the James family were also displayed in various athletic endeavors—basketball, football, baseball, track and field. The James family held some athletic genes, and Rankins was obviously proud of its athletes, as it should be, Tate thought. There were a few photos of him scattered around his little hometown in Colorado, too.

He made his way back to the register. "Sorry, I was checking out your wall back there. Love it."

Ian nodded proudly. "Mr. Bradbury—the owner, he's a huge supporter of community sports and stuff. He's awesome like that."

"Do you know why Hannah James quit skiing?"

Ian combined a grimace with a nod and supplied, "Injury. Major bummer. She was wicked good. Hannah is the coolest. She was—"

The phone rang. He glanced at the display and said, "Speaking of my boss. Do you mind?" He pointed at the phone.

"Not at all," Tate answered.

Injury, huh? He silently speculated about how bad it had to have been that she'd quit the sport completely. He wanted to ask, but he could tell this call was going to take a while.

He paid, then waved goodbye to a still-talking Ian and decided to stop at Snowy Sky on his way home. He suddenly had an urge to speak to Hannah. Surely she'd had time to calm down and think things through by now.

OF COURSE SHE had to be on the roof. Clearly, the woman had no concern for her own safety, making him wonder again about the accident that had caused her retirement.

Tate felt a strange mix of amusement and fear as he watched her shoveling the snow from the roof. Freddie was on the opposite end, both of them working their way toward the middle of the building. He took a moment to appreciate her lithe, graceful movements before she caught him watching.

Pausing for a few seconds, she seemed to be talking to herself. She went back to scooping.

He moved closer until he was standing next to the ladder they had propped up against the building.

"Hey," he called. "I know you saw me. What are you doing?"

"Baking cookies," she replied sarcastically. "What does it look like I'm doing?" Freddie's laughter drifted down to him.

Okay, clearly he needed a new approach. "Can I come up and talk to you for a minute?"

Rustling ensued and then her face appeared above him, gold-brown eyes staring down at him from beneath her stocking cap. She looked so pretty with her cheeks tinged pink from the cold. But her scowl, clearly directed at him? Not so pretty.

"No. What do you need?"

"Why are you up there shoveling snow? It's dangerous."

She scowled more fiercely. "Oh, so I should pass all the dangerous jobs off on someone else?"

Her logic had a way of making him feel so...dense.

"I just don't want you falling off or something."

"How sweet," she drawled out the word before rolling her eyes and adding, "I'm not reckless. Freddie and I are both wearing harnesses. Did you stop by to lecture me on my safety again? Because I can assure you, my shoveling snow doesn't concern you."

This wasn't going the way he'd anticipated. He needed to change tactics. "You know that Festival of Trees?"

"Uh-huh."

"What do I wear to an event like that? I forgot to ask when I RSVP'd and the flier doesn't say. Do people usually dress up?"

"They *usually* do, yes. But I'm not sure if you have the right clothes for—"

"I'll figure something out—" he interrupted. "Hannah, I didn't really come here to talk to you about that. I was just… If you could spare a few minutes I'd like to go over what happened at the board meeting."

"I don't see the point."

"I do." He went on before she could argue, "You probably don't believe this, but I only want what's best for Snowy Sky. And for Lucas, for my family. My recommendations make perfect sense and if you would take the time to get past your disdain for snowboarding you would see that. You're a smart woman and—"

She let out an impatient sigh. "Don't patronize me. I know I'm smart. And I have no *disdain* for snowboarding. I just don't think it's necessary to structure the resort around it, not to mention take on the added expense, which we clearly interpret differently. But what does any of this have to do with Lucas or your family?"

"Would you please come down here so I can explain?"

"Explain what? How you ambushed me? I may be young, I may not have a college education, I may not *look* the part of a businesswoman to you, but my only mistake was in giving you the benefit of the doubt and believing your Mr. Nice Guy routine."

"Mr. Nice Guy routine? I wasn't… Would you please listen to reason?"

"Reason? I thought you were just giving your opinion? I thought that's what you were hired to do—consult. Give your opinion. But I guess that was before you decided to take over my resort, which in essence answers your question about why I'm not reasonable on this topic. Snowy Sky is mine."

An exasperated sigh escaped him. "Except, that it's also mine now, too. And a few others', as well. All of whom should have a say in what happens with it."

"You've already had plenty to say. And I haven't stopped you from saying any of it, have I? In fact, I kind of helped you out there. A heads-up would have been nice, you know? I wasn't anything but accommodating to you. And then you stabbed me in the back."

"Stabbed you in the back?" he repeated incredulously. "I did not… That's ridiculous. If you would have asked me what I was going to bring to the board I would have told you. In fact, I was a little surprised you didn't. That confirmed my initial impression that you were rather ambivalent about the whole thing and I…" His neck hurt so he looked toward the side of the building as he kept explaining.

When he looked back up again she'd disappeared.

"Hannah?" he called out, only to be hit directly between the eyes with a snowball. He sputtered and took a step to the side, wiping his face before looking up again. "Did you just hit me with a snowball?"

She peeked over the side of the roof. "Yes, I did. Anything ambivalent about that, Tate?"

HANNAH WATCHED HIM walk away, already regretting the spontaneous display of temper. Dr. Voss would not be pleased by her loss of control. He would remind her that such a demonstration was counterproductive. But ambivalent? How could he…? She couldn't possibly have given off that impression, could she?

She flung a shovel full of snow off the roof, and then another, hoping the physical exertion would calm her down.

She couldn't get past how wrong she'd been about him and the job he'd been hired to do. So much for the here today, gone tomorrow visit that she'd hoped for.

What was she going to do?

"Hannah, are you okay?"

She looked up to find Freddie watching her intently.

"No. I mean, yes. Yes, I'm fine." But she wasn't. No, she wasn't fine at all.

CHAPTER EIGHT

To say he felt conspicuous would be a dramatic understatement. Complete idiot would probably suffice, Tate decided as he wandered around the room in his nicest suit. He'd even worn a tie. A cursory perusal of the crowd gathered in the Faraway Restaurant's dining room for the Festival of Trees fund-raiser hadn't revealed a single other tie-wearing individual, unless you counted the giant plush Christmas bear sitting on the prize table with a red satin bow crookedly positioned around his neck.

Studying the crowd, he realized that overdressed didn't exactly describe the manner in which his attire was lacking. He'd specifically asked, but Hannah hadn't mentioned that he was supposed to wear...

"Hey, why does Addison get to wear regular clothes?" Jonah Cedar, Shay's husband and Hannah's brother-in-law, flipped a thumb in Tate's direction. Jonah was wearing a blue and silver sweater featuring Rudolph sporting his own tiny Christmas sweater and holding an American flag. Tate decided the only sweater worse than Jonah's was the one Hannah's cousin-in-law Aidan Hollings was wearing.

His sweater was red, white and green with little yellow-and-black bees all over it. A giant bee with a kind of demented grin graced the front. The bee was wearing a Santa hat and holding a candy cane in each of his front— what did you call them on a bee? Legs?

Shay studied Jonah with narrowed eyes. "Obviously Tate's not participating in the contest. Give him a break—he's new in town."

"Or he didn't want to humiliate himself."

"Jonah—"

Jonah interrupted with a grin and an "I love you, Shay."

Shay moved closer to her husband as Tate marveled at how her expression went from mild irritation to goofy love struck in an instant.

"Participating in what?" Tate asked.

Bering James, Hannah's cousin and the owner of James Guide and Outfitter Service let out a hearty chuckle. He pointed at his own kitschy-looking knitwear, featuring a moose with a bright string of Christmas lights tangled in its antlers.

"There is an ugly Christmas sweater contest tonight. A lot of us guys are happy about it because it means we didn't have to dress up in monkey suits like yours—no offense."

Tate executed an easy shrug. "None taken."

"A number of the women," Bering continued, "like to see us—for some crazy reason—strung up in fancy garb. Folks don't have much of a chance to dress up around here. Weddings, funerals, and the Rotary Club fundraiser were pretty much it until the festival began last year."

"Ah, I see. I wasn't aware…"

Jonah chimed in, "Yeah, well, consider yourself lucky."

"What's the prize?"

"I don't know exactly. A basket of Christmas stuff maybe?" Bering gestured toward one side of the room where the table with the Teddy bear also held assorted colorful gift bags and cellophane-wrapped baskets for which Tate had purchased raffle tickets when he'd first arrived.

Hannah's brother Tag jumped in. "If you win you get to choose from any basket up there, but it's not really about the prize. It's about—"

Tate thought he understood. It was about supporting your community—helping, participating and not caring about looking silly for a good cause.

"Community pride?" he asked.

"No. Cake," Jonah quipped. "I mean, yes, community pride is important but—"

"Baked goods are a close second around here," Bering said, "especially where my wife is concerned."

Aidan joined them looking extra ridiculous in not only the bee Christmas sweater but also Christmas—could you call those pants? Tate had never seen Christmas-themed pants on a man before and they appeared to be made out of velvet or some other weird fabric. He also had a pair of felt antlers positioned on his head. Tate thought he should win for that alone.

Bering explained, "People really want to win because the winner also gets a cake baked by Lilah. Lilah Brooke from the Donut Den. Have you met Lilah?"

"I've met the Donut Den."

Bering chuckled. "Then you understand."

"Indeed. I bet that's some cake."

Then Tag asked him, "You do know about the tree auction, though, right?"

Tate did know about that. Various businesses, organizations and individuals had donated decorated Christmas trees, which had been displayed throughout the Faraway Inn for the past week. After dinner the trees would be auctioned off one by one. The winning bidder of each tree would also be treated to delivery and set up of the Christmas tree they'd purchased.

After his botched attempt to ask Hannah out at the inn, he'd learned the trees were on display and brought Lucas to have a look. His nephew had been quaking with excitement, hustling from one decorated masterpiece to the next.

The tree donated by James Guide and Outfitter Service was covered with tiny hand-carved canoes and paddles. A tree featuring silly cats had made Lucas laugh hysterically. The one from the Faraway Inn was hung with moose and bear ornaments along with tiny impressively realistic replicas of the inn.

But it was the tree donated by an equipment hauling company that had left Lucas in a state of speechless awe. It was covered with little dozers, track hoes, cranes, trucks, and other equipment and vehicles in various shapes and sizes. All made as scale models and of superior, and obviously expensive, quality.

Tate planned to win that tree.

HANNAH ENTERED THE dining room and spotted Tate immediately. He wasn't the only man in the room who wasn't wearing an ugly sweater, but he was the only one in a suit. She wished she would have told him to wear a sweater because his tall, fit form looked way too good in that flattering, charcoal-colored ensemble with a tie. A silver-and-white snowflake-embossed tie no less.

With his black hair neatly tousled across his forehead, he was extraordinarily good-looking and a little intimidating. And probably more than slightly irritated with her.

Talking and laughing as he was with her brother, cousins and friends, anyone would think he'd lived here in Rankins forever. Except that he stuck out like a sore thumb. He could have been going to the opera or to a formal wedding instead of a Rankins fund-raiser.

She hadn't seen him since she'd pelted him with the snowball. After she'd had some time to calm down, she felt an apology might be in order. That didn't mean she wanted to take back what she'd said, however, but she would apologize for the snowball.

Might as well get this over with, she thought, and bravely headed his way. His purposeful stride in her direction told her he'd been waiting. The cool, intent look on his face agitated the butterflies already swarming in her stomach.

"Hello, Tate. You look very handsome, for a snowboarder."

"Thank you, Hannah. You on the other hand look just as festively silly as everyone else in the room. Everyone except for me that is."

She glanced down at her own holiday-themed tunic-style sweater she'd paired with wool leggings and tall shiny leather boots. She'd added a necklace and earring set constructed of tiny twinkling Christmas lights. She forced out an awkward laugh. "Thank you."

"Why didn't you tell me about the ugly-sweater thing? I specifically asked you if people dress up."

"No, you asked if they *usually* dress up, and usually they do. This year is different because of the ugly-sweater contest. Honestly, I didn't really expect you to attend. I assumed you were just being polite." She offered another explanation, "Besides, I wouldn't want you to feel awkward—"

"Really?" he returned flatly, obviously not believing her lame excuses. "I appreciate that, I really do because there's nothing at all awkward about wearing an expensive suit in a room full of blue jeans and goofy sweaters. I'm trying to fit in here in Rankins in case you haven't noticed."

She tried to quash her guilt. "Tate, it's a contest for community members to—"

"Of which I'm not?"

"You are, temporarily, I suppose."

He smiled tightly. "Maybe you should accept the fact that I'm here to stay?"

The words flew out of her mouth before she could stop them. "I will accept that around the same time I accept the recommendations you've made for Snowy Sky."

"Hannah—"

Interrupting with her hands, palms up in a conciliatory gesture, she said, "Okay, I'm sorry. I wasn't going to get into this again. I want to apologize for the snowball. I don't lose my temper very often."

"Good, because I don't want to fight with you either."

Something hitched in her chest as his voice

went low and smooth and his eyes were pinned on hers.

"Quite the opposite in fact."

Her face went hot and her pulse began to pound fast and hard, because the opposite of fighting was...

He brought his hands up to tug on his lapels and his voice went flat. "But this kind of passive-aggressive behavior isn't going to change anything where Snowy Sky is concerned, you know that, right? Passive-aggressive behavior is, at its very core, unproductive."

Her eyes widened and she took a step backward as embarrassment mingled with a twinge of remorse. "Thank you for that insight into my psyche, Dr. Addison. I'll be sure and let Dr. Voss know he has some competition."

"Who?"

She tapped a finger to her forehead, regretting the mention of her therapist. "Never mind."

He whooshed out a noisy breath. "Maybe I deserved this somewhat. I can see where I could have handled things differently, where maybe I misread you. But I'm thinking, if we're going to disagree over the future of Snowy Sky, why don't we just do that?"

She stared blandly and gave her head a little shake. She thought that was precisely the problem.

He added, "Let's lay it all out on the table. Literally."

"What are you getting at?"

"At the special board meeting, we'll both present our ideas and arguments. Give it our best shots and accept whatever the outcome might be."

She narrowed her eyes suspiciously. "How is that any different than what we're already doing?"

"Well…it's not really, I guess." He pulled a shoulder up into a shrug and then added a boyish grin. "Except maybe in our attitudes?"

Hannah squinted menacingly because clearly he meant *her* attitude. *Who's being passive-aggressive now?* she wanted to ask, but he kept talking.

"I like you, Hannah, in spite of our differing opinions. And Lucas is obviously crazy about you and that means so much to me."

"He's a great kid."

"I think so, too, even with everything… So I feel like I should tell you, I intend to have my way where Snowy Sky is concerned. You see, this is about more than business to me. This venture means so much and I…"

She stared. Was he serious with this shtick? This audaciousness? Calling Snow Sky a venture? Her dream, her salvation, her chance to finally make something of herself and her life—a *venture*?

Her pulse pounded in her head for a different, far less pleasant reason now, but she managed to keep her tone level. "Are you somehow implying that it doesn't mean a lot to me? Because I can assure you that it does."

"No, not at all. I can see how much work you've put into Snowy Sky. I just… I don't want you to think that I'm taking it lightly. The resort is coming along nicely, but it could be a phenomenal place. And that's what *I'm* trying to achieve."

Her jaw dropped open.

Later she would be grateful to the mayor, because he was the only thing that saved her from losing her temper with Tate Addison in front of the entire town.

Mayor Cummings stepped up to the microphone, grinning from ear to ear. The ugly-sweater contest had been his idea and undoubtedly he was pleased as punch with the buzz he'd created. After thanking the donors, the volunteers, Shay and the staff at the Faraway Inn who were donating their time for tonight's event, and praising various other deserving individuals, he finally announced the winner.

The crowd erupted with clapping and cheers as a beaming, antler-wearing Aidan popped out of his chair and jogged forward to accept his prize, which included the first annual "Ugly Christmas Trophy"—a weird-looking doll wearing its own ugly sweater that Hannah had to laugh at.

The mayor then recommended that everyone take their seats as servers suddenly appeared and began placing meals in front of the patrons. The auction was scheduled to begin immediately after the meal, so she made her way to the table where her parents were already seated, along with Tag, Adele, Shay and Jonah, Jonah's grandfather Caleb, and his friend Doc.

As luck would have it, she had a perfect view of Tate at the table next to theirs where he was chatting away with Janie, Aidan, Bering, Emily and Cricket.

Tate appeared enthralled by the events of the evening, completely at ease in his beautiful gray suit. Hannah was a bit irritable and distracted, which just made matters worse because she really didn't do irritable and distracted very well.

The bidding began as dessert was being served. As usual, she was blown away by the extent of support in the community. Jonah's grandfather bid an exorbitant amount on a tree donated by Bradbury's that was covered entirely in fishing gear.

As the next tree was wheeled into place beside the mayor, he announced.

"Can I get one hundred dollars for this amazing tree donated by Revel Heavy Equipment and Hauling?"

She saw Tate's hand shoot up. Bering also began bidding against him as well as a few other patrons. As the bidding continued it was apparent that Tate was very determined to get the win.

She picked up her phone to text her friend Piper who hadn't attended tonight due to a mild case of strep throat. Hannah knew she was home marathon-watching the last season of *Mad Men*.

She wrote: Put Don Draper on pause. I've got a job for you.

Passive-aggressive, huh? Tate hadn't seen anything yet.

CHAPTER NINE

THE NEXT MORNING Tate lounged on the sofa in the living room and contentedly admired their new Christmas tree. He'd had to pay mightily for the toy-covered creation.

"How much for tree?" Viktor asked as he came in from the kitchen and joined him on the sofa. Tate could already smell the cinnamon from the muffins he was baking.

"A lot." He grimaced and relayed the story of how he'd thought he was going to win it for far less until the mayor announced that a call-in bidder was on the line. Bering and a couple others had initially been in the mix but when the phone bidder entered the arena, an all-out bidding war had ensued.

Tate had been so happy to win that he'd tacked on an extra donation for the hospital. Last night had marked his first ever auction. If it hadn't been for such a good cause, and the perfect tree for Lucas, for the first time in his life he might have regretted his competitive spirit.

But any such thoughts had been banished when the tree had been delivered early that morning and set up by an industrious crew of Faraway Inn employees. It was fantastic and he could not wait for Lucas to see it.

"Worth every penny," Viktor responded. "This is what you work so hard for, for so many years. You can have and give Lukie whatever you want."

"You worked just as hard," Tate responded, his way of letting Viktor know how much his belief and dedication had meant to him all of these years.

Viktor grinned. "Yes, and I enjoy tree, too. It looks nice there."

"I thought about having them put it in the foyer, but I like this room. This is where we always end up, and I want Lucas to be able to enjoy it as much as possible."

Large windows stretched from nearly floor to ceiling in the living room, showcasing a snow-covered wilderness view worthy of an oil painting. A huge, cushy U-shaped sofa took up miles of space while a large stone fireplace made up most of the interior wall.

Lucas shuffled sleepily into the room, a puffy panda bear tucked under his arm.

His eyes lit on the tree and he froze.

"The tree." He whispered the words as he studied the lit creation, the toy trucks and equipment reflecting the colorful twinkling lights. "It's… Uncle Tate, it's that tree."

He turned to look at Tate.

"Yep, it's that tree. That's our Christmas tree. What do you think?"

He faced it again and his tiny shoulders slumped.

"What's wrong, buddy?"

"We'll give it back after Christmas, right?"

"No, we get to keep it. You get to keep all the toys hanging on it, too. They're yours."

"For how long?"

"Forever."

He tipped his head skeptically as if he couldn't quite believe it. Then he turned beseeching eyes on Tate, who could tell how desperately the child wanted to believe his words.

"Really?" the boy asked.

"Yes, Lucas. Really." Then he added, "I promise."

He scampered toward Tate and crawled up onto his lap. He wrapped his skinny arms around Tate's neck and held on. Tate was reminded of Lexie. He battled with the guilt as he hugged him in return; comforted in the notion he would always be here for Lucas and could always keep him safe.

"It's the best tree ever," Lucas said.

"Listen, you can play with those trucks, all you want. And then after Christmas we'll put them in your room upstairs."

He pulled away, stared at the tree for a few seconds and finally scooted off his lap. He handed Tate the bear "for safekeeping" and walked toward the tree.

Tate's memories of Christmas before Viktor had come into his life were pretty stark. Penny would give him a second-hand toy of some kind and mostly leave him alone.

He hadn't really realized what he was missing out on until he was older. And by then, he and Viktor had begun their own traditions. They were always together, but usually traveling over the holidays. They would venture out to most often the ski village they happened to be staying in and buy enough candy and small, silly gifts to fill each other's stockings. Viktor would make crispy fried latkes and brew his special hot cider. They'd tell stories, crack jokes and meet up with as many friends as they could, not to mention Viktor's family when they were close enough to visit Ukraine.

He was grateful for every moment, and now he was determined to start some traditions for Lucas.

Lucas tentatively removed an ornament from its position on the tree, trailing his fingers over the shiny yellow surface. "This one's a backhoe," he informed Viktor.

"How does that one work?" Viktor asked.

Lucas moved closer to show him.

Tate didn't want to spoil Lucas too much, but he wanted him to have a real Christmas— a truly happy Christmas fit for a six-year-old who'd never had a stable family or a real home. How, he wondered, did he do that? The family and the home bit? For some reason the thought coalesced in his brain that Hannah would undoubtedly know exactly what to do.

THE DOORBELL RANG at her parents' house where Hannah and some of the family had gathered to help with holiday preparations.

"Mom, where do you want the tree?" Hannah called out. She'd answered the door and motioned the tree-delivery crew inside.

Last night, her parents had purchased the tree Snowy Sky had donated to the auction. But Hannah's mom, Margaret, already had a tree decorated with the traditional assortment of family ornaments. Even though they were all grown, Margaret insisted on hanging every ornament her children had ever made over the years. With six kids, there were enough Popsicle-stick, cotton-ball and canning-jar-lid creations to fill nearly every inch of the nine-foot tree.

Her triplet siblings, Hazel, Iris, and Seth, were home from college for the holidays and also helping to finish the decorating. Later, her mom, Hazel and Iris were going to do some baking. She planned to do some sampling. Shay was coming over to hang out, too, and they were going to plan the menu for the Christmas Eve bash her parents held every year.

Margaret gestured at the volunteer crew, Ian, who worked at Bradbury's, and Nick, a part-time busboy from the Faraway Inn. "We're going to put this tree in the family room. Your father and Seth just moved the foosball table downstairs for the holidays. They've got a space all ready for it."

"Nice. Okay, guys, this way." Hannah motioned at the two teenagers.

She followed. They passed the stairway where Hazel and Iris were now busy giggling and hanging lighted garland along the rail of the landing that stretched across the second floor. Ian nearly ran into the wall, he was so busy gawking at her sisters.

"Careful there, Romeo," she muttered as she reached out and snagged him by the back of the shirt, righting his path before he fell over. Clearly embarrassed, he slipped her a grateful grin.

They continued to their destination where Hannah noticed a mound of boxes piled high, a looming symbol of her next task.

"Do you want the entire village set up, Mom?" She calculated her mom's miniature Christmas village took up roughly two acres of space. Her dad and Tag had constructed special tables for the village years ago.

"Yes, your dad and Seth are getting the tables out of the storage room right now."

"How about just the core of the downtown area this year? The cute shops and town square?"

"Hannah, you know it doesn't look right without the country church, the school and all the houses. Not to mention the farm and the ice-skating pond."

"Okeydokey, farm it is," she muttered. She steeled herself for a very long day. Sometimes her mother's decorations felt a bit excessive, sometimes Christmas festivities in general felt a little over the top to her. But it meant a lot to her mom and really, she couldn't imagine Christmas without her mom's enthusiasm. She made Christmas special for everyone, especially Christmas Eve.

She watched the boys setting up the new tree and smiled to herself as she thought about the tree Tate had won. He'd set a record with his purchase. The "mystery bidder" had sure kept things interesting.

Hannah had been texting Piper the entire time, encouraging her to keep bidding no matter how high it got. Hannah knew Tate would bid whatever it took, so it was a win-win as far as she was concerned. Lucas would have an awesome Christmas tree, the hospital would have the added windfall and Hannah had a bit of satisfaction. In fact, she thought with a grin, that technically made it a win-win-win.

CHAPTER TEN

IN THE END Hannah couldn't bring herself to cancel dinner at Tate's. Each time she had picked up her phone, Lucas's hope-filled expression flashed through her mind. She couldn't do that to Lucas, or to Viktor for that matter. She'd seen Lucas in the atrium several mornings in a row. Tate had joined them a few times, but they hadn't spoken about anything business related. She was fine with that.

The special board meeting had been scheduled for two days after Christmas. With the ease of teleconferencing, the general consensus had been to hold the meeting as soon as possible after the holiday. She couldn't shake the sense of foreboding as she suspected this meant board members were eager to begin initiating Tate's "new direction."

She'd been spending extra hours coming up with a response to counter the proposal she predicted Tate and Park were going to present. She wasn't sure exactly how they would structure it, but as Tate had pointed out their intentions weren't really a secret.

The biggest, most expensive changes concerned adding the half-pipe and the snowboarding terrain. After speaking with their accountant, she believed she had stumbled on the avenue with the most promise to shut them down.

Pulling into the driveway of Edith's house—she still couldn't quite think of it as Tate's—she gave herself a quick pep talk. After gathering up the shopping bag from the backseat, she headed for the porch where a beaming Lucas opened the door before she could even knock.

Tate stood behind him, all gorgeous male in a pair of worn jeans and a blue flannel button-down shirt that made his eyes shine like cobalt glass. She loved cobalt glass. And the hopeful, somewhat repentant look on his face that seemed to be asking her not to be mad at him made it difficult to retain that emotion.

She was terrible at holding a grudge. Also, the striking child with black hair that matched his uncle's, who was quickly stealing her heart, didn't help matters either. Especially when he was standing in front of her, bouncing excitedly on his toes like a tiny boxer before a fight.

He reached for her hand. "Hannah, come

and see our Christmas tree. You're not going to believe it. It's so great."

"Perfect, because I have a gift for you to put under your tree."

"For me?" His tone held surprise, and his shy, hope-filled expression had her wondering if he was not used to getting gifts? How could that possibly be the case with Tate as his uncle? The love he felt for his nephew was obvious and his generosity evident.

"Yes, my young sir, for you."

Lucas led her straight to the tree and she pretended as though she didn't already know that Tate had won the tree at the auction. She exclaimed about its beauty and then spent several minutes examining the toy decorations and quizzing Lucas about the various pieces of equipment hanging from the branches.

"When I get done playing with them, I put them back on the tree. But after Christmas is over, then I get to put them all in my room. It's a lot of toys, but Uncle Tate says I can keep them."

His eyes darted toward his uncle. Something about that serious tone with the hint of disbelief and that wide-eyed, searching look at his uncle filled her with concern.

Viktor walked into the room. "Dinner is

ready. What can I get you for beverage, Hannah?"

She asked Lucas, "What are you having?"

He grinned. "I like milk. And you know what? We always have lots of milk here. I got milk sometimes before my mom died, but not much after."

Viktor reached out and tweaked Lucas's ear. "Big glass of milk for you, Lukie, already on table."

From the corner of her eye she saw Tate squeeze his eyes shut as he tipped his head to one side. He opened them on a nod as if to reassure himself, and a picture began to form in her mind. There was a story here with this little guy and she suddenly desperately wanted to know it.

"Milk for me, too," she said enthusiastically.

The grin Lucas turned on her felt brighter than the sun. He reached out, tucked his hand inside hers and led her to the table. Where she proceeded to stuff herself on delicious pierogi, spicy sausage, a flavorful beet dish she was surprised she liked and the best stuffed cabbage she'd ever eaten.

After dinner she played with Lucas and his fleet. There were backhoes, various trucks, a forklift, a track hoe and many other assorted pieces of equipment. He was impressed that she knew their uses and how to "drive" them properly.

Picking up a shiny yellow bulldozer she said, "This guy reminds me of your uncle."

Tate appeared puzzled while Lucas grinned and asked, "Why?"

"Because it runs over everything in its path to get to where it wants to go."

Tate narrowed his eyes, opened his mouth to respond and then quickly shut it again. Then he grinned at her.

Lucas popped to his feet. "Hey, I'll be right back." He briefly disappeared up to his room and returned with a plastic bin full of Legos, whereupon they assembled a "building site" and put the equipment to proper use, including "bulldozing" a ten-inch high Lego wall.

Another hour passed quickly before Tate informed Lucas it was time to stow his toys so he could get ready for bed. Hannah helped him tidy up and handed him the toys one at a time so he could position them just so on the tree.

After he'd put the last one in place, he stood a few feet away from her where she was seated on the floor. He pinned his gaze on her the way she'd noticed he did when there was something he wanted to say. She waited, wishing she could lighten this child's heart somehow.

She smiled and impulsively opened her arms.

He lunged toward her and threw his arms around her neck. "Good night, Hannah. I'll miss you."

She hugged him tight. "Good night, sweet Lucas. I'll miss you, too, but we'll see each other soon." She kissed him on the top of his head. "Yum, you smell good—like bubble gum."

He nodded as he pulled away. "It's special soap Uncle Tate bought me just for kids. And it won't sting my eyes if I accidentally get it in there. I don't like soap in my eyes."

"Me either," she said. "That's the worst. Then you have to go like this." She squinted and made a funny show of rubbing her face. He doubled over laughing. Then he stilled and gave her another sideways glance. "Can you babysit me soon?"

"I sure can." She smiled and added a kiss on his cheek. "I'll talk to your uncle about it."

He skipped over toward Tate and they headed for the stairs.

Tate returned to the living room several minutes later as Viktor excused himself to take a phone call. Tate removed something from his back pocket and lowered himself onto the sofa a few feet away from her. Leaning forward he placed a red-and-black walkie-talkie on the coffee table in front of him.

"Are we part of a covert operation?" she joked.

A gentle smile softened his features. "It's so I can hear Lucas if he gets scared. I wanted to put one of those baby monitors in his room, but he said it made him feel like a baby, so we settled on these. He has nightmares and my room is right next to his so I can hear him then, but we have these for when I'm not in my room."

Sympathy made her wince, but she took his comment as an opening to ask, "What happened to him, Tate?"

He placed his hands on his thighs, splaying his long fingers over his knees. "I'm not sure exactly. I have a pretty good idea, though, and he's...he's had it pretty rough."

"I've picked up on that. He told me his mom died. That would be your sister?"

He shifted in his seat and Hannah could see the sorrow in his eyes. "Yes, my sister, Lexie. She was quite a bit younger than me and a drug addict. She overdosed a year and a half ago. I was granted custody of Lucas last month."

"I'm so sorry about your sister. Custody from his father?"

"No, his dad is dead. From his grandmother—our mother. She's an addict, too, and treated him much worse than Lexie did. At least Lexie loved him, and before she relapsed I had thought—I'd hoped…"

"Oh, Tate." Hannah couldn't imagine a mother—a grandmother, an aunt, or any family member for that matter—that didn't love the children in her life with all of her being. "I can only imagine how difficult this has been for you, for Lucas. Poor little guy."

"Lucas really likes you. You don't know how much that means because for some reason he took to you right away, but he's very distrustful of new people. The fact that he held your hand was amazing, and then when he hugged you…" He looked up at the ceiling as if searching for words. When he met her gaze again his eyes were shining brightly.

Running a hand over his jaw, he seemed to be gathering his emotions. "It's unusual to say the least. He's shy and he doesn't trust people. For good reason. I've taken him to two different psychologists and neither one of them could get him to open up. Eight sessions and he barely said a word."

A spike of concern flowed through her. "He's obviously a great kid in spite of everything. Of course, I can see the sadness in him, and there's this hesitancy about him, too, as if he's afraid to just jump in and be a kid."

He nodded his agreement. "That's it exactly."

"Do you want to tell me about it?"

"I do, but I don't want you to think I'm trying to win you over with sympathy where Snowy Sky is concerned."

"Please don't insult me. That's business. We're talking about an innocent child here. I adore him. You know that's genuine."

He appeared relieved and satisfied with that response.

"He got into trouble a lot with his grandmother. I'm sure for normal things kids do. She did the same with me, but then other times she would be way too lax. That kind of inconsistency makes you wary. I'm sure she used any excuse to lock him in his room, to get him out of her hair—whenever she was hungover, or so she could party with her buddies."

He continued talking and by the time he was finished, she could feel unshed tears burning behind her eyes along with a deep simmering anger. He shared Lucas's experiences peppered with his own firsthand knowledge, the latter relayed very matter-of-factly.

"Bits and pieces are still trickling out… His life with Lexie was better. At least she looked after him properly and kept him fed, and for the first few years when she was still sober I think things were okay. But then, gradually Lexie was pulled back into that life. At first I didn't recognize it because I was away competing. When I talked to her she would lie and tell me everything was fine. Then I quit hearing from her. That's when I found out she left Lucas with Penny. A few months later she was dead. Lucas was stuck with her for almost two years."

He brought his hands up and linked them behind his neck. He grimaced and she felt herself softening toward him yet again.

He was obviously trying very hard to give Lucas the best life he possibly could. Hannah didn't believe he was attempting to "win her over" with sympathy, but she felt it nonetheless. She was going to have to be very, very careful to keep her feelings for Lucas separate from her feelings for Tate.

"He's terrified of the dark. I know a lot of

kids are, but his fear is extreme. Penny's neighbor at the tenement they were living in told me that one night Penny told Lucas she'd be right back. Went out to buy some Cocoa Puffs… She hadn't paid the power bill, ended up taking off on a bender, and Lucas was left alone in the dark and cold for three days. The neighbor knew this because on the fourth day Penny called and asked her to check on Lucas."

Hannah squeezed her eyes shut as a burst of rage shot through her bloodstream and left her hands shaking. "Why didn't the neighbor call the police?"

Tate brought his shoulders up into a helpless shrug, but she could see the angry tension radiating from him, as well. "I have no idea. The woman said she didn't feel like it was any of her business, although she had plenty to say about that episode and a few others."

She knew it wouldn't do any good to rehash the hows and whys. All that mattered was that it wouldn't happen again. "What are you doing now? To…to heal? To…" To what? Move on? She didn't even know for sure.

"Even though it was pretty much a bust as far as the one-on-one sessions for Lucas went, I consulted a few doctors in Colorado before we came here to get some ideas on how to proceed. We have a recommendation for a child psychologist in Glacier City, too, if we need one. And a couple names in Anchorage. For now we're just doing the best we can."

She nodded.

"And Christmas—I want him to have a Christmas. He's never had one. Gifts…" He gestured at the tree. "A home with a tree, Christmas movies and music, food, and a family. He's never had any of that. I sent him stuff of course, but she…"

Gifts. A horrible, unfathomable thought filtered through her brain. "She sold them, didn't she?"

"Yes. I sent her a check every month even while we were fighting for custody. I sent Lucas boxes of gifts and school stuff and clothing…" He trailed off with a disgusted shake of his head. "He barely saw any of it. The pawnshop owner she frequented told me sometimes she didn't even open the packages until she brought them into his shop."

He kept his head down for a few long seconds before meeting her eyes again. "He said she would walk out the door with the money she got from Lucas's packages and buy alcohol next door or meet her dealer across the street. The guy would watch her out the window."

"I'm so sorry. I can't even imagine." But, in a sense, she could imagine. The anger she had felt for the drunk driver who'd caused her accident had been so intense, so consuming, she had believed she'd never be able to forgive.

Eventually, with Dr. Voss's help she'd come to understand the cruel, iron-clad hold of addiction. And she'd realized forgiveness was the only way she would ever truly heal and be able to move on. So she'd forgiven the alcoholic who'd nearly killed her and then left her for dead—as much as she could anyway. But she'd not forgotten.

No, she'd never forget.

But how could a grandmother choose her addiction over her own grandchild? How could she not treasure that precious child? How could anyone not want to see happiness shining in his eyes instead of that heart-wrenching trepidation that was so often reflected there?

She suddenly felt guilty for taking even one millimeter of her mom's Christmas spirit for granted.

Impulsively, she found herself asking, "Why don't you guys come over for Christmas Eve? To my parents' house? My mom does Christmas like you've never seen before—games, food, baking, a white elephant gift exchange. Lucas would love it. You would all love it."

He remained silent and Hannah felt her spirits sink. She hadn't meant to put him on the spot; she just felt compelled to help with Lucas in some way. Then a light seemed to flick on in his eyes while his mouth slowly furled upwards into a smile. She felt this sensation deep inside of her, and as their eyes met she wondered if he felt it, too.

"That would be great. We'd love to come. Just the thought of showing Lucas how Christmas should be... To be perfectly honest, I'm not even sure how it should be. I bought him a bunch of gifts but..."

The feeling grew stronger, like a magnet urging her toward him. She wanted to wrap her arms around him and tell him that she would be there for him, and that she could— she would—help him with Lucas and give them all a wonderful Christmas.

A practical thought nudged its way into her brain; a sobering, cruel, rational thought that had to do with Snowy Sky. How much of herself could she really give to him with this business between them? Would compromising with Snowy Sky mean compromising everything she'd worked so hard for? Would it mean sacrificing her dream to have a chance with Tate? *Okay, Hannah, getting a little ahead of yourself here.*

"What did you get him?"

She felt her eyes widen as Tate began to recite the list.

"So, essentially the entire inventory of a toy store?"

The way his mouth curved upwards when he was fighting a smile was just…

"Well, he didn't have anything when I got him. One tiny suitcase, a few books and a stuffed bear."

"Let me see."

"What?"

"The gifts? Where did you hide them? Let's go take a look."

She followed him upstairs, through his room and into the enormous walk-in closet, which was currently stacked with a colossal array of boxes, bags and loose items. She resisted the urge to make another joke because she knew how much love he had put into this endeavor. But…

She looked around, trying to decide how best to say it, finally deciding on honesty. "Tate, this is too much."

"You think?" He scratched his head, seemingly perplexed.

She gave it to him straight. "Yes. I do. This is more than any child needs."

She sat on the floor and patted the ground next to her. "Sit."

He lowered himself beside her and Hannah wondered why the closet suddenly seemed smaller, more intimate, while huddled on the floor close to him. His knee grazed hers and she tried to distract herself with sorting the toys.

"We'll put a pile of smaller things here for Lucas's stocking. You did get him a stocking, right?"

"Yes, I bought one your cousin knitted. Lilah has some for sale in the bakery."

She had to admit he was serious about showing his support for the community. "Oh, how sweet, and I'm sure it's beautiful. So, let's go over the things Lucas has talked about, or expressed an interest in, or that you know that he'll love."

She picked up a big stuffed lion. "I think we can safely place this in the 'keep" pile."

He agreed and they began sorting, talking and laughing—putting some gifts aside for Lucas's birthday, a few for his Easter basket and a few more to surprise him with over the coming months.

Tate studied the giant stack of gifts piled up on one side of the closet. "What do I do with the rest of these?"

"You can return them or you could donate some. There are so many kids out there, right here in our valley, in fact, who would love even one of these toys."

Hannah flashed him a cautious smile. "Which reminds me. I have a confession to make."

Tate narrowed his eyes at her. "Yeah?"

"Um, remember how you accused me of being passive-aggressive?"

He grinned. "Don't worry about it. I already know you knew I was coming to the Festival of Trees."

"Not that," she said. "But I don't regret that, because you look really nice in a suit."

He chuckled even as the air seemed to thicken between them.

She nibbled on her lip, wondering how this would go over. Would he be angry?

"What?" he asked.

"The phone bidder at the auction? That was me. Well, it was a friend. I had her drive up the price on the tree."

He quirked a brow. "Really?"

She nodded and tried to look contrite. "Yes. I'm sorry."

"Are you?"

"Should I be? I wouldn't have done it if it wasn't for a really great cause."

He tipped his head back and laughed. "It's fine. It was worth every penny. You should have seen his face when he saw it. Priceless."

Hannah wasn't sure what she'd expected. But this easygoing reaction and the love he had for Lucas just endeared him to her more.

She needed to get out of this closet before she not so passively-aggressively confessed all and threw herself into his arms.

She stood to stretch out the kinks that had begun to accumulate in her muscles.

"Is there a local toy drive?" he asked as he rose to his feet.

"There is." She relayed the details as they returned to the kitchen. Where she also half-jokingly warned him about what to expect at a James family Christmas Eve get-together, both the good and bad.

"I'll sum it up for you—an overload of holiday decor, some atrocious singing, lots of teasing, a squabble or two and food. Enough food to feed roughly a thousand times the number of people who will be there. But the leftovers are one of my favorite parts. We're very lucky."

Tate laughed, asking questions while he prepared some kind of herbal tea smelling faintly of cinnamon and flowers. The conversation moved on to other things, lighthearted things, until it was way past time for her to call it a night.

He insisted on going outside to start her car so it could warm up because her older model didn't have remote ignition. A dusting of snow covered his jacket when he came back. After shrugging out of it, he shook it off outside and then hung it on the banister.

"We've got a couple inches of new snow out there. I cleaned it off your windows."

She opened the closet where she'd seen Viktor stow her coat earlier. She pulled her stocking hat from the pocket and slipped it on her head.

"Thanks. I'll pick Lucas up on Tuesday, okay? We'll feed the koi and then I'll take him for part of the day?" She reminded him, "It's *babysitting*, so maybe pretend like you guys have something to do?"

"Okay, but he'll be so excited to hang out

with you, I doubt he'll notice us. Thank you, for your help and for spending time with him."

She felt his eyes on her, wondered what he was thinking. She couldn't seem to stop this attraction. And it was growing fast, at least on her part. Because she liked him; she'd liked him before the board meeting and in spite of his misguided attempts to alter Snowy Sky, she now saw him in yet another light. And right now that light was shining brighter than any other.

How could it not after this evening? After witnessing this man trying desperately to be a father to a child who'd never had one, with no example to follow because he'd never had one himself? She could also see that he was something like a son to Viktor, and their relationship stirred up warm and fuzzy feelings inside of her, as well.

Behind that smooth, often too-serious exterior lurked something a bit melancholy and unsettled that was so difficult to resist. She found herself yearning to get in there and somehow make it all better and…and she really needed to change this train of thought because that wasn't her responsibility.

The difficulty in continuing this battle with

him over Snowy Sky flared in her mind. If the resort didn't mean so much to her on a personal level, if it wasn't such an integral part of her continued healing process, then maybe. Just maybe she could bend. But then there was her health, the uncertainty of her future, which made her want Snowy Sky's success even more.

Tate reached over and rearranged one side of her hat. His fingertips lingered and lightly brushed the skin of her cheek. Her pulse leaped as a shudder ran through her.

"Sorry, my hands are probably cold, huh?"

"No," she whispered without thinking. "They're not."

He smiled slowly, sweetly, and she realized that she'd given herself away. She felt a flush warm her cheeks. "Oh, I…"

"Hannah," Tate whispered her name as he took two steps closer. Close enough to…

He bent his head and kissed her lips and she felt a rush of emotion so intense she couldn't think. The kiss held the perfect amount of gentle pressure. A low moan escaped from her lips as she felt something click into place inside of her. She imagined a lost piece of her soul that had been drifting around aimlessly since the accident had finally found its home.

Her eyelids fluttered closed while her hands traveled up to wind around his neck and suddenly there was so much heat and all these… feelings. She'd never felt like this in a kiss. Like she might have—finally—found all she really needed in the world.

When their lips parted, he let his forehead rest on hers. She could hear his rapid breathing and she smiled because it seemed to match her own. Her heart ached with emotion—real emotion, and for the first time in so long she wasn't pretending to be happier than she really was. Or hoping that the acting would make the happiness real. She wasn't pretending about anything at all. She needed to get out of there before it started spilling out and she said something, or did something, that neither of them was ready for.

She stepped back and smiled up at him, trying to rein in her feelings but knowing it probably showed all over her face. She felt a nervous giggle coming on.

Instead she reached out with both hands and tugged playfully on the hem of his shirt. "Good night, Tate. Thank you for a lovely evening."

He quirked a brow in the way she noticed he

did when he was about to laugh at her. "Night, Hannah."

And then she walked out into the frigid winter night, but she didn't feel cold. Not even close.

CHAPTER ELEVEN

TATE HADN'T BEEN exaggerating Lucas's shyness with new people. After picking him up, Hannah took him to her cousin Janie's house to meet her four boys who were out of school for the winter holidays. He spent the first half hour glued to her side. She sensed he wanted to participate, that he was enjoying absorbing the interaction, so she waited, hoping he'd join in on his own.

To her extreme appreciation, it was Aidan who finally managed to lure Lucas out of his shell. Aidan hooked up his laptop to the big-screen TV and presented a jungle slide show—including numerous photos of a green anaconda. Lucas scooted off her lap to get closer to the screen. By the end of it, he and Aidan were chatting about the jungle and Lucas was asking questions.

He hesitantly agreed to do a craft that Janie arranged. All the boys participated, even the older two, and by the time they were through they would each have a pair of reindeer antlers to wear on their heads.

"Did you make the ones Aidan wore at the Festival of Trees?" she asked Janie.

"Guilty," her cousin said with a grin as she hot-glue-gunned a few more sequins to Gabe's pair.

"You realize you probably sealed it for him with those, right?"

Janie chuckled. "I do. Here you go, Gabe. He really wanted to win that cake."

She laughed as Gabe took the antlers, closely examining his mother's work.

"Awesome, Mom." He positioned them on his head.

Lucas seemed giddy with his efforts, wearing his crooked, glittered antlers proudly. They gathered the boys together for some photos. Lucas joined in with the others to make silly faces for a few of the pictures.

Snack time came next and Janie presented a stunning array of Christmas cookies. While the kids attacked the treats like a pack of hyenas, Lucas allowed Hannah out of his sight long enough for her to help Janie whip up a batch of her famous homemade hot chocolate.

A cauldron of milk already sat on the stove top when she came into the kitchen.

Jane gave her a beseeching look. "Oh, Hannah, what a sweet little guy."

She grinned. "I know."

"He adores you."

"The feeling is mutual. I'm telling you, Janie," she said, lifting one hand and pointing at it with the other, "he's got me wrapped around this finger."

"I can see that, too. But that shyness is heartbreaking and I don't want to say he's awkward, but it's like he's insecure, maybe? Is there something…?"

Hannah explained as well as she could, careful not to break any confidence of Tate's.

Janie listened as she whisked the rich chocolate concoction into the steaming milk. Hannah kept talking while retrieving an assortment of Christmas mugs from the cupboard in the corner.

"Wow," Janie commented when she was through. "How incredibly sad and criminal."

"That's true. It probably is criminal in some regards. But what do you recommend? I know I can't change the past, but I want to help him. I don't know anyone who has more experience with children than you."

"Trust me on this one, having them doesn't guarantee you always know what to do with them. I mean there's definitely something to that maternal instinct as far as keeping them alive and all. But as for the rest..." Janie paused, seemingly lost in her thoughts.

Hannah handed over a cup for her to fill. Janie ladled in the chocolate. Hannah took the full mug and replaced it with an empty. They did that a few more times and Hannah's mind had started to wander when Janie said, "Love."

"Hmm?"

"Love," she repeated. "Love is the answer for Lucas. I know it sounds overly simplistic, but when the boys lost their father I tried everything I could think of to make us all better—crying, not crying, talking, not talking, grief counseling. In the end it was just love that got us through. Aidan's love in particular. I don't know what the situation is between you and Tate, but for whatever reason Lucas has taken to you. And that means a ton. It means you can help him. He needs kindness and patience and consistency. Kids like to know what's coming next. You're great with him, so listen to your instincts—your heart.

"Poor little guy..." Janie paused to sniffle. "Sorry, pregnancy. I'm always a heartbeat away from tears."

Hannah smiled gently and reached out to

give her elbow a light squeeze. "That's quite all right. How are you feeling?"

"Great, actually. Aidan is so wonderful." She gave her head a shake as if she couldn't quite believe it herself. "Other than gaining a little too much weight, which I tend to do when I'm pregnant, I'm also retaining so much water I can't even wear my wedding ring. Look at these little sausages." She held up her fingers and wiggled them. "I'm now borrowing Reagan's snow boots because my ankles are the size of a baby elephant's. But the boys are so excited to have a little sister. Gareth and Reagan are already making plans."

"What about the twins?"

She gave Hannah a wry look. "The twins are four. They're excited when I make pancakes shaped liked Mickey Mouse."

Hannah busted out a laugh. Then thought about her rambunctious, silly, fun-loving little cousins and couldn't help but compare them to the shy and subdued Lucas.

Love.

She hoped Janie was right, because love she could do.

"THAT'S GREAT, LUCAS. Bend your knees a bit more. Arms forward… That's it," Tate called out a few days later as Lucas glided down the bunny hill on his snowboard. Hannah had generously arranged for them to use the magic carpet on the beginner hill so he and Viktor could start Lucas's snowboarding lessons.

He looked over at Viktor. "What do you think?"

He lifted a shoulder. "There is potential. An athlete like you comes along only one time in one million. But, I've seen kids who cannot even stand upright on board at first become champion. Sometimes, with much practice, something will click. So we will see."

This had to work. It had worked for him, and Lucas needed this as much as Tate had, if not more. For Tate, snowboarding had been something to look forward to, something to be proud of, something to work hard at and then relish in the results. For a long time it had been his reason to live. And snowboarding was something Tate could do and teach him—a way for him and Lucas to bond. Like Tate had with Viktor.

Lucas skidded to a perfect stop near them. Tate felt a moment of elation before Lucas tipped over backward into the snow.

He stepped toward him, reached down and

slipped his hands under Lucas's shoulders to stand him upright.

"What do you think, buddy?"

He smiled and Tate could tell he was trying to be brave. "It's pretty fun, Uncle Tate, but it's kind of slippery."

Tate chuckled and gave him a hug. "It is pretty slippery, but it gets better, I promise. Do you want to try again?"

"Sure." He nodded solemnly.

"Okay, here goes." He let go and Lucas slid down the hill about twenty feet, but this time he took a hard fall, his helmet slapping against the ground.

Tate knew falling was part of learning, yet he felt a speck of alarm when Lucas stayed put. He ran toward him. "Lucas? Are you okay?"

"Yes, I'm just resting." Reaching out a gloved hand, he scooped up some snow. He took a bite. "Uncle Tate, is Hannah coming over tonight?"

Tate grinned. "Would you like to invite her?"

He nodded. "Yep. That would make my day."

"You know what?" Tate unzipped his pocket and removed his phone. "Mine, too."

HANNAH FLIPPED OVER the card with the gray shark on it. She remembered where the other card was but pretended that she didn't. She stifled a smile, feigning puzzlement as she watched Lucas squirm with excitement.

"Darn," she said as she turned the alligator card back over.

He quickly flipped over one shark and then the other.

"Ah, there it is!" She slapped a hand to her forehead, earning a giggle from Lucas.

He turned an elephant card. She remembered they'd only seen the other elephant once, so she was thrilled when he picked the match. Tate had shared that he wasn't sure where Lucas stood academically. He'd only gone to school sporadically and Penny certainly wasn't one to emphasize learning.

She knew Lucas was bright; he knew the alphabet and could write his name. He could barely read, but she and Tate had started working on that. Lucas was both quick and eager to learn.

Now she flipped over the cat card and covered up the image so only the word remained. "What does this card say?"

"Cat," he said confidently.

"You got it." She high-fived him and smiled at Tate who was watching them from his spot on the floor. Leaning against the sofa, one leg outstretched, the other bent at the knee, he had a lazy, satisfied grin on his face. The way he watched her turned her insides to mush. She was beginning to crave these times when he seemed to live in the moment, forgetting his troubles and whatever dark thoughts plagued him.

Lucas won the game and then promptly announced that he was hungry.

Tate made a pizza from scratch. He'd prepared the dough that morning. Delicious yeasty flavor filled the air as he showed Lucas how to roll the soft dough onto a round stoneware pan. They smeared the crust with sauce, sprinkled on the cheese, and topped it off with sausage and pepperoni.

She was impressed with Tate's skill and told him so. She felt compelled to confess, "I can't cook. I'm like the only person in my family who doesn't cook. Even my cousin-in-law Emily who could barely make coffee when she met Bering, cooks better than I do—way better in fact."

"Viktor insisted I learn. It comes in very handy. We're teaching Lucas, too."

Twenty minutes in the oven and the pizza was done. After eating their fill of the delicious cheesy dish, Lucas asked to be excused so he could pick out a movie.

Tate's lips curved up slowly, a playful expression on his face as he watched her. He reached for her hand, entwining his fingers with hers. Her heart began to race as he leaned toward her and then his soft lips were gently kissing hers. She felt a wave of affection—and happiness. The combination was intense and left her breathless.

Pulling away with a satisfied grin he said, "Thanks for coming over."

"Thanks for inviting me," she somehow managed to return.

Lucas called from the next room. Less than halfway through the film, he fell asleep curled up between them on the sofa. When Tate carried him to his room, Hannah stood to tidy up a bit. She picked up Lucas's coat to hang it in the closet.

In the habit of checking kids' pockets, she reached inside one of Lucas's, pulled out the contents and felt her stomach drop as she examined what she found. She walked over and sat on the sofa, clutching the item in her hand.

Tate came back into the room a few minutes later. "He's doing so well, don't you think? Thank you so much. I—" He stopped, undoubtedly concerned about the look on her face. "What's wrong?"

"I don't know how to tell you this, so I'm just going to say it—I was cleaning up a little and I went to hang Lucas's coat in the closet and I found this in his pocket." She tipped her chin toward the coffee table.

He walked closer. "What is it?"

"It's my cousin Janie's wedding ring."

THE NEXT MORNING Tate watched as Lucas finished the last of his pancakes. Tate and Hannah had discussed the situation at length the night before. He wondered if he should call a therapist. Hannah had recommended a direct approach of asking Lucas in a nonthreatening manner. *Don't accuse*, she'd said, *just ask because kid logic can be very surprising sometimes*.

"Lucas, I need to ask you something, okay?"

He nearly broke down as Lucas bobbed his head, his black hair sleep tousled, a spot of syrup dotting his race-car pajamas. Could this little guy, this child of his heart, be a thief? Didn't he have enough going against him as it was?

"Last night I found this ring in your coat pocket." Tate had decided not to let him know that Hannah knew what he'd done. At least not yet. "Where did you get it?"

Lucas stopped twirling his fork in the remaining syrup on his plate. "I found it at the boys' house when I went with Hannah."

"What do you mean, you found it?"

"It was sitting on the window ledge in a little dish."

Found it? Okay, maybe that meant he didn't really understand what he was doing.

"Why did you think it was okay to take it?"

"That's what Grandma would have me do. It was hard sometimes finding stuff at the places she took me, but I knew this was a good one when I saw it. You can sell it, Uncle Tate, and then we won't run out of food so fast. It's not fair that you have to buy all the food and I don't help. That's what Grandma would say."

Of course, Tate thought. Penny. He inhaled a long, slow breath; he couldn't let Lucas see his anger. His lying, alcoholic, drug-abusing thief of a mother hadn't bothered to teach her grandson how to read, but she'd taught him how to steal. Perfect. Was there no end to her selfishness and manipulation?

He explained to Lucas the best he could that in spite of what she had told him, stealing was wrong. He also took the opportunity to explain how some of the ways his grandmother had treated him were also wrong and he could talk to Tate about them anytime. He would never get into trouble for telling him anything.

Lucas seemed to understand. But then he burst into tears and climbed onto Tate's lap.

"I'm sorry, Uncle Tate. I thought taking it would make it so I could stay with you longer."

Swallowing his own sob, Tate hugged him tight, rocking him gently in his arms. "You don't have to do anything to make me keep you. Adults are supposed to take care of the kids in their life—that's the way it works. I'm keeping you forever and I'm going to take care of you. That's another promise. And remember, I always keep my promises, right?"

VIKTOR DROVE LUCAS into town for his swim lesson, while Tate waited in the atrium for Hannah to arrive.

She waved as she as came in, quickly retrieved food for the fish and didn't waste any time on her usual joy and ceremony in feeding them. Instead, she took a seat next to him on the garden bench, a look of concern stamped on her face.

He handed her Janie's ring.

"How did it go?"

"Fine, I think." He relayed the conversation as she listened intently. He didn't see any judgment on her face, and he realized how incredibly grateful he was for that.

"It sounds like you did great. I can't think of anything I would have said or done differently."

"I'm worried."

"What are you worried about?"

"I'm worried that I'm not doing the right things, saying the right things."

When she reached over and took his hand, he instantly felt better. Being able to share his concerns with her—a normal, functioning woman he could trust—was reassuring. Tate had never trusted a woman before in his entire life. He realized how much he wanted to not only trust Hannah but to rely on her. He smiled at her and relished the feeling.

Tate wasn't one to foist his problems off on someone else, but now he found himself wondering if that was what he was doing where Lucas was concerned?

CHAPTER TWELVE

ON CHRISTMAS EVE, Tate, Viktor and Lucas walked through the wreath-and-garland-swathed door of Margaret and Ben James's home. Tate felt a surprising, potent moment of claustrophobia at the sea of bodies and the riotous noise level, but thankfully Hannah had seen them arrive. As she hurried toward them with her brighter-than-the-sun smile, he not only felt himself smiling in return, he was struck with an immediate sense of calm.

Lucas, who had been standing tense beside him seemed to feel it, too. The Hannah effect, he thought, as he watched Lucas's shoulders relax and a happy smile spread over his face. He folded his little hand around hers and Tate found himself wanting to do the same.

She set about making introductions, starting with her parents, and Tate thought she bore a strong resemblance to her mother. But those sharp, caramel-toned eyes she'd definitely inherited from her dad.

Ben and Margaret were warm and kind and seemed genuinely excited to have strangers joining their festivities. They moved farther into the house as Burl Ives sang out his wish for them all to have a holly jolly Christmas this year. Tate tried to soak it all in. It even smelled like how he imagined Christmas should smell; evergreen and peppermint with hints of cinnamon and vanilla.

Hannah led them into the spacious great room where holiday knickknacks took up nearly every inch of flat space; snowmen were arranged along the top of a long bookshelf that stretched across much of one wall, a collection of Santa Clauses were displayed atop the fireplace hearth and a large nativity scene had its own shelf.

Lucas was grinning from ear to ear while firmly latched to Hannah's side. He tapped on her arm and she bent to listen to what he had to say.

Tate couldn't hear him over the din, but Hannah said, "Sure."

She smiled at him and Viktor. "Lucas wants to go see Mom's Christmas village." She pointed across the room toward the elaborate display.

Tate was relieved that Lucas wanted to

be with Hannah, yet a pang of alarm sliced through him as he watched him go. He knew he was in good hands—it wasn't that. He wasn't sure exactly what was going on, but his palms were sweaty and the uncomfortable tightness in his chest was back and escalating to a full-blown squeezing pain.

Tate welcomed the distraction as Margaret introduced him to some friends. Next he met Hannah's younger sisters Iris and Hazel, two of the triplets. The resemblance among all the sisters was striking, although he thought none of them had Hannah's level of magnetism. Hannah just seemed to shine. He and Viktor chatted with Iris as she led them to the appetizers and beverages.

He filled a small plate and accepted a cup of hot, spicy cider before settling in the great room where he discussed fishing with Hannah's dad, Ben, for a while. He chatted with Tag and met the remaining triplet, Seth, who began asking him about snowboarding.

Tate managed to keep an eye on Hannah and Lucas at the same time. They'd been playing a noisy dice game with a group of kids and he couldn't help but notice that all of the children seemed enraptured by her. She was like the

Pied Piper of children, and adults, too, from what Tate could discern.

After the game she and Lucas disappeared through the doorway leading to another room. He waited for a break in the conversation and then followed. He found a new crowd in the kitchen where he met an older woman he learned was Hannah's aunt Claire, her cousin Janie's mom.

Claire and Janie were roasting chestnuts. Tate had never seen anyone roast a chestnut before; he didn't realize people did more than sing about that activity in this day and age. The kids gathered around as Claire showed the older kids how to carefully score the surface and warned them about the importance of their technique so they didn't cut themselves.

The nutty smell made his mouth water and when Lucas brought him one he declared the warm buttery nut one of the most delicious things he'd ever tasted. Lucas was literally bouncing with joy and chattering a mile a minute—something else he had never seen before.

He stood in front of Hannah and held his arms aloft. She lifted him easily and swung him upward high in the air. Then, pulling him close and hugging him tight, she whispered something in his ear.

As Lucas giggled wildly another wave of uneasiness began to inhabit him, like a block of dry ice settling inside his core, its cold fog creeping through his body. It reminded him of the feeling he used to get when he didn't immediately get the hang of a new trick on his board—a hopeless sense of inadequacy. Hannah was so good with him. Their bond had forged so naturally.

She always seemed to know what to say, what to do, while Tate constantly questioned himself and felt like he was missing something, like he wasn't doing enough. Would he ever achieve that easiness that Hannah had with him?

She set Lucas back on his feet and he scampered off with some other kids. She turned her smile on him and Tate tried to return it but suspected he'd done a pretty poor job of it judging by the questioning look she gave him in return.

Ben walked into the room and announced that dinner was ready. A chaotic line began to form around one of the three tables arranged in the dining area. One table was covered with homemade treats—cookies, pies, pastries and cakes. Bowls of nutmeg-sprinkled eggnog and holiday punch sat chilling on another smaller table. Cups were stacked alongside a gleaming silver ice-filled bucket.

The long rectangular table featured an array of dishes arranged buffet-style. He thought he could identify the scents of garlic and rosemary and fresh-baked bread of some kind. Just then, Hannah's sister Hazel walked by and set a heaping basket of rolls on the end of the table. Iris joined her, placing a huge red bowl filled with some kind of salad in the only empty space remaining in the middle of the table.

Iris and Hazel flanked him, chatting and introducing him to various other family members and friends. Iris handed him a plate decorated with a wreath and birds in flight. He studied the design, trying to get a grip on his inexplicable anxiety.

"The birds are decorating the wreath," Hannah explained a moment later as she peeked over his shoulder. "See, this one is carrying a ribbon in its beak, this guy's got a button or something and this one is fastening a flower here." Her arm grazed his as she pointed and he could smell her sweet Hannah scent, like rose petals and vanilla. He suddenly found himself wishing she wasn't so…perfect.

He tipped the plate. "Ah, I see. You're right."

"You doing okay?"

And the fact she knew something was bothering him bothered him even more. "Of course," he managed to say. "How could I not be? It's like the Claus family reunion here."

She eyed him carefully. "Because this family is big and we can be a lot to take in all at once. I know you're not used to this kind of thing and probably not sure what to make of it all."

"It's great. I'm fine." He knew he sounded defensive, prickly even, which wasn't fair because he was a guest here, and she and the entire James family had been nothing but welcoming to him and Viktor and Lucas. He tried to hide it by changing the subject. "Lucas is having a great time."

"He is," she replied quietly, her eyes all soft and filled with a concern that added guilt and edginess to his already-overloaded emotions.

Gesturing toward the table she said, "Why don't you fix your plate and go eat with him?"

He watched her disappear into the kitchen. People were filling their plates and heading into the great room where portable tables had been set up and covered with festive Christmas cloths and baskets of napkin-wrapped flatware. Tate joined them even as he wanted to follow her—to apologize, but what could he say when he didn't even know exactly what the problem was himself?

Besides he wanted to be with Lucas, too.

Viktor had already helped Lucas with his plate, so Tate settled next to them and tried to enjoy the best Christmas meal he'd ever eaten.

Near the end of the evening, Lucas climbed into Hannah's lap and fell asleep. Across the room Viktor was visiting with Tag, Iris and a couple of Hannah's cousins. Tate caught his eye and tipped his head toward the door. He nodded and soon rose to his feet. After thanking Ben and Margaret for their hospitality and saying their goodbyes, Tate gathered Lucas from Hannah's arms.

She walked them to the door.

"Thank you guys for coming. I think Lucas had a great time."

Viktor chuckled. "That is understatement. I had wonderful time, too, Hannah. Your family—truly special bunch of people. You are very lucky."

"Thank you, Viktor. I think so, too. You guys are pretty lucky yourselves. Merry Christmas."

Hannah tried to catch his eye, but Tate

avoided it, mumbled his own thank-you and goodbye.

A cloud of despair officially settled over him as he carried Lucas to the car and strapped him in his booster seat. What was wrong with him? It really had been a great evening. Truly perfect. And then Tate admitted to himself that was exactly the problem—in his heart he knew he could never compete with perfect.

AFTER EVERYONE HAD LEFT, the dishes washed, and the rest of the house mostly cleaned, an exhausted Hannah settled on the cushy sectional sofa with her sisters and Adele. Ben, Margaret and Seth had gone to bed. In typical nice-guy fashion, Tag had left early because he'd volunteered to work Christmas day so his fellow paramedics who had children could enjoy a day off.

Hannah, Shay and Adele had decided to sleep over at her parents'. Since the triplets were home for Christmas, the sisters thought it would be fun to wake up together again on Christmas morning as they had when they were kids. Adele had been raised by a single mother who had usually worked double shifts waitressing through the holidays, so she'd embraced the opportunity to be a part of the festivities.

The women sipped eggnog and nibbled on desserts as they discussed the evening's success.

"That Lucas is one darling little boy, Hannah." Adele took a bite of her coconut cream pie.

"I know." She grinned. She'd had plenty of second thoughts after inviting Tate, but as soon as they'd arrived and she'd seen Lucas's face, every doubt had disappeared. She'd never forget the wonder on his face as he studied the Christmas village and asked so politely if he could touch the tiny glass horses pulling a carriage through the porcelain town.

"Why does he live with his uncle and that cute Russian dude?" Iris asked. "I like him."

"Viktor is Ukrainian and he was Tate's snowboard coach. He's like a father to Tate. And Tate's sister passed away so he has custody of Lucas."

"That's a modern-day family right there," Hazel commented, then bit the head off of a frosting-and-sprinkle-covered snowman cookie.

Hannah felt Shay's eyes studying her. "And how do you feel about Tate?"

She responded with a questioning look.

"You've never invited anyone home for Christmas. You've never invited anyone for any other holiday either. In fact, you've never invited anyone home period—not even for dinner."

"That's not true. Troy Porter—"

"Was your prom date," Shay smoothly interrupted. "You went out with him three times in high school and on prom night you brought him inside the house only long enough for Dad to take some photos. And even then you stood there awkwardly, fiddling with the straps on your dress and looking like you had cramps. Don't even bother trying to deny it. Mom has the photographic evidence."

She snapped her mouth shut. They all laughed, and Hazel and Iris added their own recollections of Hannah's less-than-exciting love life.

Iris said, "Remember the time you went out with that guy from Glacier City? The competitive archer or whatever? He drove all the way here to pick you up and he was going to teach you how to shoot his bow. So you guys went out to Bob Clemson's shooting range and then he brought you home after like an hour because you embarrassed him."

She barked out a laugh at the memory. "Hey,

I didn't know I was going to outshoot him. He bragged about how great he was. I thought I was going to learn something."

Adele snorted with laughter as she reached over and patted her hand. "Good for you. I don't buy into that letting-a-guy-feel-manly crap either."

Hannah shrugged and finished off her pie. "Thank you, Adele. I can't help it if I'm competitive."

"It's not really that, Adele," Shay chimed in with a grin. "I'm competitive, too. It's Hannah's *way* of winning that can be a little off-putting. She shows no mercy."

Being athletic had always been her way of standing out, even within her own family of athletes. It had served her well on the slopes, too, and now she felt a fresh twinge of hurt at the reminder of that loss. She missed competition. The challenge of building Snowy Sky had filled some of that void. Now she couldn't help but wonder how much longer that would be the case?

Hazel took mercy and pointed out, "But to be fair Hannah was always really busy skiing and training. Not much time for boys."

Hannah thought about Spencer. She would have brought him home. Had planned to bring him home before the accident. He'd broken up with her standing beside her hospital bed, and she remembered staring at him and wondering how he could have professed to love her the very morning of the accident when she'd still been whole. Three days later after she'd regained consciousness in the critical-care unit, unable to feel her legs and knowing her left one may have to be amputated, he'd confessed that he couldn't "handle it." The recovery she was facing and the possibility that she might not ever walk again had been too much.

Even heavily medicated as she'd been at the time, she remembered making a joke about it being only fitting that he go ahead and break her heart, too, because it had been about the only thing left of her body that wasn't broken. In spite of her Herculean efforts to banish them, thoughts of Spencer still got to her. The fact that *she*—just her alone—hadn't been enough.

But this wasn't a matter of bringing home a guy she was involved with, a man she had thought might be the one. Tate was not Spencer and this situation was in no way the same.

"This is different. Tate and I aren't seeing each other that way. We're…"

All eyes were glued on her, but for the life of

her she couldn't come up with a suitable word. She thought they were becoming friends, but that kiss—two of them now if you counted that sweet grazing of the lips. She decided she did. Those moments had shifted her feelings for him into something more. And although they hadn't talked about what that might be, and even though they were at odds when it came to Snowy Sky, she was willing to see where it would lead. But then, tonight he'd been...

She slowly became aware of the women waiting for her response. "We're business associates. Friends, too. I guess."

There was a lengthy pause as her sisters and Adele looked at one another and then burst into a loud chorus of laughter.

She could hear the defensive, unconvincing tenor in her tone. "What? I invited Tate for Lucas's sake, and Viktor's. I like him, too. Tate wanted Lucas to have a real Christmas."

Hazel smiled and patted her shoulder. "Then what better place to have a Christmas than here?"

Hannah had thought so. She had thought it was a great evening, except something had been bothering Tate. And as much as she didn't want it to be true, she couldn't shake the fear that it was her. His actions tonight had left her thinking they were no longer on the same page. She couldn't help but wonder if once again she wasn't quite enough for the man she was so desperately falling for.

TATE SAT IN front of the Christmas tree, watching the light bounce off the backhoes and bulldozers and dump trucks. He thought about the evening. Lucas had slept all the way home and barely stirred as Tate settled him into bed.

He had stood beside his bed for a long time, watching him sleep and listening to him breathe. He was filled with both joy and unease as he realized he couldn't remember Lucas ever sleeping this soundly or looking so content.

Operation Awesome Christmas Eve had been a total success where Lucas was concerned. But it had left him with a gaping feeling of inadequacy, although he realized that had been brewing for a while now.

He tried not to dwell on the past, but the fact was that a person's experiences shaped them and gave them the tools to navigate through life. But what happened when those experiences were so negative that they left very little to build on?

Tate was terrified he didn't have the ammunition in his emotional arsenal to give Lucas the kind of family he deserved—the kind of family Hannah had.

And along with that realization came the sinking feeling he wasn't capable of giving Hannah the kind of love she was so clearly accustomed to either—the kind she definitely deserved.

FOR HANNAH, one Christmas celebration followed another, including the Christmas morning gift exchange at her parents' house. They'd simplified the event years ago by engaging in a name draw with a dollar limit.

She was touched by the photo Hazel gave to her of the triplets on the ski lift at the resort.

"Hazel, I love this! How did you…? Freddie must have helped."

"He did." Hazel gave her a happy smile. "We're so proud of you, Hannah. Freddie gave us a quick tour, too. Snowy Sky is just magical."

She felt a surge of pride, followed by the nagging reminder that she would be finding out exactly how much of that magic Park and Tate intended to take away in just a couple days.

Forcing thoughts of Snowy Sky out of her

head, she enjoyed a big breakfast with her family, relaxed and then later headed to a huge gathering at their aunt Claire's house with some extended family and friends.

She didn't hear from Tate.

As the hours ticked by, the fact weighed heavier and heavier on her, even as she reminded herself that he didn't owe her anything. So they'd kissed a couple times, which had led her to believe they were heading for something. Obviously, he'd changed his mind, and so what? She was a grown-up. She could handle a little rejection, right? It wasn't as they were in a relationship. She could handle it.

So why was her heart thumping like a scared rabbit's the day after Christmas as she went to take care of the koi? Lucas greeted her, but Tate was conspicuously absent. She refused to let his behavior interfere with her plans or her relationship with Lucas.

Lucas talked about Christmas as they fed the fish. She could tell he'd loved every moment. After describing each gift he'd received, every game they'd played and each dish Viktor had prepared for their holiday meal, Hannah asked, "So, do you want to go sledding with me and Janie and the boys today?"

"Sledding! Really? Yes!"

"Okay, should we go ask your uncle?"

A fresh swirl of nerves churned inside of her as she followed Lucas into the house. They found Tate in the den bent over a pile of paperwork. His eyes collided with hers when she walked through the door. Hannah thought he looked a bit alarmed at the sight of her.

Managing to keep her voice light she said, "Hey, sorry to interrupt."

"Uncle Tate, can I go sledding with Hannah and the boys?"

Tate had a smile for Lucas, before asking her, "Sledding?"

"Yes, Janie and I and the boys are going sledding at Snowy Sky."

"Sure. Why don't you go put on your snow pants? Viktor is in the kitchen, he can help you if you need it."

He turned and scampered off.

Tate's voice was low and quiet. "It's really nice of Janie to include him after what happened with the ring."

"She understands, Tate. Especially considering what he's been through. I don't know anyone with more compassion for children that Janie."

He scoffed. "I'm not sure anyone can really understand what he's been through. When you've gone through things in life like Lucas and I have…"

My goodness, Hannah thought, that sounded an awful lot like a pity party.

"Well, we all go through tough times. Janie lost her first husband while she was pregnant with the twins and then suffered a horrible bout of postpartum depression. Meanwhile, her boys lost their father and they all struggled. She was a single mother for a long time and it wasn't until Aidan came into their lives…"

She needed to get to the point. "Tate, are you okay? Did something happen on Christmas Eve? Did I do something?"

He pressed his palms together and bent his head to rest on his hands, like he was gathering his thoughts. He looked up and she felt her heart lurch at the anguish—the distance in his expression.

"No. No, you didn't. I'm sorry if I gave you that impression. We had a good time on Christmas Eve, and that's sort of the problem. It's just… It's not you, or anything you did. It's me. I never should have kissed you. I'm sorry about that, too. I can't have a relationship right now."

Hannah felt the already dull ache begin to sharpen inside of her. She'd heard it all before.

Flashbacks from Spencer's breakup whirled around in her head. About how he couldn't handle what she was going through. He wasn't strong enough to help her, to be there for her. It wasn't her, it wasn't anything she'd done. Hannah knew what that really meant. She wasn't enough. She wasn't worth it.

Tate went on, "I can't get involved with anyone. It's not fair to Lucas. I need to focus all my energy on him. I need to make sure he's okay first and figure out what kind of family *we* can be."

"I see."

"I hope there are no hard feelings. I really like you, Hannah, and I hope we can still be friends."

Not fair to Lucas? She adored Lucas and she'd done everything she could to help him. And it was working. She'd thought Tate wanted her help. And why *wouldn't* he want help? Hannah didn't understand what that last statement meant either, but the picture was clear enough as far as she and Tate were concerned.

Lucas galloped back into the room, a smiling Viktor trailing behind. A duffel bag was thrown over his shoulder and he quickly ticked off all the items he'd tucked inside including extra gloves and a change of clothes.

Hannah thanked Viktor and then waited, her heart bruised and aching, disappointment seeping into her soul, while Lucas doled out his goodbye hugs. She could only be grateful that she hadn't known Tate better, fallen any harder, because the damage could have been so much worse. And it was already bad enough.

CHAPTER THIRTEEN

HANNAH SHUFFLED PAPERS and recited the speech one more time in her mind—the speech that would put an end to this hostile takeover once and for all. Yes, she knew that wasn't the proper terminology, but she thought it sounded fitting. Just as Al Capone had been taken down by taxes, Park Lowell would be done in by numbers, as well.

She tuned in as the chairman, Terry, called the special board meeting to order. She was ready for whatever Park was going to propose. Terry went on to say that since the meeting had been called for a specific purpose they would proceed straight to the relevant business.

"Park, you wanna go ahead?"

Park stood up and began passing around copies of a slim bound booklet to each board member. He announced that those participating remotely had been sent the information in a pdf file. "As you will see in the proposal I'm presenting, these are basically the recommendations that Tate brought up to the board at the last meeting in written form. The proposal includes the construction of a half-pipe, a snowboard-cross course and a terrain park." He stopped to smirk at Hannah. "With plans for the construction of a second half-pipe in three to five years."

Hannah bit the side of her cheek to keep from interrupting. She had a neatly typed handout for the board members, too. She sat back and listened to the rest of his spiel.

"This is nice, Park and Tate," she commented when Park finally sat down and the chairman acknowledged her turn to speak.

"Outstanding photographs," she gushed at Park, and by the look on his face she was sure he didn't know whether she was being honest or facetious, which had been her goal.

"So, as much as I know *some* of us here would like to adopt your proposal—" she couldn't help slipping in the slight emphasis on *some* "—there's a problem."

"Problem? What problem?" Park shot back.

She stood and began passing out the documents she'd brought along. After everyone had a copy, she turned and faced the room.

"Insurance." She paused for dramatic effect. "We can't afford the insurance. If we install a half-pipe and a terrain park like this, our insurance costs nearly triple. Even if we could afford the initial investment and the substantial upkeep, which I also feel would dramatically push our financial limits, the figures I've compiled show the number of customers we'd have to generate in order to pay for the ongoing insurance costs. It won't work. I spoke to both our agent and the insurance company directly. These numbers are industry standards. Unfortunately, Snowy Sky is just too small to take on the liability of a much larger mountain."

Hannah couldn't help but add, "But great work, guys. I can see you've put a lot of time into this." She tapped the cover of the shiny bound booklet.

She paused to look around the room; and wondered why this revelation wasn't being met with quite the impact she'd been anticipating. The room remained silent, and she couldn't help but think she was hearing the glaring sound of disappointment.

Tate rose to his feet. "Mr. Chairman, may I address the board?"

"Of course, Tate, and please call me Terry. We're pretty informal here."

"Thanks, Terry." Brushing his palms together, his eyes skimmed over the board members.

Not for the first time, Hannah admired his style. It would be so easy for him to be full of himself—arrogant and condescending. But he didn't come across that way at all; he was confident, yes, but his demeanor was also rife with a kind of humble respect.

"Before we begin discussion on the proposal, I'd like to make a more, um, informal proposition."

Informal proposition? Hannah had no idea where this was headed but felt a surge of nervous tension anyway.

"As you will all probably recall from conversations we've had, I've taken the time to do a casual poll as to whether most of us ski or snowboard. I'm happy to report that nearly every member of the board participates in one or the other, and as a group, we're pretty evenly split with skiers outnumbering snowboarders by only three. So, what I'd like to do is for us all to take a research trip to a resort that caters fairly evenly to skiers and snowboarders, with stats roughly equal to Snowy Sky as per population base and projected demographics. So you all can see firsthand how we can make this work here. Could the board table this discussion until we return?"

She felt her jaw drop open. He couldn't be serious? This was even more preposterous than his two half-pipe pipe dream.

He paused, apparently to let his suggestion sink in.

She didn't waste any time. "Excuse me, Tate, but what you're proposing is impossible. On so many levels. Number one—a trip like that would be very expensive and Snowy Sky does not have the funds to whisk the entire board off on a ski vacation. And number two—what you're suggesting, about finding a resort equal to Snowy Sky seems very implausible. And number three—what is the point?"

"The second item on your list is already taken care of. Big G Basin in British Columbia, Canada, fits the bill with stats nearly identical to Rankins—small, remote town with limited additional industry and a growing reliance on tourism in both the summer and winter.

"And as to the first point…"

Hannah didn't like the look on his face. She snuck a glance at Park who was proudly watching Tate like some kind of loyal subject pledging fealty to his liege lord.

"I feel so strongly about this that I'd like to

pay for the entire board of directors and their families to participate in this snow-sporting getaway. Big G is having a competition in a couple weeks—the Super Big G Ski and Snowboard Event. We could be there to see how they conduct that while we spend some time hitting the slopes ourselves. I intend to show how the additional revenue from opening Snowy Sky up to competitions would cover the added insurance costs, as per your third point."

The room erupted with a buzz of chatter, questions thrown out about accommodations, airfare, event tickets and logistics. All of which Tate had answers for and would be handling on the board's behalf through his employee, Stacey.

Stacey? Hannah didn't even know he had an employee named Stacey. Listening to him rattle on, she once again felt as if control of her resort—of her life—was slipping from her grasp.

Tate was bribing the board with a ski vacation? Or a—what had he called it? A snow-sporting getaway? How very diplomatic, she thought cynically. Skiing, snowboarding, snowball fighting—no matter what you called it the idea was outrageous. Was this even legal? she wondered. Despair and anger fought for the top spot on her emotional tier. How in the world was she supposed to compete with this?

HANNAH WAS BUSY pacing in front of her fireplace. If the knock hadn't been so loud on her door she probably wouldn't have heard it. Only one person she knew knocked like that and thankfully it was one person she wouldn't mind seeing right now. She needed to vent.

"Come in, Adele." She yelled, but Adele was already opening the door.

Hannah heard her cousin stomp the snow from her boots. Adele came in and removed her dark gray down jacket. She looked stunning in a soft clingy sweater in shades of pink and gray. Tight blue jeans disappeared into tall gray boots that stretched up to her knees.

"You look gorgeous," Hannah told her.

"Thank you," she said. "You look frazzled. I'm guessing the meeting didn't go well. Are you ready? You don't look ready. You can tell me about it on the way."

"Ready? For what?"

"The bonfire."

Slapping a hand to her forehead, she realized she'd totally forgotten. Bering and his wife, Emily, were having a bonfire to celebrate Emily's birthday.

"Give me five minutes."

"Of course. I'm actually a little early anyway. How did the meeting go?"

"Terrible. Tate is taking us all on vacation."

"A vacation? That *does* sound terrible," Adele quipped, her lips twitching with a teasing smile.

"Yep, the entire board and their families. I don't have a family—do you want to come with me? I'll tell you about it in the car."

Hannah raised one hand, fingers spread wide. "My five starts now."

She scurried into the kitchen and poured some kibbles for the cats and changed the water in their dish. When Shay married Jonah and moved into his house in town, she had inherited three of Shay's six cats who didn't care for Jonah's dog—or any dogs for that matter. Hannah was thrilled to keep them and happily spoiled them rotten.

She stepped into the bathroom, ran a brush through her hair, and pulled the messy mass away from her face and secured it with a rubber band at the base of her neck. A touch of balm to protect her lips from the biting cold and her primping was done.

In her room she slipped her feet into a pair of chunky snow boots, grabbed her hat, scarf, gloves and down jacket out of the closet, and reappeared.

"How did I do?"

"Three minutes, forty-three seconds," Adele said. "I don't know how you do it."

She gestured at herself with a head-to-toe sweeping motion. "Well, I don't try very hard for one thing."

Adele chuckled.

She grinned. "Speaking of trying—nice eye shadow. Is Cricket coming tonight?"

Adele's cheeks turned pink as she muttered, "Um, I think so. He mentioned he might be there."

"Mmm-hmm. I can see right now we're going to need a longer car ride."

After climbing into Adele's sporty SUV, Hannah briefed her on her Tate troubles. Adele admitted that "something" might be forming between her and Cricket—if he would stop being so high-handed and bossy.

They could see bright orange flames from the bonfire shooting toward the sky as they neared the end of the long driveway leading to Bering and Emily's home. They parked and piled on their cold-weather ensembles, Adele's looking much more coordinated than Hannah's.

Cricket met them when they were about halfway toward the group of people already gathered around the large fire pit Bering had constructed. The roaring blaze crackled and sparked. Hannah found herself looking forward to roasting marshmallows with the kids.

"Hey, Cricket." Hannah smiled.

"Hi, Banana." He was the only person outside of her family who still used that childhood nickname.

He grinned at Adele, who suddenly looked fidgety on her feet. "Hi, Adele."

"Hello, Cricket." Her voice sounded so prim that Hannah nearly laughed.

He looked back at Hannah. "You know how we've been talking about hiring another pilot? To fill in for me?"

"Yeah."

"I found someone. He's great. And he's got plenty of experience. So I'll work with him this week, then I'd like to take next weekend off."

She nodded. "Sounds good. You deserve a break." Hannah trusted him implicitly. If he thought the pilot was good, she knew he would be good. Cricket had logged hundreds of hours since they'd started JB Heli-Ski. To her knowledge, he'd never turned down a single trip, with the exception of inclement weather.

"Big plans?" she asked.

"Yes, actually. Tate invited me to go to Big G with you and the board."

"That's great! Adele is coming with me." Hannah meant it. Even though Cricket and Tate were friendly, she knew his loyalty lay with her. The idea of having this support system along on the trip further buoyed her mood.

Cricket was already looking at Adele with a satisfied grin. Her cousin was staring at her feet, both of which left Hannah wondering *What the heck?* And thinking they should work it out, she headed for the crowd, greeting family and friends, and giving Emily birthday wishes.

A while later she was browning yet another marshmallow on the end of her metal roasting stick when she felt someone walk up behind her. She knew it was Tate before she even turned around because she smelled his tantalizing mix of soap and spicy cologne.

Ignoring him, she shifted her marshmallow away from the coals and moved it toward her cousin. "Here, Reagan, do you want this one?"

"Awesome, yes. Mom wants me to make s'mores for the twins." He sandwiched the gooey marshmallow between two graham crackers already full of chocolate and slowly pulled it off of the roasting stick.

"I'm taking this one to Gabe. I'll be right back."

"I'll start another one for Finn."

She retrieved a marshmallow from the bag and carefully arranged it on the end of the stick.

"Hey," Tate said, moving to sit in the now-empty seat beside her. "How mad at me are you?"

"What do you mean?" she asked, keeping her eyes on the marshmallow.

"How mad about the Big G trip? On a scale of one to ten—one being an irritating mosquito bite and ten a criminal offense?"

Hannah felt her lips twitching with humor. Tate being his troubled Heathcliff-like self was difficult enough to resist, but Tate being funny was impossible.

"Hmm." She looked up thoughtfully toward the sky for a few long seconds before latching her eyes on to his. "I could do bodily harm but not a felony. More like a body slam or a good hard punch. So, that would be like…what? An eight?"

She finally met his eyes and swallowed nervously because they seemed to be asking her something, but she had no idea what. His lips curled up into a grin as he softly replied, "I don't know. The body slam sounds okay."

She felt her limbs go weak. Because Tate being flirtatious was way, way too much. Not to mention crossing the line *he'd* laid down. She narrowed her eyes. "I thought we were going to be just friends."

"Believe it or not, that's what I'm going for here."

She dipped her chin and delivered a flat look. "I have a news bulletin for you—your friend skills need some work. You can flirt with your friends, but not the ones you've already kissed. You know what? Scratch that. I don't care if you flirt with them. Just don't flirt with me."

She looked back at the fire and let out a huff of frustration. "Now my marshmallow is burned." She blew on the end of her stick to cool the marshmallow and then plucked it off the end of her stick and tossed it into the coals.

"Hannah—"

She let out a tired sigh. "I'm sorry, Tate.

It's just… I can't take it. I'm having a hard enough time keeping my feelings for you separate from what you're trying to do to Snowy Sky. I get that it doesn't matter to you because this is your business—it's what you do, but Snowy Sky is my…" She stopped herself.

She wasn't going to whine and try to make him feel sorry for her. What good would that do? But at the same time she couldn't keep this up. She wished he never would have kissed her, because then maybe her emotions wouldn't be all muddled like they were, although she had a feeling that wouldn't matter.

She went on. "I love Lucas. I want to do whatever I can to help him. But I can't do this flirty thing with you. You set the boundaries, remember? So, let's adhere to them, okay?"

His jaw went tight, his mouth a grim serious line, like the Tate she'd first met. And that was fine with her. She didn't like that Tate nearly as well, and would find him much easier to resist.

She saw Lucas approaching with Viktor.

"Hey, Lucas! Have you ever made a s'more?"

He shook his head, the expression on his face pure curiosity. Hannah thought, *Poor kid, he needs me more than I even realized.*

And so did his uncle. Too bad Tate couldn't see that.

She flashed Lucas a bright smile and it felt good to mean it. "Well, come here, buddy, and I'll show you how these little pieces of heaven are done."

HANNAH PICKED LUCAS up the next morning. They hadn't decided what they were going to do for the day, so she took him up to Snowy Sky. A shipment of rental equipment she had ordered to cover the soft openings and a few "Rankins Ski Free" days had arrived the day before. Freddie had been going through the gear in the rental shop. He had some questions and Hannah wanted to check out the equipment anyway.

Lucas began eyeing the skis, playing with poles and just generally exploring. Hannah liked how he was beginning to act more engaged and confident every day.

"So," Freddie was saying. "There's a mistake on the packing list. It doesn't match up with my order here."

He explained the problem as she studied the papers. "I see what you mean. I have the original on my computer. I'll go get it."

Lucas was across the room playing with the

buckles on a pair of ski boots. "Hey, Lucas, I'm going to run over to my office and print something off of my computer. Do you want to come with me or stay here with Freddie?" Heeding Janie's advice, Hannah always tried to let Lucas know the schedule, and she tried to give him options if she thought a situation might make him uncomfortable.

He eyed Freddie, whom he had taken to almost immediately upon meeting. They'd spent a bit of time with him since and she was sure it was Freddie's laid-back manner that attracted Lucas. The kid just oozed friendliness.

"I'll stay."

"Okay, I won't be long. And you know where I am if you need me. Just have Freddie text me."

He nodded.

His answer felt like more progress and she ran the errand with a happy heart. Fifteen minutes later she returned to find Lucas standing on the fitting table wearing a pair of tiny ski boots atop a shiny new pair of skis. Freddie was explaining how to tell if a boot fit properly.

"Hannah, look at me—I'm skiing like you."

Freddie grinned. "Isn't this cool? This little guy offered to help me out getting some of these bindings set."

"It is." She smiled and pulled out her phone to snap a photo. "Thank you, Lucas. That's awesome. This photo can go on our website if your uncle Tate agrees."

"The boots are tight, not like snowboard boots."

"I know it feels kind of funny, but they are that way so your foot feels connected to the ski. Then, when your foot moves, even a little bit, the ski knows what to do."

He nodded solemnly, fixing his wide dark eyes on hers. "Hannah?"

"Yeah?"

"Could you teach me how to ski?"

She hadn't seen that one coming. Tate had been busy teaching him to snowboard. But kids were curious. She remembered trying snowboarding a few times herself.

"Sure. What do you think, Freddie? You want to fire up the lift and take a few runs?"

"You know it."

WHEN LUCAS TURNED and executed a near-perfect stop next to her, Hannah asked him, "Lucas, you're sure you've never skied before, right?"

He shook his head. "Nope."

"Well, holy cow, mister. You're a natural. What do you think?"

"It's awesome," he gushed. With each and every one of his smiles he seemed to capture a bigger chunk of her heart.

Feeling his helmet again to make sure it was secure, she said, "Okay, I'm going to show you something. Are you ready? Watch me."

He nodded, so she took off down the hill, making a big wide S-shaped turn. She stopped and turned to look at him, ignoring the ache in her leg.

"Do you want to try that?"

He nodded confidently, something he didn't do often. Then, to her complete astonishment, he followed in her tracks, stopping beside her.

"How was that?" he asked.

"Perfect," she stated and meant it.

"Can I keep going?"

"Absolutely."

They made several more runs and Lucas continued to improve. She wasn't sure what to think, other than the kid truly had something special.

She had skied to the bottom to watch him

when she heard a noise behind her. She turned to discover it was Tate.

"What do you think you're doing?"

An angry Tate if his tone was any indication.

"What are you are talking about specifically?"

"I'm talking about Lucas, what else? Why does he have skis on?"

She expelled a relieved breath. "Oh, that."

"Yes, that," he returned coldly.

"He asked me if he could try skiing and I said yes. Don't worry, I'm a great teacher. I used to show kids all the time. And, Tate, he's absolutely amazing. Your nephew could be a downhill phenomenon someday."

"There's no doubt in my mind that you're an excellent teacher. That's not the point." Along with the angry furrow on his brow, there was a look in his eyes that she'd never seen before. What was wrong with him?

"What is the point, then?" she asked carefully.

"I don't want him to be a downhill phenomenon. I want him to be a snowboard freestyle champion. Is this your way of getting back at me?"

She felt her own brow creasing with confusion. "Back at you? For what?"

"For my proposal to the board, for this trip, for what happened between us?"

"Are you...?" She shook her head as if she couldn't believe what she was hearing, because she couldn't. "You must be joking. You honestly think I would take Lucas skiing to spite you somehow? Get over yourself. You're always accusing me of being prejudiced against snowboarding, but now I can see that maybe that was coming from your own place of bias. He asked me if he could try it. I didn't—I don't—see the harm." She added a shrug, hoping to dispel his angst.

It didn't work. His agitation was obvious. Looking down, he placed a gloved hand on his forehead and then removed it with a sigh. "You don't get it."

"Get what?" She inhaled a deep breath of frosty air and met his eyes, which were still shining with hostility. "I am honestly shocked that you're upset about this."

They heard a voice and simultaneously turned to see Lucas gliding down the hill. He shifted his skis to one side, skidded to a stop and dashed off a happy wave. Hannah smiled and returned the gesture, incredibly pleased with his progress. She had thought Tate would be, too.

"I can ski, Uncle Tate," Lucas called out proudly.

She glanced at Tate, who seemed to be watching his nephew with new eyes.

"I see that. Good job, buddy," he yelled back. "Have fun. I'll see you later."

Without another word, he turned away from her and headed back to the lodge.

CHAPTER FOURTEEN

ON NEW YEAR'S EVE Hannah actually found herself looking forward to a night out. She needed a distraction. She'd been spending entirely too much time thinking about Tate. They'd barely spoken since the ski episode, not about anything meaningful anyway.

By silent, mutual agreement, they were careful to keep things friendly for Lucas's sake. Something she seemed much better at than him, which didn't seem fair, because although she knew he was angry with her, she wasn't too pleased with him either.

Now she and Adele walked through the door of the Cozy Caribou, which had been decorated in shimmering silver and black for the evening. A stage had been set up at the far end of the bar, and twinkle lights had been wrapped around the posts and strung across the ceiling.

"Wowza," Adele exclaimed. "This party is fit for…I want to say New York, but with the moose head on the wall and the antique fishing and logging gear I'm thinking maybe…"

"Seattle?" Hannah offered.

"Definitely."

"Tess used to have a nightclub in Seattle years ago." Tess was the owner of the Cozy Caribou, which she operated with her longtime companion, Mack.

Rankins's very own band Rushing Tide had come home to perform and the entire town was abuzz with excitement.

"Look, there's Shay," Adele pointed toward the bar where Shay stood talking with the musicians among a group of people.

As they made their way through the crowd, Hannah felt herself relaxing. She was sure she'd never seen so many people inside the Cozy Caribou at once, and that's what managed to circle her thoughts back around to Tate. Surely he'd be overwhelmed by the number of folks here tonight?

"Have you seen Tate?" she suddenly blurted to Adele. "Cricket said he was coming. In spite of everything, I can't help but feel sorry for him. He doesn't know very many people. I was thinking about asking Cricket to introduce him around a bit."

"Oh, I wouldn't worry about that," Adele

pointed across the room. "Your snowboarder seems to make friends pretty easily."

She spotted him and felt her stomach sink to her toes. He was literally surrounded by people, talking and laughing as if he'd lived here forever.

Before long the band started and Hannah was amazed by how incredibly talented the musicians were. She'd always been away skiing the times they'd visited their hometown to perform. She did her best to enjoy the evening, but for some reason Tate's presence was spoiling her efforts.

Apparently Adele had been correct and she'd worried about him for nothing because little more than two hours into the evening he'd yet to say a word to her. And the more she thought about that, the more it hurt.

She'd done an excellent job of keeping their differences with regard to Snowy Sky out of their personal dealings. She loved Lucas. She'd gone out of her way to help Tate out where he was concerned. And this was how he repaid her? She didn't care, she reminded herself, she wasn't sorry that she'd taken Lucas skiing so she wasn't about to apologize for that. Lucas had enjoyed every minute of it; he'd been asking to go again.

Forcing herself to try to have some fun, she caught up with old friends, yet in spite of her efforts to ignore him right back, she was aware of Tate no matter where he went; seemingly at ease in a sea of people who until a few weeks ago, and some probably even until tonight, had been strangers to him. Hannah was talking to Cricket on the edge of the dance floor when the music suddenly stopped.

"Hey, everybody! Having a good time?" shouted Clark, the band's lead singer. The crowd broke out in applause and cheers. "We want to thank you all for coming out to see us tonight. I can't tell you what a blast this is for Ezra and me. It's like we're back in high school and practicing in one of your garages. Ouch, did we manage to tick off some parents back then." The room erupted with laughter, many of them remembering that very thing.

"We're getting ready to take a quick break, but before we do it's a policy of ours when we play a local club to drag someone up on stage to sing a few tunes. Anyone have any suggestions?" The crowd went wild as names were shouted out amid hoots and cheers.

After a moment he held up a hand, quieting the crowd again. "Okay, okay," he said. "The rumor mill tells me there's a new, uh," he looked down at a slip of paper in his hand and said, "professional snowboarder in town. And it's about time, too, huh? Because Rankins has been in serious need of one of those for years." More noise blasted from the audience.

"And," Clark went on, "several young ladies have informed me that this dude is hot, hot, hot. So, in deference to our hometown boys I think we should try to embarrass the new guy. What do you say?"

No. A surge of horror rose within her. If he did this he would be a laughingstock. In a small town like Rankins, this was the kind of disaster that stuck with a person for life. People would never forget it.

She could see his tall form moving through the crowd toward the stage—and he was smiling. Tate obviously didn't understand the implications of being humiliated like this in a small town. He would be branded as the guy who made a fool of himself that one New Year's on the stage at the Caribou—like a bad reality-show audition. And he needed to be taken seriously if he was going to truly make this place a home for Lucas.

"Wait!" she yelled, turning some heads but not quite projecting over the noisy crowd to the front of the room.

She yelled again, "Wait!"

Cricket, who had been clapping and cheering along with the rest of the crowd stopped to look at her.

"Hannah? What's the matter? Are you okay?"

"No, Cricket." Grabbing his arm, she shouted the words to be heard over the din, which suddenly quieted to a murmur. "We have to do something! Tate can't get up there." The screechy fear in her voice carried this time, more heads turning their way. She didn't care.

Taking a step forward, Cricket reached out and snagged her elbow.

"Hannah, hold on. What are you—?"

"We can't let him be humiliated like this."

"Will you relax." He slid an arm around her shoulder and grinned down at her, effectively holding her in place.

"But, he, Tate—"

"Tate is a big boy. Hannah, listen to me."

He was squeezing her shoulder to get her attention, but she couldn't listen because it was too late. She put her hands on her cheeks as she stared dumbly at the stage. She muttered, "No, oh no."

Soulful music began and after a few beats, which stretched on like an eternity, Tate began to sing and he was…good. Really good. Not

Clark good. But his voice was rich and smooth and totally in tune and pitch—or whatever those musical terms were. Hannah couldn't even carry a tune, but she knew one when she heard it.

A sense of relief flowed through her, only to be followed by an immediate and powerful embarrassment. Her cheeks felt hot as she stared at Cricket who was peering back at her as if he'd just figured out something very important. Which, to be fair, he probably had. She hadn't exactly been quiet about it. Apparently she was the one destined to look like a fool tonight.

Quiet laughter spilled from between his lips. He dipped his head to her ear. "Clark and Ezra never choose anyone who can't sing. I realize now that you didn't know this because you told me earlier that you've never been to one of their concerts."

She looked up toward the stage, her gaze locking on Tate's. She saw, felt, the intensity in his expression. It was as though he'd pinned her in place with his eyes and she felt herself tremble with so many emotions that she couldn't have moved even if she'd wanted to. Desire, longing, wanting—were those the same? Affection and a nearly overwhelming sense of loss.

He needed to stop with the mixed signals. She wasn't equipped to play these kinds of games. She thought she'd made that clear.

Tears clouded her vision, but she refused to let them fall. She didn't cry. She'd never been a crier. Reaching over, she gripped Cricket's wrist as Adele suddenly appeared at her side.

"How bad is it?" she whispered. "How badly did I embarrass myself here?"

He winced. "Mmm… I'm not going to lie to you. Moderately. People are undoubtedly talking, but it's also loud and busy."

Adele added, "Plus, it's New Year's Eve, so someone is bound to top you on the make-a-fool-of-myself scale before the evening is over."

She gave them both a weak smile. "Thank you, guys. I'm going to go home."

"I understand." Cricket bent and kissed the top of her head. "I'm sorry, Banana. And for the record, I think he's an idiot."

Stupid tears pressed their way forward again. She swallowed them down. "Thanks, Cricket. Make sure Adele gets home safe. No drinking and driving."

"I will." He nodded. "I'm not drinking. And

neither is Tag. Tag borrowed the fire hall's wagon and I've got Janie's Suburban. We're driving anyone home who needs it."

She hugged them both and slowly navigated toward the door avoiding curious glances and managing to keep things lighthearted. Finally finding her coat, she was ready to open the back door when someone stepped close behind her.

"You look gorgeous." Tate's voice next to her ear sent a shiver skittering across her skin.

She turned and his eyes flicked down the length of her and then back up again. And this time she could read the look loud and clear. He stepped even closer and a sizzling awareness surged through her.

"Absolutely stop-the-heart gorgeous," he repeated.

Why would he say such a terrible-wonderful thing after she'd specifically requested that he not flirt with her? "Have you been drinking?"

"What?" A look of surprise transformed his features as he let out a chuckle. "No. I don't drink. Considering my family history, I've never had the desire."

"Oh." She hadn't known that. The revelation made her happy in spite of her current muddled state of mortification and sadness. "Neither do I."

"I know."

"You do?"

Narrowed, piercing eyes studied her. "Yes, Cricket told me. Because he said you were leaving and I was worried about you driving on New Year's Eve."

She tried not to read anything into that. "Well, that's nice. But now you know I'll be fine, because I don't drink either, so..." She trailed off because she hated how nervous and frazzled she sounded.

"I do know, but I wanted to thank you for looking out for me tonight."

Any hope that he hadn't seen her display faded like a puff of smoke on a breeze. She didn't respond, fantasizing that she, too, could disappear in the same manner.

Hannah confessed, brushing a hand over her face and letting out a tired sigh, "Clearly I watch too much reality television."

"I liked it." His mouth formed into a teasing smile and she felt another flush creeping over her skin.

"I did it for Lucas," she returned, hoping without much hope that he would believe that. It was partly true. She went on to explain, "The stigma of something humiliating like that in a town this size…"

He grinned, obviously seeing through her half-truth. "Uh-huh, Lucas and I both appreciate it."

"Okay. Lucas is welcome. I have to go now."

"Hannah, don't be like this, please. Don't be mad at me."

"Me? Be like this? I'm not mad at you, Tate. You're the one who is mad at me, remember?"

He exhaled loudly. "I'm sorry about the skiing thing. It… I have my reasons for wanting Lucas to snowboard."

Her voice was gentle when she said, "Your reason is pretty obvious. You're not the first parent in history to dream of having a child follow in their footsteps. Just remember that sometimes kids' feet want to travel in entirely different directions than what others may have planned for them.

"Besides, a little skiing doesn't mean he's going to give up snowboarding. What are you going to do, keep him from trying any sport but snowboarding? What if he decides he likes baseball or lacrosse or…badminton?"

His mouth tightened into a straight, grim line. "It's more complicated than that."

"I doubt it," she answered, because she really didn't see how it could be. "I think you're the only one making it complicated."

"We'll talk about this later."

She shrugged, as if it didn't make any difference to her one way or the other.

He leaned an arm against the wall so she was enclosed in kind of a semicircle of Tateness. Her heart began to beat wildly.

"Hannah, I am sorry. I do care about you. Just like you obviously care about me." He cupped his other hand on her shoulder and she felt the breath catch in her throat as his fingers shifted, his thumb moving toward her neck as if seeking the crazy fluttering of her pulse there. The feel of his skin against hers was so wonderful it was almost cruel.

She desperately wanted to deny his words, but in light of her little display that seemed rather pointless.

She drew in a shaky breath. "But nothing has changed in that regard, so what do you want from me, Tate?"

"What do I want?" He rested his head on his forearm for a few seconds before saying, "What I want...I'm afraid I can't ever have."

The pain in his voice managed to dissolve every remaining bit of anger she'd been harboring. She knew she could make him happy. And Lucas, too, if only he would let it happen.

She placed a hand on his shoulder. "Tate…"

He hissed in a sharp breath as he pushed himself away from the wall, away from his feelings. She could see him mentally shifting once again—away from her. She wanted to reach out for him, but the idea of further rejection kept her planted in place.

A chorus of shouts, whistles and laughter rang out as the band began to play "Auld Lang Syne." Hannah stared at him—waiting. Finally she turned, pushed open the door and walked out into the night, letting the cold air of another lonely year seep into her.

CHAPTER FIFTEEN

HANNAH LET HERSELF into the spacious suite she and Adele were sharing at Big G Lodge. Stepping forward, she lowered her bag and spun a slow circle, absorbing the lush surroundings; dove-gray and light blue walls perfectly complemented the dark wood furnishings. There was an extra-big-screen TV and a fully stocked minibar. Her spirits sank as she made her way toward the bed and examined the luxurious pillow-top mattress beneath the fluffy white down comforter and soft-as-silk sheets.

Large framed black-and-white photos featuring dramatic panoramas of the Canadian Rockies and charming scenes of the mountain town of Garner in the "old days" hung around the room.

She crossed the expanse, stopping before the picture window to take in the stunning view of the resort surrounded by beautiful white-capped mountain peaks. She let out a depressed sigh.

Big G was gorgeous. Tate was right. Everything about this place was comparable to Snowy Sky. The little town of Garner sat in a valley at the base of the ski mountain with a population even smaller than Rankins. Garner wasn't quite as remote as Rankins geographically, but it may as well have been. It was many miles to the nearest city of any significant size, making Big G a destination resort, also like Snowy Sky.

"This place!" Adele gushed, breezing into the room a few minutes later and dropping the bag she'd had slung over her shoulder. Mimicking Hannah's earlier action, although with perceptibly more enthusiasm than she had displayed, Adele twirled. Hannah couldn't help but wonder how many guests before them had executed the same move.

Adele said, "I'm not trying to make you feel worse or anything, but wow."

"I know," Hannah said with another sigh. "I'm sure some of the board members are already calling for my replacement. Park is probably printing new business cards as we speak."

Adele's face scrunched with concern. "They can't do that, can they?" She moved to inspect the bedding. "You said you had a counter argument for the money Tate and Park want to spend?"

Tate had emailed all the board members a summation of how much revenue professional competitions like this Super Big G Ski and Snowboard event brought in for the resort and the town of Garner every year. The number was substantial.

"I do, but I can't deny that if we managed to get Snowy Sky up to competition regulations, events like this would bring in a considerable amount of money. The initial investment coupled with the added insurance costs would be a burden and a risk, but I don't know…"

She gave a helpless shrug before continuing, "I think most board members will see both sides. And we've got those business mavericks on the board—self-made entrepreneurs and risk takers who will like the idea of gambling like this. And now that we're here, making this comparison in person? I have to admit this was a brilliant move on Tate's part."

Adele removed two plush white robes from the closet. "You want to know what I think?"

"What?"

Slipping into one robe, she wrapped the other around Hannah's shoulders and gave her a tight sideways hug. "I think you should relax and enjoy a five-star vacation on Tate Addison's dime. Deal with the rest of it as it comes up."

Adele moved away, unzipped her suitcase and began removing articles of clothing. "Let's get our swimsuits on and try out our hot tub."

Hannah stared thoughtfully out the window, beyond the hot tub, to where soft snowflakes were now floating from the sky like tiny feathers from a pillow. She loved to watch it snow. She remembered the feeling when she was a little girl of that first snowfall of winter and asking her dad over and over again how long it would be until there was enough snow to ski.

"At the very least it'll drive Park crazy. If you act like none of this bothers you, he'll wonder what you're up to."

Even the weather had cooperated with Tate, dropping five inches of powder on top of a base that was already about as perfect as it could get. At least she could look forward to doing some skiing. She wasn't going to let the pain in her leg spoil some time on the slopes, so why should she let Tate and Park ruin the rest of what could be a lovely vacation?

Maybe Adele had a point.

TATE HAD RESERVED a private room for dinner that evening for the entire board and their families. Wanting to make sure everyone got the most out of the weekend, he'd asked his employee, Stacey, to give the group an overview of the resort and all the activities that were available. If anyone needed rental equipment, or lessons, or a list of things to do or places to eat in the town of Garner, Stacey was the person to talk to.

Stacey had just finished her presentation when the waitstaff arrived with a filet-mignon dinner and a black-bean-and-quinoa alternative for any vegans in the party.

She added, "I'm sticking around for dinner, so I'll be available to schedule any activities you'd like to partake in or answer any questions you might have. Don't forget the party Saturday night in the Cascade Ballroom. We'll all have a great time. The first couple hours are for everyone, but tailored to families with a host of neat activities for the kiddos. Trust me, Mr. Addison has gone all out. The adult party will start about nine thirty when the DJ begins to play. The details are in your handout, but feel free to ask me anything."

Lucas had asked if he could sit next to Hannah, and Tate had acquiesced. He knew he would be up and down mingling and answering questions anyway. He'd asked Hannah if she minded and of course she'd said no. She seemed so good at compartmentalizing her feelings, which just strengthened his belief that Snowy Sky didn't mean as much to her as it did to him, or more to the point, that the meaning it held was different.

From where he stood across the room, he watched her pick up her napkin, expertly twisting and shaping the cloth into some kind of critter puppet. He could hear Lucas's giggle as the creation seemed to come to life and dance around. No one could make him giggle the way she could.

Then again, no one could make Tate feel like Hannah did either. He missed her. Kissing her had been unlike anything he'd ever experienced; he'd never *felt* so much in a kiss—so much promise and hope. He'd also never experienced these kinds of feelings for a woman before Hannah.

With Hannah everything had felt so right. He'd purposely stayed away from her on New Year's even though he'd watched her all evening. But when she'd tried to "save" him something had shifted inside of him, and he hadn't been able to stop himself from approaching her—from touching her. He wasn't used to having someone look out for him like that.

She'd been ready to storm the stage—for him. Cricket was right, she was brave.

Viktor spoke from beside him. "She is natural mother, your Hannah."

Tate ran a hand over his cheek. "Yes, she is. But she's not my Hannah." Why couldn't he be a natural father?

"It bothers you, this bond she has forged with Lukie, yes?"

Tate winced, silently acknowledging the statement. Surprising how much it bothered him to hear his problem spoken aloud. He had no idea how Viktor always seemed to know these things about him. He just did, and now Tate didn't even try to lie. Their relationship had always been based on reality and honesty—even if that honesty was sometimes painful.

"Yes," he answered softly. "It does."

"Why is this?"

"I'm not sure. I'm a little jealous I guess, but happy at the same time. That sounds weird. I guess it bothers me that everything seems to come so easy for her. She's so…perfect."

Viktor tipped his back and laughed. "You think life has been easy for Hannah? You think is easy now?"

Tate shot him a surprised look. "Pretty

much. You don't? I mean she comes from this amazing family of real people—normal, good people, who adore her. She's so loved, and she has so much love to give. She has everything I want."

"Everything?"

Tate couldn't think of anything else he'd rather have.

Viktor wrapped an arm around his shoulder and squeezed. "Do you remember what I used to tell you so often when you were competing?"

Tate belted out a laugh. "You told me lots of things, Viktor. Lots and lots."

Viktor chuckled. "This is true. Is why you were champion of the world. But I am talking about the one thing I would tell you when you performed well but would weigh your success too much against another's?"

Tate remembered. Viktor had always told him to never be pleased with just winning, with just doing enough to get the win. He always wanted Tate to perform at *his* highest level. If that meant first place then great, but if it meant third or fourth or tenth, that was fine, too. As long as he was doing his best. And somehow, Viktor always knew exactly what he was capable of and he would say…

"Do you remember?"

"Viktor, I don't think this applies to personal relationships and—"

"Ah, but it does. So much of competition of any kind is like life." Viktor looked him in the eyes. "You may have the odds stacked against you at the onset, but you take those odds and you work, and you learn, and you practice until you achieve what you want."

Tate didn't see how he could learn to love and give love when he didn't seem to have the innate skills. His foundation and Hannah's could not be more opposite. "But—"

Viktor turned a finger inward to lightly tap Tate's chest. "I would say—you are capable of more, Tate. I would say—you deserve exactly what you earn and you can *earn* whatever you want."

AFTER SPENDING THE next day on the slopes Hannah and Adele ventured into the enchanting little town of Garner for dinner. Colorful scroll detailing decorated the storefronts, lending the town a Bavarian-village kind of feel. Unique shops and boutiques lined the main street selling everything from ski and snowboard gear to gourmet cooking supplies, knickknacks and fancy chocolates. Hannah's favorite was the shop dedicated to clocks; there must have been a hundred cuckoo clocks chirping in the windows.

Agreeing on a quiet pub for dinner, they enjoyed delicious sandwiches piled high with shaved roast beef, caramelized onions and a deliciously melted combination of cheeses. Afterward they continued their stroll down the main street of town.

"I'm having so much fun imagining Rankins with this kind of tourism in the winter." Adele pointed to a shop featuring authentic German collectibles: ceramic figurines, dolls, handmade plush animals. "It's going to be a different place in the winter. It'll be so great, Hannah."

Hannah knew providing this visual had been part of Tate's intention, yet when she thought about it, it worked in her favor, too. "I was just thinking the same thing."

Adele went on, "And we don't need to come up with a theme. We already have our own rustic kind of flair."

Rankins consisted of a mix of historic old buildings in a variety of styles—timber frame, log, brick, and eclectic mixes of weathered wood and stone and metal. And thanks in great part to encouragement from the Tourism Bureau, the townsfolk were showing their pride in Rankins's colorful history by donating antique logging equipment, fishing paraphernalia,and mining gear, which was being artfully arranged around the town. Summer tourism was already at record highs and she felt a current of excited anticipation as she thought of what was now in store for Rankins in the winter.

Her mood plummeted as she imagined how Tate's proposal would give Snowy Sky a more modern feel. Couldn't he see how well the theme worked here in Garner? How the lodge complemented the town? She had to get him to compromise on this point at least.

Music drifted from a bar up ahead on the block.

"Hey, let's go in," Adele suggested. "I'd love a glass of wine and I'll buy you a hot chocolate."

Hannah didn't want to, but she knew Adele was trying to boost her spirits and Hannah appreciated her coming along this weekend. There was no reason why Adele shouldn't have some fun.

"Okay, sure."

A small group of people was packing up, so they were able to snag a table and a waitress immediately took their orders. The band was fantastic and surprisingly enough Hannah soon found herself having a nice time. Drinks were delivered as the band began playing one of Adele's favorite songs.

"We have to dance to this," she yelled. She stood and motioned for Hannah to follow. "Come on."

CROWDED PUBS WEREN'T exactly Tate's idea of a good time, but Cricket had talked him into hearing a band. He claimed it was one of his favorites, but Tate suspected he was tired of watching him mope around.

Cricket was drinking a beer and chatting up a professional snowboarder and her friends who had come to town a couple days early for the competition. Tate was sipping his tonic and lime while one of the women tried desperately to get his attention. He wasn't interested, but he could only sit silently for so long before he started to look like a jerk.

He twisted around on his stool looking for an excuse to get away...

Hannah.

He spotted her easily, despite the crowded dance floor. She was just so...radiant. He suffered a flash of embarrassment at even thinking the word, but it fit. He couldn't take his eyes off her, and he knew he wasn't the only one.

Smiling, waves of brown hair falling down her back. She looked so happy. Hannah almost always looked happy, he had learned, even when she really wasn't. He'd picked up on that, too. But most of the time her contentment seemed genuine, and he liked that so much. It balanced his tendency to take life so seriously. And suddenly he realized the unhappiest moments he'd witnessed from her had all been because of him.

Viktor's words came to him and all the stupid reasons he'd decided they were better off apart flashed through his mind. He discarded them in one fell swoop. Because he needed her. It was that simple. And Lucas needed her, too. He hoped Viktor was right that if he tried hard enough, he could actually deserve her, too, because he was going to try. He stood and moved toward the dance floor, toward Hannah.

She was all he could see, all he could think about, and suddenly he had to get to her as quickly as he could and tell her exactly how he felt.

HANNAH DANCED A couple more songs and then caught Adele's eye. Thirsty, she mimed a drinking motion and pointed toward their table. Adele waved as a nice-looking guy swept her into his arms. Good for Adele, Hannah thought. She'd been pining over Cricket way too much lately.

Standing beside their table she drained her glass of water. Wanting a refill, she spun around to search for the waitress only to find a wide, firm chest blocking her path. Her eyes flicked upwards and she started to move around him, until she realized she was staring into the face of the only man to ever break her heart.

AND THAT'S HOW Tate ended up with beer spilled all over his shirtsleeve and down half his back. He wasn't paying attention and he stepped into a guy whose hands were gripping the handles of four mugs of beer. Tate apologized, backtracked to the bar and fished some money out of his wallet, including a huge tip. He told the cute bartender that the guy's drinks were on him. She flipped him a towel and a sweet smile.

He waved a thank-you and sopped up the mess the best he could. The guy was grateful and impressed with his generosity, and unfortunately he knew who Tate was. He was a snowboarder himself in town for the Super Big G. Was Tate competing again? Did he have any insight about the cross course? Tate politely visited for a few minutes before continuing on his mission, and that's when he saw Hannah talking to Spencer Kitt.

SPENCER? HANNAH THOUGHT she might throw up.

"Hannah, hey. How, uh, how are you?"

"Fine, Spence. How are you?"

Three years ago she'd been ready to bring this guy home to meet her family. Three days after her near-fatal accident he'd shattered her heart and crushed her spirit, and now they were how-are-you-ing? This was surreal.

His eyes traveled up and down her frame. "You look incredible. You're just totally hot, but you always were. I'd heard that you'd made a full recovery, but I can't believe you're here standing right in front of me."

He lifted a hand as if he was going to touch her. She gave it her best get-that-spider-away-from-me glare, and he lowered it back to his side.

"As opposed to what? Being in a wheel-chair?" She couldn't help her cynical tone. No, that wasn't true—she didn't *want* to temper her anger.

He winced, nodding as he replied, "I deserve that, and more. You probably hate me, but, Hannah, I'm so sorry about everything." He inhaled deeply and went on, "Sorry sounds ridiculous now that I'm saying it. So many times I've wanted to call, but I was such a fool."

With his green eyes fixed firmly on hers, he sounded as sincere as he looked. And he looked really good; muscles very noticeable beneath his close-fitting T-shirt, blond hair neatly trimmed with a touch of honey-golden stubble covering his jaw. How could someone who was so good-looking be so cruel? Why hadn't she considered that he might be here for this event? The Super Big G was a very big deal.

"Spence—"

"No, wait. I'm sure this speech sounds practiced and that's because it is. I promised myself that if—when—when I ran into you someday I wouldn't waste the opportunity to say everything I've wanted to say. I was such a stupid coward, and I—"

TATE WATCHED FROM across the room and he knew. He just knew there was something between Hannah and Spencer Kitt. A painful knot began to form in his chest at the thought that he might be too late. Because his feelings for Hannah were clear as crystal now. He briefly pondered what to do. Another man might throw in the towel, a nice guy would probably back off.

But something about the way she was standing, her posture and her movements, or lack thereof, called to him. Her lips were curved up into a smile, but he knew her well enough by now to know that she didn't mean it because… Because the rest of her wasn't smiling, and she did that—smiled with her face while the rest of her didn't match the moment. He wondered if she knew she did that.

He walked up and joined them.

"Tate." She met his eyes and he hoped he wasn't imagining the relief he saw there.

"Hannah, there you are."

"Tate, hey, man!" Kitt cried, reaching out a hand. "Great to see you."

"Yep, here I am," Hannah replied in a dull, slow, very un-Hannah-like manner. Something wasn't quite right here.

"Spencer." Tate shook his hand. "Haven't seen you in a while. How's it going?"

"Good. Here for the Super Big. Are you competing again?"

"No, actually I'm here on business. I don't know if Hannah mentioned it, but she's here with me."

He watched Spencer's face fall and wished those words were true in the sense he was assuming.

"…for the same business."

Spencer brightened again. "No, we hadn't gotten that far. We were just, um, catching up. We used to know each other a long time ago." He turned a meaningful, hopeful smile on Hannah.

She continued to stare blankly. Tate thought she looked ill. Something told him this was all Kitt's fault.

"That's nice," he somehow managed a polite smile along with the words. "But unfortunately I need to interrupt." He reached out and gave her forearm a gentle squeeze. "Can I steal you away, Hannah?" Why hadn't he done this already—weeks ago? Stolen her away, or at least stolen her heart, like she'd stolen his?

"I want to introduce you to some people," he lied.

"Sure." Her voice was barely audible.

Spencer looked disappointed but sounded

eager, "Hannah, we'll talk later, okay? Tomorrow? I'll call you and—"

Tate led her away without giving her a chance to respond.

HANNAH WAS SHAKEN. No, shaken didn't even begin to cover how she felt—like someone had stuck her in a giant clothes dryer and left her tumbling for days.

Tate stopped near the bar where Cricket and Adele were huddled close.

"Cricket, Hannah and I are leaving. Can you make sure Adele gets back to the hotel safely?"

He grinned. "Yep, I won't let her out of my sight."

Adele scowled. "I can get myself back to the hotel. Hannah, are you okay?"

She nodded. "Tired, and just a little out of sorts." She shivered and brushed her hands over her arms.

She heard Tate mutter something to Cricket before he stepped away. Where was he going? She kind of wanted to follow him…

Adele took her by the hand. "Sweetie, you are really pale? Are you coming down with something?"

She opened her mouth to respond but nothing came out, and the next thing she knew Tate was standing beside her again. He'd somehow found her jacket along the seemingly endless line of pegs and cubbies against the wall. How had he managed that so quickly? He held it while she slipped into it. He linked the fingers of his hand through hers and the warmth from him somehow began to melt the icy cold that had settled through her body. She smiled weakly at Adele, who promised not to be late, and allowed Tate to lead her outside.

She inhaled deeply, hoping the frigid air would bring her back to her senses. Tate continued to hold her hand and she let herself be comforted by the feel of his skin against hers, allowed herself to wish he would take her in his arms and tell her… What? She didn't even know.

They walked a ways in silence before he asked, "How do you know Spencer Kitt? From your competition days?"

She glanced in his direction without making eye contact. "Yes, we were… We used to be…"

"In a relationship?" he supplied.

"Yes."

"Do you want to talk about it?"

"No."

"I do."

"What? Why?"

"Because, I… Hannah, I'm sorry about what happened between us. I royally screwed up and I know it. I kissed you and then on Christmas Eve I realized how little I have to offer you. I got scared. Your upbringing—your family, is so…perfect. And I didn't have that. I don't even know what a real family means—or does, or even talks about. But I'd like to try and figure it out. I'd like to try again—with you."

She couldn't speak. This was too much. Rejections from the only two men she'd cared about in her entire life and then apologies from them both on the same night? What was wrong with her that they couldn't just…*not* hurt her in the first place?

Tate stopped walking and only then did she realize they were standing in front of the lodge.

"Thank you for escorting me back. I'm, um, a little out of it. And my leg hurts. Can we talk about this later?" She forced the words out of her painfully dry throat as she looked up to meet his eyes. Why was this happening to her? She extricated her hand from his and immediately felt the cold begin to seep back into her body.

"Of course. Your leg hurts?"

Had she mentioned her leg? Why had she

said that? She didn't want him to know. She forced out a smile, but it felt more like a grimace. "It's nothing. Just an old injury that flares up once in a while. I'm sure you have some of those, too."

He didn't answer, just stared with warm, pleading eyes that she couldn't deal with right now. It was a look she would have loved to have seen a couple of weeks ago on Christmas. What had changed? she wondered. She suddenly wanted to scream at him for playing with her emotions in this way. But Hannah wasn't a screamer either.

She shivered. "Good night, Tate. I'll see you tomorrow."

TATE WATCHED HANNAH jog up the stairs into the lodge and felt a brutal mix of longing and regret and love.

Love?

Yep, he was in love with her. He'd been in love with her almost from the first. Why had he waited so long to admit it to himself? Because if he hadn't he could go to her right now.

She was clearly miserable and he couldn't stand it. It was so rare to see anything but happiness radiating from her. He'd seen anger a few times, had the snowball memory to prove it, but never this sadness. He wished he could go after her and make her smile.

He loved her smile. Hannah's smile made him feel as though everything was right in the entire universe and when she directed it at him, he felt like a better man—a better person, like anything was possible. No wonder Lucas adored her so much. The thought of not seeing that smile anymore made his heart hurt.

Cricket's words from that day in the Faraway Restaurant floated through his brain about Hannah being "tough." And brave. Tate had assumed Cricket meant that in the business sense.

If he was going to try and… What was he going to try and do where she was concerned? Win her back wasn't quite right because he hadn't exactly had her to begin with. And whose fault was that? he asked himself. He wanted her in his life, he knew that, and if he was going to stand a chance he would need more information—information he should have sought long ago. He just hoped it wasn't too late.

He sent a text to Viktor to let him know he was back at the lodge but wouldn't be back in the room for a while. Instead he walked over to the concierge desk, handed the young man an outrageous tip and asked if he would order him a large black coffee from the restaurant. Then he took a seat in the lobby and waited.

CHAPTER SIXTEEN

HEAD POUNDING, EARS RINGING, leg aching, and with a vague sense of nausea still plaguing her, Hannah finally made it to her room. It seemed like a chore even to remove her clothing; she only managed to kick off her boots and peel away her outer layer before collapsing on the bed.

Hours, minutes, she had no idea how much time had passed when she heard Adele sneaking into the room. A moment later she felt a soft hand touching her forehead. She opened her eyes and smiled weakly.

"I'm sorry, did I wake you? I was worried you might have a fever."

"You're sweet." Hannah tucked a hand beneath her cheek. "No, I'm just lying here. Thinking."

"Cricket said he saw you talking to a guy in the bar. He said he thought it was Spencer. He's your old boyfriend, right? That cretin who broke your heart while you were still in the hospital?"

Hannah exhaled wearily. "Yes."

"That explains your odd behavior. I even feel a little sick myself now. What did he say?"

"Everything. Everything I would have loved to have heard him say three years ago."

"You've told me before that you don't have feelings for him anymore. Did seeing him make you realize that you do?"

"Yes, no, maybe…sort of."

TATE WAITED ALMOST an hour in the lobby before Cricket had finally shown up holding Adele's hand tightly in his. He waited some more while the couple appeared to argue. Finally Cricket pushed the button and the doors slid open. Adele stepped inside—alone. Tate hurriedly sent him a text.

He pulled his phone from his pocket and then scanned the lobby. Tate waved.

Cricket walked over and sat in the adjacent chair. "What's up?"

"I was waiting for you."

"I'm flattered, but hopelessly infatuated with someone else."

Tate laughed.

"If you're wanting a night out on the town, I'm done, man. I think I'm getting old."

"Don't feel bad—I've always been old."

"You don't drink at all, do you?"

"No. Too much addiction in my genetic makeup."

"Smart. I've got some of that, too."

"I need you to tell me about Hannah."

Cricket's entire body took on a defensive posture; menacing scowl, hands raised, head shaking. "No way. If you want to know something about Hannah you need to ask her yourself. No way would I betray that girl."

Tate grinned. "I know she's your partner and a good friend, and I respect that. I'm not asking you to give me proprietary information. And I'd love to ask her myself but I'm afraid time is of the essence here."

Now he looked curious. "What do you mean?"

"Do you know Spencer Kitt?"

Cricket fell back against the fluffy cushion behind him as he let out a sigh. "I told Adele I thought I saw him in the bar. He was talking to Hannah, right?"

"Yep. I want to know what he means to her."

"I can't say for sure what he means now, but I know he meant a lot once upon a time. Before he broke up with her."

Tate couldn't imagine why a simpleton like Spencer Kitt would give up a woman like Hannah. "The reason?"

"You heard about the accident, right?"

Tate tilted his head. "Accident?"

"Hannah's accident?" Cricket's eyes widened with surprise. "Man, you are behind the curve. I'll tell you what I know because it's information you could get from almost anyone in Rankins. That stunt she pulled on New Year's kind of leads me to believe that she, uh, likes you."

Tate couldn't help the satisfied grin that erupted across his face. He'd been thinking about that, too. Holding on to that possibility. He lifted a hand, motioning for Cricket to continue.

"So, the accident... She was on her way home from a day of training at Squaw Valley when a drunk driver crossed the center line..."

As Cricket relayed the story as he knew it, Tate experienced alternating bouts of horror, grief, sadness and relief.

"She's lucky to be alive. I can't even remember how many bones were broken."

Tate continued to listen, dumbfounded at the challenges she'd overcome during her long recovery.

"So," Cricket said when he'd finished, "you can see why Snowy Sky is so important to her. After losing her skiing career and everything she'd worked so hard for, and nearly her life, she views that resort as her shot at redemption— her second chance at success."

Tate nodded slowly, trying to let it all sink in. Finally he said, "Thank you. I really appreciate this."

Cricket smiled. "Good luck, man. No offense, but you're going to need it to get Hannah."

Tate stayed put in the lobby for a long time after Cricket left and considered everything he'd heard. Hannah had been through so much. How could he have been so blind? So self-absorbed? She had quit skiing because she'd been in a terrible accident, which had nearly killed her. Her recovery had taken many months, physical as well as mental.

Frustration made his skin crawl as he thought the situation through, feeling like a complete imbecile. Despite Viktor's observations and not-so-subtle comments, he'd been so focused on his own life, *his* wants and needs, that he hadn't stopped to think that there might be more to Hannah than what he saw—what she let anyone see.

The assumptions he had made about Snowy

Sky being just a business proposition to her. The kid in Bradbury's had told him that she'd been injured, but he'd never dreamed it had been so severe. Why hadn't he taken that as a cue to find out? She'd even made a joke about her therapist that night at the Festival of Trees fund-raiser. Tate could only imagine how losing everything like she had would mess with a person's head.

And Kitt? *What kind of a louse breaks up with a woman so soon after she's suffered that kind of trauma?*

His heart hurt to think about everything she'd been through. In spite of all of that, here she was, giving her time and energy and love to Lucas. And to him. He'd reciprocated by... by bulldozing his way into her life, wreaking havoc and threatening everything she'd worked so hard for. Then he'd kissed her only to be frightened away by the demons of his own past and fear of his shortcomings.

He couldn't believe he'd blown a chance with the most amazing woman he'd ever met. No, that wasn't true; he was pretty sure Hannah was the most amazing woman on the planet.

He'd screwed up even worse than he realized. If he still had a shot he wasn't going to blow it this time.

HANNAH AWOKE THE next morning to a firm knocking on the door. She heard Adele come out of the bathroom and watched her jog toward the door. There was some mumbling and then a young guy in a navy blue jacket came in with a huge bouquet of peach-colored roses.

After handing him a tip and seeing him to the door she hustled back and flopped on the end of Hannah's bed.

"My goodness, what a way to start your morning, huh?"

"Those are for me?"

"Who else would they be for?"

"You."

"What?"

"From Cricket."

"That man," she huffed with a roll of her eyes, but Hannah could tell the malice just wasn't there. "We're not quite to the flower stage yet."

There was a card with the flowers. "What does the note say?" Hannah asked, propping the pillows up behind her.

"I wonder what orange roses signify?" Adele pondered as she tore open the card.

Hannah knew the color didn't mean anything in this case. Well, nothing in the sense Adele suggested.

"'Will you please have dinner with me tonight?' It's not signed."

"They're from Spencer. He sent me this color of roses once when we were dating. I told him they were my favorite."

LATER THAT MORNING Hannah placed the toe of one boot into her ski binding, clicked the heel into place and then repeated the action with her other leg. It still felt a little strange to ski without gearing up to race. For some reason it hit her hard this day.

She tried to think of something positive; one nice thing about skiing recreationally was that she no longer had to wear her boots quite so tight. She swallowed down the lump in her throat. Who was she kidding? She missed those boots that made her feet ache and her toes numb. Missed them with a desperation that nearly left her breathless.

Some things are not meant to be, Hannah, she told herself, pulling her goggles down from their perch on her helmet and securing them in place over her eyes. Like her and Tate. Pushing outward from the center of her boot with one ski, and then the other, she glided toward the lift.

Several lanes were roped off at the top of

the rise like the line for an amusement-park ride. There wasn't much of a crowd and no one else in the single-rider line, but when it was her turn to enter into the main queue, a snow-boarder joined her. Something hitched in her chest when she realized it was Tate. *An entire mountain and here he is journeying up the lift to the beginner runs?* Interesting coincidence.

"Good morning. Mind if I join you?"

"Good morning. Nope, that would be fine."

She shuffled her skis along. They were only a few spots away from their turn.

"Lucas is riding with Viktor."

She moved forward and positioned her skis on the platform. He manipulated his board into place beside her. They both looked over their shoulders and grabbed the chair as it smoothly slid in place behind their knees, lifting them as they leaned back and sailed up into the air.

"How is Lucas doing?" Hannah asked after she'd settled her skis on the metal bar that acted as a footrest. She loved the foot-rests that a lot of the newer lifts were equipped with these days. Snowy Sky would have them and it was so nice to be able to rest your legs after hours of hard skiing in heavy, tight boots weighed down with skis.

Especially if you were cursed with a bum

leg. She subtly shifted her weight to ease the pain from the pressure now on it.

"He's having fun."

"Good. I saw him at breakfast. He seemed excited about his lesson with Viktor this morning. I told him I'd spend some time with him after lunch."

"Ah…that explains it."

"Explains what?"

"Explains why he just asked me how much longer till lunch?"

She laughed.

"I watched him eat two plate-sized pancakes, four strips of bacon, and about a pound and a half of strawberries less than an hour ago, so I knew he couldn't really be hungry."

"Well, I'm looking forward to it, too."

She could feel Tate's eyes drilling into her, but she kept staring straight ahead.

"He was wondering if you could give him another ski lesson?"

Her stomach tightened. Was this his idea of an apology? She turned her head then and felt confident her look conveyed her general feeling of hurt and confusion.

"I'm so sorry, Hannah. I overreacted about the skiing thing. I'd like to explain about that. You were basically right when you accused me of wanting Lucas to snowboard for my sake. I…I thought it was the one thing I could teach him. A way for us to connect."

"There are a million things for you to teach him. A million ways to show him you love him. I see you doing both all the time. And you're doing a great job by the way."

He cut his eyes away and then brought them right back. "Thank you. I know. I know that now. I mean, I've come to realize that. Thanks to you."

She nodded. It was a good apology. She smiled at him and he smiled back and Hannah felt her heart skip a beat. Why did he have to be so irresistible?

"I'd like to discuss this some more and there are other things I'd like to talk to you about, too. Can we maybe have dinner tonight? Just the two of us?"

"I can't. I have plans."

"With Adele? Because Cricket wants to take her—"

"No, with someone else."

"Spencer?" By his tone he may as well have said Attila the Hun.

Spencer had called to follow up on his dinner invitation. He said he wanted to talk, too. Suddenly everyone wanted to talk to her. Her first instinct had been to decline. The idea of spending time with him like that felt too painful, but he'd been so earnest, so convincing. Amazing how his voice, his sweetness had catapulted her back to the past. She'd eventually agreed.

"Yes, with Spencer."

"I could tell there was something between you two at the bar last night."

"There's nothing between him and I. There used to be—a long time ago. I don't know…"

They'd reached the top of the lift and she was glad because she'd had no idea what she was going to say. They both bailed off and moved to one side so Tate could secure his one loose boot to his board. Which he did quickly, then he stood upright again, clapping his gloves together, shaking off the bits of snow he'd accumulated in the process.

"Can I see you after?"

"After what?"

"After your dinner."

"After dinner is the party. We told Lucas we'd go together."

Lines of frustration appeared on his forehead, but apparently he wasn't discouraged because they were quickly smoothed away with a grin.

"That's right. Okay, I'll see you there, then—at the party."

TATE WATCHED HANNAH and Spencer Kitt from his own table across the restaurant. Kitt's body language told him everything he needed to know—the hand at her elbow when they were seated, reaching across the table to touch her hair, leaning-over-the-table type of conversation. Kitt wanted her back.

Had Tate started calling the nicest restaurants in town until he found their reservation? Had he arrived early and tipped the waitress beforehand to seat them at a certain table? Did he feel like a stalker? Yes to all three disturbing questions, but now was not the time for introspection.

A man wearing a black suit and shiny gelled hair delivered a bottle of wine to their table that Tate knew for a fact Hannah wouldn't drink. Strike one, he thought with satisfaction as he deduced that Hannah must have drank before the accident. That moron Kitt didn't know her at all anymore.

The sommelier handed the glass to Kitt who swirled it around and sniffed it and acted like he knew what he was doing, before taking a sip and nodding his approval. The guy topped off his glass and then picked up the one sitting in front of Hannah. She shook her head, obviously declining. Kitt looked a little annoyed but quickly squelched it. He'd probably hoped to impress Hannah with an expensive bottle of wine, and now here he was stuck with it when he probably would have been just as happy with a cheap beer.

Tate smiled when the waiter soon returned to the table with a cup of Hannah's favorite— hot chocolate. He recognized the mound of whipped topping and chocolate sprinkles because it was the same thing he was drinking. For some odd reason that fact made him very happy.

ONCE UPON A TIME, a dinner like this would have left Hannah starry-eyed. But now, as she sat across the table from Spencer, she tried to be honest with herself.

After he had broken up with her it had been so painful to deal with the realization that he hadn't really loved her—not unconditionally. Then later a part of her was glad because what would have happened as time went on?

There was a myriad of circumstances that could occur in life that forever changed a person. What if they had gotten married right before the accident? Or if they'd been married and she'd later been diagnosed with cancer or some other life-altering disease? Or even now if she ended up losing her leg? Would he leave her? Hannah couldn't help thinking that she already knew the answer even though he'd been saying all the right things, and doing them, the entire evening.

"Spence, thank you again for the flowers, they're gorgeous."

His ready smile had been one of the traits that had first attracted her to him. He'd turned that smile on her at a competition in Aspen—across a rack of skis. She'd been on her way to the lodge for lunch after a morning of hard training. He'd commented on her goggles, which had turned out to be his preferred brand, as well. He'd joined her for lunch where they'd both ordered the special without looking at the menu. Hannah thought she'd fallen for him the second he'd recited her personal best in the giant slalom event.

He reached across the table and held her hand. "Hannah, can you ever forgive me? No, I don't even want you to answer that right now. I'm just asking that you give it some thought. I made a terrible mistake. I realized a long time ago how special you are and what we had. By then it felt too late. But thinking about you and now seeing you. I miss you…"

Hannah listened to his heartfelt soliloquy,

but her eyes kept drifting to their intertwined fingers. Why didn't the feel of his hand on hers make the cold go away? Sitting here with him she felt as if she'd swallowed a block of icy concrete.

"Are you sure you won't have a glass of wine? It's a nice vintage." Hannah knew it was an expensive bottle, yet she stared in disbelief. Was she crazy to think Spencer should be sensitive enough to ask if she wanted wine before ordering it? She'd rarely consumed alcohol before the accident—just an occasional glass of red wine. But after the accident just the thought, the smell, made her nauseated. She didn't begrudge anyone else drinking sensibly, but it wasn't for her. She tacked on a small smile. "No, thank you. I already told you I don't drink."

"At all?"

She sighed. "No. Not at all."

"Okay," he said. "I understand."

But she thought she saw a trace of irritation, of displeasure.

"Spencer—"

"Maybe I can talk you into it. I used to be pretty good at that. Remember the time we went swimming in that frozen lake in the

Alps? You enjoyed a glass of wine then, didn't you?"

He added a wink and that was the moment when Hannah knew this reunion with Spencer was truly futile.

TATE WATCHED AS they finished their meal. Hannah declined dessert and he wondered if it was because she was too full of the Bolognese she'd ordered, but only picked at, or too full of Kitt's lines.

Finally they both stood, Hannah gave Kitt a quick hug and left the restaurant. Even though he would have preferred to get her alone, he was glad they'd made plans to attend the party with Lucas. At least Kitt wouldn't be with her all night.

He decided to wait for Kitt to depart before he did the same, but Kitt resumed his seat and now held his phone in his hand.

Tate was settling his bill with the waitress, including another tip for tying up the table for so long when he saw Park Lowell emerge from the bar at the back of the restaurant and walk straight to Kitt's table.

Hmm. Park and Kitt were friends? He watched the two shake hands. It was obvious that they did indeed know each other.

Then a thought that had been a nagging question all night surfaced in the forefront of his brain; why *hadn't* Kitt tried to patch things up with Hannah years ago?

Tate rubbed a frustrated hand across his jaw. Not that he hadn't made his own mess of things with her, by being so, so…obtuse. Hannah was right—he had been like a bulldozer.

But how in the world was he going to fix it now? The only thing he knew for sure was that he wasn't going to wait to try and fix it. Not like Kitt had done.

Tate thought for a second and then a slow smile spread across his face. He picked up his phone and placed a call to Stacey.

"Stacey? Hey, it's me. I need you to see if you can find me something—a gift actually."

CHAPTER SEVENTEEN

THE LAST THING Hannah felt like doing was going to the party. She was tired—tired and confused and overwrought. But she'd promised Lucas, and Adele was excited, so she was determined to make the best of the evening.

Hannah and Adele walked into the Big G Lodge's Cascade Ballroom to find that Stacey had been spot-on about Tate going all out; a long buffet set with gleaming silver servers graced one end of the room while sparkling, powder blue tablecloths covered at least a dozen large round tables, each with a different snow globe centerpiece.

A barrel-sized jar stood at one end of the buffet line along with ballots for guests to guess how many glistening snowflakes had been placed inside. The partygoer with the closest guess would win the snow globe of their choice.

Carnival-style games had been set up along the other end of the ballroom. From where they stood she could see a basketball hoop shoot, a pop-the-balloon-with-a-dart booth and some kind of fishing game. That piqued some enthusiasm within her. Playing games with Lucas would undoubtedly be the highlight of her evening.

She greeted several of Snowy Sky's board members, wives, husbands and other family members. Some skiers and snowboarders already in town for the competition had been invited as well, and she knew a few of them, too.

Tate had said he'd see her here, that there was something he wanted to talk about. And this morning on the lift he'd seemed…different. More like the Tate she'd come to know before Christmas Eve. But what did that mean? She didn't want to open her heart—again—to someone who wasn't sure what he wanted or if he wanted her. She hadn't yet recovered from the disappointment of their first go-around.

She was standing near the buffet when she saw Viktor and Lucas enter the ballroom without Tate. She waved and Lucas made a beeline toward her. They filled their plates and a short time later they were all settled around a table enjoying their meal—Hannah, Lucas, Viktor, Adele and Cricket.

She noticed Tate the second he came through

the door, but she pretended not to until Cricket pointed him out. Spotting them, Tate held up a finger indicating he'd be right over.

He arrived with a full plate, taking a seat in the empty chair next to hers. He smiled warmly, so warmly it made her insides flutter. She returned it with a lukewarm smile of her own and was proud of herself for maintaining her dignity. Then he leaned close to her and she felt her resolve begin to melt like a crayon in the sun.

His breath was hot on her ear and he smelled really good, like mint and lemons.

"Is your dance card full?"

"My dance card? Um, no, but I'm not dancing," she managed to utter. "I'm going to bed. I told Lucas I'd take him upstairs and tuck him in, and then I'm going to my room." She didn't mention that her date with Spencer had completely zapped her mentally, or that her leg was complaining after a day of skiing. The pain was stirring a fresh batch of worry even though she kept telling herself not to until she knew she had something to worry about. Easier said than done. She was exhausted inside and out.

"Please?"

"Please, what?"

"Please dance with me. I saw you dancing last night at the pub and now it's on my bucket list."

"Dancing is on your bucket list?" she asked wryly.

"Dancing with *you*—my bucket list is very specific." There was a playful note to his tone that she found difficult to resist.

"Oh? Well…that's…" Her voice sounded kind of husky and surprised, like a bad Marilyn Monroe impersonation. She felt a warmth at her cheeks because that was actually really sweet—and pretty romantic. She loved to dance and the idea of holding Tate that close left her a bit light-headed.

"I'm not dancing," she managed weakly. Then changed the subject. "Lucas and I are going to go play some games. Do you want to come along?"

At the word *games*, Lucas had jumped out of his chair. Tate stood and they all three headed toward the other end of the ballroom.

After a respectable effort, Tate and Lucas won a prize in the hoop shoot. Lucas tried his hand at fishing, which consisted of casting a line over a huge tarp decorated like the ocean. Clearly having a ball, he "caught" several plastic animal figurines. It warmed Hannah's heart to see him so happy.

Next they made their way to the fish frenzy—a game where the objective was to toss ping-pong balls into small cups, the kind often seen at carnivals in the old days filled with goldfish for prizes. There were no goldfish here; instead the prizes were plush jungle animals. Successfully landing the balls in certain cups scored points rewarded by difficulty. Points were accumulated and you could then "purchase" your prize accordingly. But the game was the same, and it was one Hannah was very familiar with.

Lucas reached over and reverently patted the large green snake the operators used to lure people in to play. It had to be at least ten feet long.

Tate asked him. "You like that snake, huh, buddy? Do you want to give it a try?"

Lucas tentatively shrugged a shoulder. He still had a difficult time asking for what he wanted. "Can you try, Uncle Tate?"

"Sure, I'll give it a go."

He bought twenty ping-pong balls. After throwing most of the balls and trying several different strategies, he managed to successfully land two.

Hannah snickered behind her hand. "Listen, Lucas, at this rate we're going to be here all night."

Tate turned and glared playfully. "You're laughing. You think you can do better?"

"Tate, no offense, but my cat Marcie could do better."

Lucas giggled.

"Okay, hotshot—it's your turn." Tate turned back to the kid running the booth. "Ten more balls."

"Don't waste your money. I only need five."

Tate's brow crinkled in confusion. "What?"

She pointed. "If you make it into the cup in the center, then you can pick any prize you want. Isn't that right—" Hannah paused to read the kid's name tag "—Devon?"

"Yes, ma'am. The lucky cup gets you any prize on the wall—including Cuddles."

"Cuddles?"

"Yeah, Cuddles the snake."

Tate gave her a patient look. "It's virtually impossible to make it into that cup. In order to win the cool prize you have to buy a bunch of tries, win like a hundred small prizes and then trade them up for the big prize."

She shrugged. "That might be *your* strategy, but that's too expensive for me. My strategy in pretty much any game has always been to just go for the gold."

Lucas nodded solemnly like this made perfect sense.

Tate rolled his eyes at her and asked Devon, "Devon, does anyone ever win Cuddles like that?"

"Oh, um, sure. My buddy Jake said someone won it once when he was working a booth last year in Juneau."

Tate gave Hannah a told-you-so look.

She returned it with one that said she wasn't intimidated.

"So, you're saying with just five ping-pong balls you can hit the lucky cup?"

A small crowd had begun to gather.

"Yes." She tousled Lucas's hair. "What do you think, Lucas? Can I do it?"

He nodded, exuding complete and total confidence in her.

"Thank you for believing in me." She narrowed her eyes at Tate. "It's nice that someone does."

He chuckled. "I would be willing to bet just about anything that nobody could win the snake that easily."

"Really? Anything?"

"Yes, let's bet. If you miss, then you have to dance with me tonight."

What was his obsession with dancing all of a sudden? Although, she had to admit she wouldn't mind losing. If her leg wasn't aching. No, it wouldn't be a good idea even then, so why was she even considering it?

"Fine, I already told you I'm not dancing tonight, though. Hand 'em over, Devon." Hannah waggled her fingers in his direction and he counted them out one by one.

"Lucas, can you hold these for me?"

He nodded eagerly and she placed four of the balls in his cupped hands.

Gearing up for her first attempt, she paused to ask Tate, "What do I get if I win?"

He shrugged. "Whatever you want."

She thought for a second and then nodded. "Sounds good. You're sure about this?"

"Positive." His total confidence in her inability would be irritating if it wasn't so amusing.

She took aim, gently lofted the first ball, and missed the lucky cup, but it landed in one just outside the center. The small crowd collectively exhaled a mix of excitement and disappointment.

"Don't worry, buddy," she said to Lucas

as he handed her the next ball. "I've got this. These cups are set a little higher…" She tossed the next one with the same result.

Tate looked impressed and also maybe a little nervous.

She offered a palm to Lucas. He kissed the ping-pong ball and placed it in her hand.

"Thank you, Lucas. *That* ought to do it."

Ready to launch the third ball she paused again to look sideways. "Something you should know about me, Tate. The story of my life should be titled—" with a flip of her wrist the ball landed with a quiet plop in the center cup "—'She Was Underestimated.'"

"She did it!" Lucas jumped up and down. "She did it, Uncle Tate. It landed in the lucky cup."

"It sure did," he managed to utter.

Hannah laughed at the stunned expression on his face.

"Whoa! No. Waaayyy." Devon stared open-mouthed for a few seconds before digging a cell phone out of his back pocket. He took a picture. "Do you care if I post this on the internet?"

Hannah winked at him. "Not at all." She looked down at Lucas. "I've got two more tries, so these along with the two your uncle made will give you enough points for a medium stuffed animal, too."

She lobbed the balls in quick succession, both of them landing in cups near the center.

Lucas was grinning from ear to ear as he chose a fluffy gray elephant as a companion for Cuddles, who was already wrapped snugly around his shoulders. Devon took a photo of him with his prizes and encouraged Hannah to join him in another.

"You've obviously played this game before." Tate commented drily when they finally strolled away.

She lifted a shoulder. "A bit, but I'm a natural at the fish frenzy. I can't tell you how many goldfish I won back in the day. We used to go to this carnival in Glacier City every summer and I would clean up. They finally asked me to quit playing and I agreed because I could only give away so many goldfish to my friends."

He shook his head like he'd been had. "What do I owe you?"

"Hmm…" she drawled, leaving him in suspense for a long moment. "I'm letting you off the hook. We'll call it even after the auction thing."

"That's not necessary," Tate said with a

smile. "I have no complaint about that. Besides, a bet is a bet."

"No, really, I wanted to do this for Lucas. I would have done it anyway."

"Maybe I'll offer a kiss as a way to pay you on my own."

She started to respond when she looked up to see Park sauntering toward them.

"Out hustling unsuspecting marks again, huh?" he asked as he stopped before them.

"Unsuspecting marks?" Hannah repeated with a laugh. She couldn't resist a sarcastic retort, "Gosh, Park, watch *CSI* much?"

Tate's gaze flicked from her to Park and back again.

Park glared, which made him seem even more weasel-ish than normal. "Hannah, you know what? You—"

Tate interceded with a raised hand, "Whoa, let's simmer down here, Park. I knew exactly what I was getting into. I should have guessed Hannah would be an expert at this game. She's apparently good at everything. And if she's not, then I'm positive she'd be smart enough not to bet that she was. That was my mistake."

She beamed at Tate and then looked at Park.

"Words of wisdom you could have used at one point in your life, huh, Park?"

Hannah took Lucas's hand and steered him around the two men. She didn't see any point in sticking around lest she lose her temper with Park. She seemed to be less composed than normal these days. Maybe she needed a session with Dr. Voss. She hadn't seen him in nearly a year, and she'd been feeling so out of sorts lately.

"I don't like that guy," Lucas said, loud enough for him to hear.

"Yeah? Well, you are an excellent judge of character, buddy." Hannah responded even louder.

Lucas informed her he needed to use the restroom, so she led him out into the hall where they were located. Steering him towards the men's room, she was surprised by the crowd until she realized there was an entrance to the bar at the opposite end of the hall. She waited, not wanting him to be confused when he walked out. There was a line for the ladies' room blocking her view, so she craned her neck occasionally from side to side to see through the crowd, keeping an eye out.

A few minutes went by and that's when an abrupt, inexplicable chill ran through her body. She looked around for the cause, but all she saw were Terry and Rita, the board chairman and his wife, walking toward her. They chatted briefly and in the next instant Lucas appeared. She exhaled the breath she'd been holding. He hadn't been gone long, yet something...

They reentered the ballroom and Lucas tugged her hand like he did when he wanted to tell her something. She knelt beside him.

"There was a woman over there who was talking to me."

Thinking about the chill she'd experienced only moments ago caused a cold hard knot of fear to settle inside of her. "A woman you don't know?"

He nodded.

"What did she say?"

"When I came out of the bathroom, she said 'hello, Lucas.' So I said hi, and then she said she wanted to show me something."

"And what did you say?"

"I was confused because she knew my name, but I've never seen her before. I figured it might be a trick. So I said okay. Then she told me to follow her but when she turned around I came over to you instead."

Hannah placed her hands on his shoulders. "You did the right thing. Don't ever go anywhere with anyone without your uncle Tate or Viktor knowing about it, okay? Even if it's someone you *do* know. You make sure you tell them first—or me, if you're with me."

"That's what I thought, too," he said with a relieved smile.

How long, she wondered, before this poor child would stop worrying about getting in trouble for the wrong things?

Wrapping him in a quick hug, something occurred to her. Continuing to hold him lightly by the shoulders she leaned away slightly and asked, "Do you know what to do if something bad does happen and you need help?"

He thought for a second. "You mean like hiding?"

"No, I mean like telling someone." She removed her phone from her pocket. "On any phone, anytime, if you are in danger—like if you're hurt or Uncle Tate or Viktor are hurt, or there's a fire, anything like that." She didn't want to scare him, but this was important.

She handed him the phone. "Do you know the number to dial on a phone if you need help?"

"Ms. Swanson talked about this at school once. Is it 911?"

"Yes, it is. And it's for anyone to use if they're ever in trouble. For emergencies—we'll talk about what things are emergencies, okay? And we'll practice. In the meantime if you have any questions about what an emergency is, just ask me."

Lucas gave her a dutiful nod.

"You're awesome, you know that?"

Tate joined them again and she wanted to tell him what had happened, but it was nearing time for the entertainment to begin. They joined the crowd getting settled in rows of folding chairs. Lively music struck up as a professional juggling troupe skipped into the room with balls and rings and bowling pins flying every which way in an organized kind of chaos. Lucas and all the children—and most of the adults—were riveted.

After the performance they chose a dessert from a long table covered with an array of elaborate, delectable-looking choices. Hannah realized how tired Lucas must be when he didn't finish his chocolate cake.

She spoke to Tate over his head. "Better get this guy to bed, huh? I saw Viktor already went upstairs so…"

"I'll get him," Tate said and scooped Lucas up into his arms, wrapping Gus around both of their shoulders.

"Can you carry Tex?" Lucas offered her the elephant he'd dubbed Tex.

"I'd be honored," she said, tucking the fluffy critter under her arm.

They had to go down the elevator to the lobby and cross through the building to another bank of elevators, which they took up to the twelfth floor. By the time they arrived at Tate's penthouse suite, Lucas was already fast asleep.

Tate laid him on the bed and slipped off his shoes.

"Should I put his pj's on?" he asked.

"I wouldn't bother," Hannah replied as she bent over and kissed Lucas on the forehead. "Viktor said he already had a bath. But be sure and tell him I tucked him in, okay? I don't want him to think I'd ever break a promise."

She felt Tate's gaze latch on to hers and then narrow thoughtfully.

"What's wrong?" she whispered.

"Nothing that I can't fix, I hope," he returned along with a grin that made her pulse leap.

He motioned toward the doorway and she followed him out. They found Viktor using his laptop in the sitting area. The television was turned on with the volume low.

"I won't be late. I'm just going to see that Hannah gets safely to her room and then I'll check with Stacey to make sure the party's going well."

Viktor happily waved them away as they exited the suite.

"You don't need to walk me to my room."

"I know. I want to, though."

Enfolding her hand in his, they walked in silence down the hall to her room. She was relieved when he didn't try to talk to her about anything personal. She took the opportunity to tell him about Lucas's strange encounter.

"It was probably someone he's met but didn't remember. He's met an awful lot of people since you guys moved to Rankins. But I still felt compelled to tell you."

Tate nodded, looking a little troubled. "No, I'm glad you did."

Squeezing her hand before releasing it, they exchanged good-nights and in spite of their casual goodbyes, she could feel the unfinished business simmering between them.

HANNAH WAS AWAKENED again the next morning by a knock on the door. She glanced at the clock, surprised to see it was nearing eight. Adele had come in late the night before, but was already freshly showered and looking cheerful as she sauntered across the room. She joked briefly with someone and then returned to Hannah with a square package wrapped in brown paper.

"Another gift from your suitor, I presume." She slid it across the bed.

Hannah picked it up and examined it, but there was no card. She ripped off the thick brown paper, opened the box, and removed... a bright yellow bulldozer? She examined it closely; the toy was heavy, constructed of metal and all the tiny parts looked authentic. She could tell it was expensive, like one of those collector's pieces. This must be some kind of a mistake, or maybe it was intended for Lucas?

Then she noticed a note had been tucked inside the box.

Hannah, I'm giving you this because in spite of the fact that we haven't had time to talk this through, I want you to know I finally recognize what you meant. I don't intend to be this guy anymore. Tate

And in spite of her weary, mentally fatigued state, it made her smile.

CHAPTER EIGHTEEN

THE QUALIFYING EVENTS had taken place over the previous two days, and the Super Big G finals were beginning this morning. Hannah and Adele bundled up and went to watch some of the competition. Hannah found she couldn't muster the courage to attend any of the women's skiing events and was relieved when Adele said she'd like to see the men's snowboarding half-pipe.

So that's where they headed. In keeping with the stats Tate had presented to the board, Hannah noted the event seemed to be drawing the biggest crowd. That didn't mean she was ready to support his proposal however, but she couldn't deny the appeal of the event. Competition was tight with one of the three final runs complete. She couldn't help but think that wouldn't be the case if Tate was still competing.

Seeing Spencer took her back to the days when she would watch him compete; the surge of nerves that would flutter in her stomach was different than the adrenaline-charged anticipation she'd feel before her own events. Because her success—or lack thereof—had been in her own hands, lending a sense of control over the outcome, it was more difficult to be on the sidelines while someone you cared about competed than to compete yourself.

She spotted Spencer in his silver and black jacket as he stood on his board, awaiting his next run. She noticed him speak to someone. It looked like…Park? That figured. Park the celebrity chaser.

And then Spencer was up—positioning his board into the entrance of the half-pipe. Picking up speed as he glided down and then along the opposite side to the lip of the pipe, he executed a flawless indy grab. He shot back down and up again—each trick seeming more difficult than the last.

Hannah could see he'd continued to improve over the past three years since she'd seen him compete. She found herself holding a breath because she knew his biggest trick was still looming.

A double-cork 1080—perfectly landed.

Easily the best she'd ever seen him on his board. The crowd knew how good it was, too, as a volley of applause erupted. That run should put him in medal contention. She was happy for him.

Both hands fisted, he pumped his arms in the air to let the fans know he appreciated the support, then directed his board toward the crowd bunched off to one side—Hannah's side. When he was directly in front of her, he stopped and flipped his goggles up onto his helmet.

"Nice run," she said.

"Thank you. I'm so stoked." He grinned, catching her eyes and holding them with his own. "Clearly, you are my good luck charm."

She tried to make light of his intensity. "Oh, Spence, I'm definitely not comfortable with that kind of pressure."

"Well, too bad. You've got it anyway. That run will put me on the podium. I'll have to wait and find out which step I'll be on, but do you want to go out with me tonight and celebrate?"

TATE WATCHED KITT flirt with Hannah and for the first time since he'd retired, he wished he was still competing. He could do tricks that made Kitt's look like child's play. His signature combination had yet to be duplicated in competition and with style gaining increasingly more respect he would have dominated this event. He knew it was juvenile, but he wanted Hannah to be in the crowd watching him.

"Hey, Tate." Park walked up beside him. "Having a great time. Thanks again for this trip. Big G is just fantastic and exactly what I envision for Snowy Sky. This will definitely do the trick."

Tate tore his eyes away from Hannah long enough to address Park. "The trick?"

"Yeah, you know, convincing the board that we're right and Hannah is wrong. This trip was a stroke of genius on your part."

Tate almost laughed at how unimportant that now seemed. He'd wanted the alterations to Snowy Sky for Lucas's sake, for his own sake. Now he realized how naive that plan had been. Snowboarding had given Tate the means to achieve his success, but Hannah was right when she'd said that it didn't necessarily mean that it was for Lucas. Ironic, his nephew being better at skiing than snowboarding—and he seemed to enjoy it more, too. No, Tate couldn't teach Lucas much about skiing, but Hannah could. She already had. She'd taught him a lot of other things, too. She'd taught both of them a lot of other things. Important things.

"You know what, Park? My plans have changed."

His eyes widened. "What do you mean?"

"My recommendation for Snowy Sky has changed. I no longer believe the resort needs to go in the direction I thought it did."

"Oh, yes, it does." Park's voice went up several octaves. "This is important. We have to have the snowboard modifications."

Tate thought that sounded a bit dramatic. "No, we don't. Hannah's numbers still work. And without that added expense, the resort will turn over a profit sooner and then we can revisit the snowboarding option."

Park was shaking his head. "No, I don't agree."

He knew Park felt strongly about this and he could understand his hesitation. After all, Tate had reached this conclusion gradually, whereas he'd just sprung it on Park. Poor guy probably needed time to adjust.

"Okay, that's fine. I have no problem with respectfully disagreeing at this time. The board has to vote on it anyway. So, we'll just see how this all plays out."

"That's right," Park said defensively, "we

will. And after this trip I'm feeling even more confident, and so are other board members. What has changed your mind? If anything, being here at Big G should reinforce everything you brought to the table."

"It has and it hasn't." He had no intention of filling Park in on his personal reasons—either for wanting the snowboarding additions initially or for now believing they weren't immediately necessary.

"This is important, Tate. There's a lot of money riding on this. We need to see this through."

His strident tone prompted something to churn in Tate's brain, but he couldn't quite put a finger on what bothered him.

"Well, sometimes, Park, and usually this is the case for me, the most important things in life are about more than money."

Park scowled. "What? That's ridiculous. Why are you getting all philosophical on me all of a sudden? You were one hundred percent for this and now you're backing out? You can't do this to me. I've got—"

"Remember, Park, it's only a proposal at this point. We haven't *lost* anything. It's all subject to board approval anyway. Don't worry, it'll be fine. It will all come down on me, not you.

Especially if you make it clear you're still voting for the proposal."

His scowl darkened. "I can't stand to think about the look on Hannah James's face if she beats me on this, too."

Tate thought that sounded a little odd, but just then Hannah began heading away from the venue and he didn't have time right now to soothe Park's worry.

"Park, we'll discuss this later, okay? I know this has come as a bit of a shock to you, but if you think it through yourself you'll see that putting these plans on hold won't make a significant difference in the long-term. And, if I'm being completely honest, Hannah's more conservative approach probably makes better economic sense."

Tate headed in the opposite direction so Park wouldn't see that he was following her, which meant he had to circle around the venue, finally catching up with her near the lodge.

"Hannah, hey."

"Hi," she answered softly.

Concern coursed through him as he took in the pale tint of her skin and the bluish smudges under her eyes. "Are you okay?"

She gave him a half smile. "Yes. Tired."

"Where are you going?"

"To get some lunch."

"Can I come with you?"

"Sure."

She opted for the small German-style deli housed inside the hotel portion of the lodge. They were seated quickly and they both ordered the "kraut dog and home fries" special as soon as the waitress finished reciting it.

Tate watched her carefully as they settled in with cups of hot chocolate. "Can I ask you something kind of odd?"

"Sure."

"Why doesn't Park Lowell like you?"

She sputtered out a laugh over her mug. "I'm glad I haven't taken a drink yet. Did you ask him about this?"

"No, I didn't figure it out until recently. I knew you guys differed on the business plan for the resort, but business is business, so his personal issue with you didn't really register until last night at the carnival. And I was talking to him again earlier today and... Well, I get it."

She bobbed her head. "Hmm, that surprises me, seeing as how you guys are friends. I'd have thought he would have made his feelings very clear before now."

"I wouldn't say we're friends, and he hasn't

hid his dislike for you. I just didn't realize it was quite so personal."

"Oh? Park would say you're friends. He has, in fact, many times. He likes to talk about all the *famous* people he cavorts with." She rolled her eyes. "Like being famous makes someone better? I don't get that. Most of the people he talks about I've never even heard of, and I think that just annoys him more." She let out a quiet laugh and he could easily imagine her goading Park with that information.

"I've noticed that about him. But you're going a little too far here." He pointed a finger at her. "I can promise you there has been no *cavorting* going on between me and Park."

She tipped her head back and laughed, and the sound was like music to his ears. Aside from some giggling with Lucas, he hadn't heard her laugh in days. Was that his fault? he wondered guiltily.

"I embarrassed him."

"You what?"

"That's why he doesn't like me. Well, it's a big part of why he doesn't like me. I humiliated him in front of a whole crowd of people at the Cozy Caribou one time shortly after he moved to town."

"How?"

She shrugged. "I'm not sure what it is about me exactly, but people tend not to take me seriously when they should. Just because I'm not all intense about every little thing, they assume I'm much more easygoing and, um—" she stopped to quirk a brow at him "—*ambivalent* than I really am."

Tate felt a prickle of his own embarrassment. Guilty as charged. He'd learned his lesson, though. He wasn't about to make that mistake again where she was concerned.

"Shortly after Park moved to Rankins, he was hanging out at the Cozy Caribou shooting pool with some guys. You know how it is sometimes—a couple pitchers of beer, a fair amount of bragging and an impromptu tournament was born. Park won his first two games, which were both against women. He started mouthing off about how women can't play pool as well as men. I'm not kidding—he actually said women were physiologically incapable of playing pool as well as men, or something along those lines."

"How could he be that dumb?"

She delicately raised a shoulder as if to say "what choice did I have?" "And so, I challenged him to a game."

Tate nodded, his lips twitching at the vision

forming in his mind's eye. "Ah, I see, with a fish frenzy kind of result?"

"Pretty much. It was worse actually. There are certain, um, sporty things I guess you'd call them that I'm just good at, in addition to the fish frenzy. I don't know why." She tilted her hands palms up as if to reiterate that she had no control over her innate athleticism. And that was probably true.

"Shooting pool is another one of these skills I'm guessing?" he asked.

"Yep, I would advise you not to play ping-pong or darts with me either. I'm also freak-ishly good with a bow. I allowed Park exactly one chance before I cleared the table."

He let out a chuckle, his head shaking in perplexity. "So he lost a game of pool, so what?"

She grimaced. "He lost five hundred dollars and suffered the decimation of his continent-sized pride."

He laughed. "What kind of idiot…?" He suddenly realized that he'd made a similar bet because he'd been just as sure as Park she wouldn't be able to deliver. "An idiot like me, obviously," he joked.

She laughed again and Tate knew he was grinning like a fool but didn't care in the least because making Hannah happy was the greatest feeling in the world. And he never thought anything could feel better than standing on top of the podium after a hard-fought competition. How wrong he'd been.

Still grinning she said, "You're so serious, so when you make a joke it's like extrafunny or something."

Tate thought this was as good of a segue as he was going to get. "I am a serious person, Hannah. Too much sometimes, and I'm beginning to realize how much of a problem that can be, thanks to you. I need to apologize to you for that, and for some other things. These last weeks—this last year really—it's been even worse than normal because of my concern for Lucas. I've felt like I had the weight of the world on my shoulders but—"

She interrupted, "Of course you have. Raising a child is a huge responsibility and the love you have for—"

He held up a hand and kept talking "—but I'm hoping to change that."

Her brows dipped down in confusion. "I'm sorry. Change what?"

"Well, I was going to try and win you over. You know—do things right—kind of gradually with flowers and gifts and dates and…"

"Tiny pieces of heavy equipment?" she asked with a teasing tone. "Thank you for that, by the way. It made me smile."

Yes, he thought, *getting somewhere.* "Good, that was my intention. I also planned on other thoughtful, albeit possibly more romantic gestures. But now I'm feeling a sense of urgency to clear the air between us. I'd like to skip some steps and move forward."

Her face scrunched with confusion and he wanted to take her in his arms and kiss her crinkled brow.

"But…why?"

"Well, Kitt for one thing."

"Spencer?"

"Yes, he obviously wants to get back together with you, Hannah. And I know you two have a history, but I'm asking you to give me a second chance before you commit to anything with him. Seeing you with him made me understand…"

As the waitress delivered their meals, Hannah's hopes plummeted from wildly soaring to crashing disappointment in the length of a few short sentences. A second chance? When had they had a first chance, really? A couple kisses did not a relationship make, although for a while there she had thought… But he was the one who had pulled back, and she was now glad he had because the heartbreak could have been so much worse.

Seeing Spencer had reminded her of that, in addition to the postaccident promise she'd made to herself to never accept anything less than unconditional love.

The French fry she'd been dredging in ketchup stilled in her hand as she peered at him intently. "So my value has increased in your eyes because someone else is now interested in me?"

He looked startled by the question. "No, that's not it. I was heading in this direction before I even found out about Kitt. I, uh, I also talked to Cricket. I know about the accident, about the injuries that ended your career."

What had Cricket said? How much did Tate know? Surely Cricket hadn't told him everything?

"Hannah, I'm so sorry. When I took the consulting job and purchased a part of Snowy Sky I was so focused on what I wanted—what I wanted for Lucas—I didn't even stop to think that you might have a story, too. That Snowy Sky might mean more to you than just a business or a job. Like you were just saying yourself, you come across as so easygoing and carefree and optimistic it never even occurred to me and—"

"Wait." Hannah interrupted with a stop-sign, palm-forward gesture. "So…what? You feel sorry for me? That's what this is about?"

"No. I mean, yes, but that's not—"

She stood, dropping her napkin on her chair, her barely touched meal now a thoroughly un-appetizing pile of sauerkraut and grease. She rubbed a hand across her forehead and felt her phone vibrate in her pocket. She pulled it out.

A rush of nerves zinged through her as she stared at the screen. "I have to take this. I'll be right back."

She answered the call as she walked toward the back of the restaurant. Listening as she continued down the hall leading to the rest-rooms and a back exit, she eventually agreed to the date and time for the appointment.

Her eyes were drawn to her leg and she couldn't help but wonder if this weekend was the last time she would ever ski on two legs? How would she teach Lucas with only one leg? Eventually maybe she'd be able to ski with a prosthetic. She'd seen people do it and the thought heartened her to a significant degree.

Swallowing down a lump of anxiety, she

tried not to think about what might be; choosing instead to focus on what she *could* control. And this situation with Tate definitely fell into that category.

She knew what she had to do as she returned to the table, but knowing wouldn't make the doing any easier. And the look of concern and sincerity on his face nearly had her chickening out.

She suddenly wanted to cry as she realized that once again she'd fallen for the wrong man, even though the feelings she'd had for Spencer didn't even begin to compare to how she felt about Tate. But that didn't change the fact she needed to be with someone who wasn't afraid of what life might bring—good or bad. She couldn't live with the fear of knowing the man she loved might not stick around when the going got rough. As Hannah very well knew, sometimes you couldn't avoid the rough patches; you just had to ski through them the best you could until you reached smoother terrain.

And she certainly didn't want to be with someone who was with her because he felt sorry for her. Continuing forward, she halted when she stood just a few feet away.

"I'm sorry, Tate, but I can't do this. I cannot have a relationship with someone based on guilt, or pity, or whatever else is going on here." She gestured between them. "But even more importantly for me is the fact that you pulled away once already when things got even a little bit rough. If I ever let a man in my life again I need to know he will face whatever life throws at him, or me, or at us, fearlessly and that he has the will to fight if that's what it takes. Fight or flight—I need a fighter. I need someone who loves me unconditionally."

HANNAH WAS STUFFING the last of her clothing into her suitcase when Adele pushed awkwardly through the door, a tall paper cup in each hand.

She started talking immediately. "I'm so glad I found you. Is your phone off? Tate told Cricket that you got a phone call and left lunch upset. I've been calling…"

She frowned at Hannah. "What are you doing?"

"Packing."

"I see that, but we're not leaving until tomorrow."

Hannah yanked on the zipper, blew out a sigh, and sat down hard on the now-closed suitcase. "I know."

Adele marched over and handed her a cup. "I brought you a hot chocolate. It has whipped cream and chocolate syrup on top. There's a muffin in my bag because Cricket said that Tate said you barely ate a bite."

Hannah squeezed out a smile for her cousin. "Thank you. You two are quite the team these days, aren't you?"

"You're welcome. And yes, I guess we are kind of…a team, now. If I don't screw it up. Apparently, according to Cricket anyway, I have commitment issues."

She managed a real smile at that news. "He has a lot of room to talk. Seriously though, you guys are great for each other. I can't believe I didn't see it sooner."

"I saw it, but I was too afraid to…" Adele trailed off with a sigh. "I hate proving him right, but I also can't deny it when it happens. Thanks, Hannah. Your blessing means everything to me. Now tell me what's going on."

Tears burned in her eyes, but she willed them away, taking pride in her self-control. At least *that* was something she could still control.

Exhaling a long breath, she tried to decide where to begin, but all she could think about was… "Adele, are you still going to love me if I only have one leg?"

"Oh, Hannah." Adele lowered herself into the cushy chair in the corner near Hannah. "Cricket and I were wondering if the call Tate mentioned was from the doctor."

"It was. Well, it was the nurse. The doctor wants to see me next week. I'm going to ask Cricket to take me. You guys are the only ones who know that I've been having problems. I don't want to tell Mom and Dad until I've found out for sure what's wrong. And Shay is too excited and busy getting ready for their baby. I don't want to upset her. And Janie is pregnant. If I ask Tag to fly me he will insist on telling Mom and Dad. And I love the triplets, but they can't keep a secret."

Adele agreed. "Cricket and I will do our best to cover for you. And to answer your question, I will always love you. Two legs, one leg, hair, no hair, hands, fingers, toes… I don't care. No one has been better to me than you since I showed up in Rankins. I don't know what it's like to have a sister, but for the first time in my life I have a real family. You epitomize the meaning of family to me—as well as friendship. My love for you is…unconditional."

Adele's answer and the use of that word

struck her like a bittersweet blow to the heart. She supposed the right words from her cousin and best friend instead of the man she loved were better than not hearing them at all.

But she wanted to hear them from Tate. More than that, she wanted to see proof of them from Tate. She did. She couldn't help it. She bent her head, cradled it in her hands and for the first time in three years she couldn't hold back her tears.

"Oh, sweetie…" Adele took her cup and set it on the dresser with her own. Then she lowered herself onto the suitcase next to Hannah, wrapping her arms around her shoulders.

"I'm…I'm…sorry…" Hannah snuffled out the apology.

Adele handed her a tissue. "Don't be sorry. That's what I'm here for. I've never seen you cry before, though, and it's scaring me a little."

Hannah laughed through her tears. "That's because I don't cry."

"You should. You're very good at it."

Which earned another sniffle-filled chuckle. "It's just… I know there are worse things than losing my leg. There are worse things than losing my skiing career. There are even worse things than giving up my plans for Snowy Sky to Tate and Park, but…I just can't seem to get a grip on what they are right now. And seeing Spencer, and knowing that if I told him that I might still be losing my leg he'd run like the wind—again. It just brings back all the feelings of sadness and inadequacy. I've tried so hard to stuff them all away. Stay positive.

"And then Tate comes prancing in, telling me, 'Oh, I changed my mind, I really am interested after all.' Clearly only because he thinks someone else might be. As tempting as it is to give it a shot with him, I can't. I can't fall in love with someone who I don't trust will stick around when things go bad. Because having a girlfriend who needs her leg amputated is pretty bad. Which reminds me, what did Cricket tell him? Does he know about my leg? I don't need him feeling sorry for me about that, too."

"I'm not sure what Cricket told him, but I can assure you he would never do or say anything that he didn't believe was in your best interest. That man loves you like a sister."

Those words brought a fresh round of tears to her eyes, reminding her of that old saying about the danger of opening floodgates. She wiped them away and muttered, "I can handle my emotions. It will not help to feel sorry for myself—"

Adele interrupted with a firm voice. "Okay, Hannah, your Dr. Voss probably wouldn't like me saying this, but I'm going to anyway. I know a thing or two about loss and life not working out the way you plan. No offense, but probably more than he learned in a classroom at whatever Ivy League university he went to. Don't get me wrong—putting on a happy face and focusing on how something could be worse in order to lessen the sting of your own situation can be an effective coping mechanism, but…"

She paused to inhale a deep breath before continuing. "Sometimes it's okay to just let go. Cry, scream, stomp your feet, kick something, feel sorry for yourself. Do whatever it takes to get that emotion out. Accept and embrace the fact that life just isn't fair, and *then* after you've done all that, and I mean really done that, then you can think about moving on."

Hannah stared wide-eyed at Adele for a moment, then finally laid her head on her cousin's shoulder and cried.

CHAPTER NINETEEN

HANNAH HAD NO idea how things would go with Tate once they returned to Rankins. He, Viktor and Lucas had flown home a day later than the rest of the party. But the evening after they returned Tate and Lucas delivered a homemade pizza to her house.

Unable to resist the matching aprons they wore or the proud smile on Lucas's face, she invited them inside to join her. As they devoured the entire pizza, laughing and reminiscing about the trip, she thought it had been wise of Tate to break the ice in this way. So they could establish a new kind of relationship for Lucas's sake.

Relieved that things seemed at least okay between them, if slightly strained, she would continue to hope for even better as time went on.

The next evening after work Lucas invited her over for a couple rounds of memory game, where he proceeded to win four out five games. Tate made popcorn the old-fashioned way on the stove top, which delighted Lucas. They settled in to watch a movie and by the end of the evening her and Tate's status seemed to have evolved to friendly. Which was what Hannah wanted—or at least that's what she kept telling herself because being around him was difficult, causing her already-tender heart to ache.

The gigantic bouquet they'd had delivered seemed a little much, but then she saw that Lucas had signed the card. A burst of affection lit within her as she imagined him carefully printing the message in his scrawling hand—"You are so great. I love you, Hannah. Lucas." Tate had added a simple, "and Tate."

Serious concern about both Tate's intentions and her willpower surfaced a few mornings later, however, when she went out to her mailbox and found a small package. After carrying it inside and peeling away the shiny foil paper, she opened the box to reveal a treasure. It was an exquisite glass fairy maybe five inches high, and in the fairy's outstretched palm was a tiny koi.

A small gasp flew from her lips. Gingerly removing it from its tissue paper bed, she carefully examined the stunning figurine; the glossy finished fish had the same black, orange and white color scheme as Bridget. The note had read, "To the most beautiful fish fairy of all. Love, Lucas and Tate."

It was the sweetest, most thoughtful gift Hannah had ever received. The fact that Tate realized and appreciated how much those koi meant to her... She squeezed her eyes shut as a wave of undeniable fondness washed over her, followed closely by a panicky feeling that tightened her chest and stole her breath.

Because this...wonderful behavior was awful. It had to stop.

HANNAH HAD PICKED Lucas up for swim lessons that morning and was trying to decide how to approach the subject with Tate when she dropped him off. Gathering her courage while waiting for Lucas to change, she saw Janie enter the community center with the twins in tow.

"Hannah, hey! Glad you're here. I was going to call you."

"Hi, Janie. Gabe, Finn," Hannah said. The twins came toward her, each with the opposite hand raised so she could fist-bump them at the same time in the way they'd devised. She peered at them closely. "What's with the switcheroo of the hats, guys? Are you trying to trick people again?" Lately, the boys wouldn't go anywhere without the hats their mom had knitted and decorated for them. Gabe sported a lime-green and yellow alien and Finn a grass-green dinosaur on an orange background.

"Ah, dang!" Gabe cried, as their little faces simultaneously fell with disappointment.

Janie chuckled. "They saw your car and wanted to try fooling you. You're one of the few people who can tell them apart."

"Pfft," Hannah said, planting her hands on her hips. "You little tricksters are going to have to do better than a hat swap to fool me. I could tell you apart from the first day I met you, which was the day you were born by the way, and every day since. A hat…" Snatching Finn's hat off of Gabe's head, she settled it on her own and pulled it down over her ears until it rested just above her eyebrows. "There, does that make me look like Finn?"

"Hannah," they cried in unison, erupting with fresh fits of giggles, which somehow caused them to start skipping around while chanting something about hats.

"These two…" Janie said with a smile and a helpless shrug. "Are you swimming today?"

"No, I brought Lucas in for his lesson."

"I'm glad we ran into you because the boys have that field trip next week to the Alaska Zoo in Anchorage?"

"Oh, that's right. I bet they're excited."

"They are bouncing off the walls, worse even than normal. But the reason I was going to call you is we had a cancellation. We have extra room, so I thought I'd ask if you or Tate, or both of you, would like to come along and bring Lucas?"

"Yes, definitely. I'll check my schedule and talk to Tate."

Lucas came out of the locker room. Upon spotting her, his face lit in a way that always made her heart swell with joy. He grinned when he saw the twins and she couldn't contain her excitement at the thought of Lucas at the zoo.

She continued to ponder the notion as she drove him home, imagining his face at seeing all those animals in real life.

After parking in the driveway, they went inside. Tate greeted Lucas, and as soon as he moved into the living room to play, she presented Tate with the zoo opportunity.

He appeared eager and enthusiastic at first, but then his face slowly fell, reminding her of the too-serious Tate she'd first met all those weeks ago. And she loved him the way he'd been these past several days—charming, attentive, funny and so attractive that sometimes when she looked at him she found it kind of hard to breathe. She loved him a little too much, that was the problem.

"What's wrong?" she asked.

"The zoo…" He trailed off with a thoughtful, distressed expression. "I can't believe I didn't think of it already."

His reaction suddenly made sense to her.

"Tate, you need to stop being so hard on yourself. No parent thinks of everything. That's why there's been a billion books written, and do you even have any idea how many parenting magazines and websites there are? We all need help and advice now and then. That's why parents get together and vent. That's what friends and family are for— Viktor, me, my brothers and sisters and my parents, Adele, Janie… We're all here to help. Use whatever resources are at your disposal. That's the way I see parenting anyway. That's what all the parents I know do—the good ones that is."

His head dipped down thoughtfully. "I suppose you're right."

"I am," she said confidently.

"Any chance you might be able to make this trip with us?"

His hopeful tone warmed her so that she couldn't contain a grin. "I'd love to and I'm pretty sure I can swing it."

He looked happy and more than a little relieved.

"And speaking of using things…I have a confession to make."

There was something in his voice that caused her pulse to leap nervously. "Oh, yeah?" she squeaked.

Hannah froze as he pushed away from the counter and moved closer to her. And closer still, right through her comfort zone until he was leaning next to her, one hip lightly grazing hers. He gripped the counter behind him and she tried not to stare at the way the muscles flexed in his arms and shoulders.

His head dipped toward her ear, and her mouth went as dry as the Alaskan tundra when she felt his hot breath against her cheek.

"Yes, I have been shamelessly using Lucas to get to you. Are you aware of that?"

"I may have figured that out," she managed with a gravelly rasp. She cleared her throat and tried to sound casual. "I'm glad you brought it up, though, because I want to talk to you about something."

"I'm not sorry."

At that she opened her mouth but shut it again, because she'd had every intention of telling him to stop, but something unexpected stirred within her in that moment.

He emitted a soft chuckle, letting his eyes rove around her face before finally settling on her lips. Her knees went weak.

His mouth twitched with humor. "I've heard that the whole single-dad thing works to pick up women. Brandy Quick invited Lucas and me to her son Ivan's birthday party this weekend. She mentioned her divorce four times in less than three minutes."

"Hmm, sounds fun," she said. Of course the single gals in town would know he was eligible. There was no doubt they'd already begun to swarm. That didn't bother her…did it? Yes, okay, it bothered her a little, but she needed to stay focused on what was important. "The socializing would be great for Lucas."

"Nothing?"

"Nothing?" She repeated, wondering if she'd misheard something.

"Yes, really, nothing? No jealousy at all? See, the way I understand this…" He gestured between them. "I mention meeting other women and you pitch a fit of jealousy and then I know you still like me."

She sputtered out a laugh. "'Pitch a fit of jealousy'? What is this—a soap opera?"

She felt her humor fade when Tate's intense gaze shifted back to her now-grinning mouth.

"I love it when you laugh and when you smile."

No words surfaced on her lips, which was odd, she thought, because she always had words—too many usually. His gaze traveling over her again made her skin even warmer. She was sure the only eyes she'd ever seen that were darker blue than his were Lucas's.

"I love how easy you laugh. Like it's always there under the surface just waiting to bubble up. And I love how you make Lucas giggle, and I love…"

His lips were only inches from hers now and Hannah felt her body reacting with a weird mix of heat and alarm. If she kissed him again she didn't think she'd be able to back away from a relationship this time. And there was just too much that was way too complicated and difficult.

There was Snowy Sky and Lucas's issues, which she knew they hadn't seen the last of, but mostly it was the uncertainty she was facing with her leg. She hated that she didn't feel confident that she and Tate could weather these obstacles. She suddenly became aware of her heartbeat, throbbing painfully.

She stepped away. "Tate, I appreciate the confession and the fact that you're not...sorry. It's very flattering. And the flowers and gifts and homemade meals are wonderful. Especially the fairy. Hands down the nicest, most thoughtful gift anyone has ever given me. I will cherish it forever."

His satisfied smile nearly halted her next words.

"But you have to stop. I want to remain a part of Lucas's life because I love him and I think it would devastate him if I backed out now. But you were right before when you said there can't be anything more than friendship between us."

His face had taken on that hard edge that she now knew was a result of too much hurt and worry. It killed her to imagine she had brought it out with her words.

"Why? Is it Spencer?"

She shook her head, almost wishing it was. "No, it's not Spencer. Spencer and I are over for good. But seeing him did make me realize some things. The most important of which is that I'm not ready for more with…"

"Me?" he finished for her.

"Anyone," she corrected softly, reminded of her leg. Because that was probably true; she would have to tell any man she got involved with about her leg. Even though she couldn't imagine thinking about anyone other than Tate.

He swallowed hard and looked away. Then his eyes latched back on to hers and she wished more than anything that things were different.

"Okay," he said quietly. "For now."

Forever, she thought, and wanted to cry. Her crying outburst at Big G had seemed to open up some kind of trapdoor of emotion that she couldn't quite get closed again.

"I need to get to work now, but can I still tell Janie we're good to go for the zoo? Think we can handle it?"

"Of course."

STROLLING THROUGH THE Anchorage zoo, the three of them joined by hands with a delighted Lucas in the middle, Tate wondered how this day could possibly get any better.

They stopped in front of the next exhibit.

"Look, sea otters." An older boy with a Seahawks cap stepped up beside Lucas.

"They're so cute." A young teenaged girl joined them, leaning her elbows on the rail beside Lucas.

"Actually those are river otters." Lucas placed his hands on the ledge and stood on his toes for a better view.

The kids shot him a curious sideways glance. "Really? How do you know?" the girl asked.

"There's lots of differences. But one thing is river otters sleep on land and sea otters sleep in water." Lucas pointed to where an otter was napping in a den with at least two pups, parts of their furry brown bodies pressed against the thick glass.

He began to explain some of the other distinctions while the older kids listened with rapt attention.

Tate and Hannah exchanged smiles. Her eyes reflected the kind of contentment he felt. And that's when he realized exactly how the day could get better; if Hannah would acknowledge her feelings for him.

He knew she still felt something. In spite of what she'd said, he wasn't giving up. She'd asked him to back off, but she'd never said her feelings had changed. And that was enough for him.

After they'd seen every single exhibit, which Lucas meticulously tracked on the folding map a safari-clad zoo employee had handed him as they arrived, they zigzagged back to check out his favorites once again. Otters, wolves and marmots seemed to be in a three-way tie and by the time they reached the gift-shop exit where the party was to meet up again, they were all getting tired.

Tate wandered closer to the information board to read about a particular bear in the zoo when he caught a glimpse of a woman walking quickly in the other direction. Something about her reminded him of Penny. He focused his attention on the board, refusing to allow anything to spoil this day.

Penny was right where she needed to be and out of their lives forever. He was determined to see that's where she stayed, so why did he feel this uncomfortable mix of doubt and guilt when he thought about her? He knew his mother had suffered a terrible childhood of her own.

He was only now fully realizing how her experiences had in turn shaped her treatment of him and Lexie. Caring for Lucas had made him see how difficult it was to raise a child when you weren't equipped emotionally in your own right. If he hadn't met Viktor he would be even more clueless than he already was.

Plus, he was learning so much from Hannah. Just watching her with kids and talking about what might be best for Lucas seemed to make the process easier. Being with her made him believe that he really could overcome some of the damage Penny had done to Lucas—and maybe even some that he had suffered, as well.

Hannah gave him hope, and he couldn't help but wonder if it was too late for Penny?

"THERE ARE SO many forms." Hannah thrummed her fingers through the stack of paperwork piled on the table in front of Tate. "You're going to have Jonah look them over when you're through?"

He glanced up from the form he was currently working on. "Yeah, he said he could handle a lot of the legal work for me. This is just the initial filing and stuff."

"Well, it'll definitely be worth it." She cast him an encouraging grin.

"I'm reading through these forms and I keep

thinking about something. You know what would make it even better?"

"What's that?"

As he focused his gaze firmly on her, her pulse began that hard, heavy thud that only Tate seemed able to induce.

"If *we* were adopting him."

"Wh-what?" she stammered.

"Marry me, Hannah."

"Tate!" She forced out a laugh because he had to be joking, didn't he? "Do you honestly believe, in your decided lack of man wisdom, that my love for Lucas would extend that far?"

He grinned at her and she felt a warm flush heat her body because he looked completely and utterly...

"I'm serious. Think about it. This would be so much easier if we were adopting Lucas together. You said you were using me to get to him, so it occurred to me if we got married we could both adopt him and quit using each other. Lucas would be ours and we could raise him together. Great idea, huh?"

Hannah had no words, a phenomenon she'd become more familiar with since he had entered her life. His suggestion was ridiculous. Yet all she could think about was what would he do if she actually said yes?

TATE WATCHED HER CLOSELY. He knew that he'd taken her by surprise, but he didn't know how else to get through to her. Whenever he suggested they go out together just the two of them—he was careful to avoid the word *date*—she politely declined. When he tried to talk to her about anything even remotely resembling the subject of a relationship she made a joke. And when he flirted she simply shut down.

He could see that he'd gotten to her and now that the question was out there he realized how desperately he wanted her to say yes.

"You're serious?" she repeated.

"Yes. But before you say no, and tell me that this would not be a good reason to get married, consider that people get pregnant and *then* get married for the sake of the child all the time. Does it always work out? No, but a lot of times it does. We already have the child and I know Lucas would be enough to keep us together.

"And okay, Lucas and I have problems and issues that you probably don't want to take on—I get that. But, Hannah, you're so...perfect. Lucas isn't the only reason I'm asking. I want to marry you. I'm in love with you. I think I've been in love with you since the first moment I saw your face peeking up at me from that snowbank. I want to—"

"Stop, Tate. Stop talking." She stood. "I can't. The answer is no, but not for the reasons you mentioned. I'm…I'm far from perfect. I'm flawed in ways you can't even imagine. And while I appreciate the proposal and am tempted to say yes on a certain level—I have to say no."

Tate watched her go with a sinking heart even as he wondered what in the world she could be referring to. Hannah knew how amazing she was, how good she had it, didn't she?

CHAPTER TWENTY

HANNAH HAD GONE into work early so she would be able to squeeze in a swim at the community center during lunchtime. Swimming was such a great workout with little impact on her leg. Checking the time—just a little before noon—she was happy to see she could catch the first few minutes of Lucas's lesson.

Across the parking lot she saw two figures emerge from the exit and begin hustling away. One of them looked like Lucas.

That royal blue down jacket and the bright yellow stocking cap on a child's retreating form would be difficult to mistake. The knitted creation Janie had made for him sported a green anaconda winding around the yellow cap so it appeared that the reptile was squeezing his head. He adored the hat, and the design and color combination made it easy to spot him from a distance.

"Lucas?" she called out because he didn't

look up as he trudged along beside a woman she did not recognize.

"Hey…" she said jogging to catch up to them. The woman fisted her hand in the back of Lucas's puffy jacket and steered him away. He stumbled sideways and Hannah felt a rush of fear. The strange occurrence at Big G flashed through her mind. What was going on here?

She hurried forward until she was ahead of the pair and then turned into their path. Recognizing a pickup parked next to the curb as Viktor's, Hannah knew he must be inside the community center. Her concern multiplied exponentially.

"Excuse me? Who are you? And where are you going with Lucas?"

"Hannah!" Lucas cried, throwing his arms around her waist. She reached down and patted his back.

The woman turned on her. "Who are *you*?"

Hannah nearly flinched as she felt the force of the woman's hate-filled sneer.

Penny. It had to be. What was her intention here? From everything she'd learned about this woman from Tate and Viktor, Hannah sensed she needed to tread carefully.

"I'm Hannah, a friend."

She snorted and said, "A friend? I'll just bet you are. I'm Penny. Lucas's grandmother. Not that I need to explain anything to you. I'm taking my grandson."

"Taking him? Taking him where?"

"Out for ice cream," she shot back sarcastically.

"Does Tate know about this? Because last I heard Viktor was bringing Lucas to his lesson today."

"Of course he does. Get in the car, Lucas," Penny snapped. Lucas tightened his hold on Hannah.

Lucas said, "I'm supposed to be at my swim lesson, but Grandma was waiting by the locker room. She said I had to go with her because Uncle Tate was waiting. But he's not here, is he, Hannah?"

"No, he's not, Lucas. But I am." She gave his shoulder a reassuring squeeze. "You're not taking this child anywhere." She spoke calmly, letting the intensity of her glare underscore the words.

Penny reached a hand in her purse which she'd been clutching tightly to her side. A flood of fear left Hannah's skin prickling as she realized the woman could have anything in that bag—mace, a knife, a stun gun, a real gun… She backed up a few steps, shifting Lucas behind her as she did so.

"Give me my grandson. You have no right to keep him from me."

Hannah could see Penny was trembling, and her tone held the sharp edge of someone very angry and desperate. She tightened her hold on Lucas.

"You're right, I don't. But Tate does, and he's told me personally that it's not a good idea for you to spend time with Lucas unsupervised." Hannah was stalling, trying to figure out how to proceed. There was no one else in the parking lot. Where was Viktor?

Penny huffed, her eyes were darting around wildly.

"I'm leaving with my grandson and you're not going to stop me."

Her worst fear materialized as the woman pulled out a gun and pointed it at Hannah's chest.

She had never been more grateful for Dr. Voss's coaching than she was at that moment. In a perfectly calm voice she asked, "Lucas, where is Viktor? Did he bring you today?"

"Yes, he watches my lessons just like you and Uncle Tate do when you bring me."

That meant Viktor should be noticing any

second that Lucas was missing. She had to keep stalling.

Penny laughed, and the sound was startling. There was a crazy, demented harshness to it. She felt Lucas flinch.

"Viktor isn't coming to save you, girlie, if that's what you're hoping for. Now, I'm taking my grandson and leaving. Lucas, get in the car or so help me, you will regret it. And you know I mean it, you little brat."

She heard Lucas gasp and then choke on a sob.

That was it.

Hannah saw red.

This woman would have to take her out before she ever harmed another hair on Lucas's head.

"Stay behind me, Lucas, buddy, okay?"

TATE WAS WORKING on his amended recommendations for the board when his phone rang.

"Hey, Viktor, what's up?"

"Tate, you must come quickly. Penny… I bring Lucas to swim lesson. She has gun… Said she'd hurt Lukie if I didn't go to equipment room…lock on door not so good, though, and I get out. But Lukie—he is gone."

Tate had started moving through the house

as soon as Viktor mentioned Penny's name. He hung up and dialed 911 with one hand and scooped up his wallet and keys with the other. The realization hit him that she had been watching. She'd been at the zoo and probably in Garner, too. And yesterday, as he walked Lucas into swim lessons he'd felt this weird tingling along his scalp. He hadn't shrugged it off.

He'd called to make sure Penny was still in rehab, feeling unsettled when he'd learned she wasn't there. Trying her Colorado number several times, no one ever answered. Then he phoned a couple of her neighbors, and they all vouched for her being back there.

But Penny was clever.

That was something people often underestimated about her—her intelligence. Tate included, obviously. Just because someone was an addict, that didn't make them stupid.

THE POLICE? Hannah heard the sirens, and wished with every fiber of her being that they were coming to her and Lucas's aid. Thankfully, Penny seemed momentarily frozen, waiting for the sirens to glide on by. But in the next instant, flashing lights appeared as two police vehicles pulled into the parking lot.

She felt a few seconds of respite before she absorbed the rage on Penny's face.

"Now you're going to smile and act like everything is fine, or I will shoot you. You hear me?" she ordered. Her hand was back in her bag, but Hannah was well aware that it still held the gun.

In her periphery she saw two officers heading their way. She recognized them—anyone who lived in the valley would recognize them. There weren't very many cops in Rankins and one of them was a friend.

"Hannah?" he called out.

"Hey, Pete." She answered a bit too loudly with a friendly smile, deliberately calling him by the wrong name.

She and Jared Berkeley had been in the same class in school, same group of friends, often hanging out together on the banks of the Opal River. Jared could turn a baseball into a rocket with a flick of his wrist, and their junior year Hannah had seen him shoot the stem off an apple at a firearms competition, defeating the then current state champion— Pete Chambers.

"Everything okay here?"

Penny narrowed her eyes at Hannah in warning.

"Yep. We're good." Hannah kept the smile on her face.

Jared kept walking, but she could see he understood because his hand had shifted toward his hip. The other officer was still moving, too, flanking them, and she knew he had caught Jared's nonverbal cue. She braced herself, planning out her next move in her mind.

It took Penny a few seconds to realize that Hannah had somehow sabotaged her. Penny looked at Jared who was still closing in. Using that hesitation in her favor, Hannah turned and enveloped Lucas in her arms. She dropped to the ground and, covering his little body with her own, she rolled right off the edge of the sidewalk until they were under Viktor's pickup. A series of loud pops ensued and she squeezed Lucas tightly as she inhaled the scent of grease and counted—one, two, three, four...

Two more pops sounded and she had no idea if anyone had been hit. She couldn't see anything from beneath the pickup where she'd rolled with Lucas. But she thought someone must have been hit because now she heard Jared calling for an ambulance and someone was screaming.

EVEN THOUGH HE'D been expecting as much, the lights of the emergency vehicles and the crowd of people caused a wave of fear inside Tate as he pulled into the parking lot of the community center. His eyes zeroed in on the ambulance where he spotted Hannah standing by a gurney with Lucas held securely in her arms. She was talking to someone as paramedics tended the patient lying there. Tate climbed out and ran toward them.

Hannah looked up and saw him, and he felt a flood of such relief that it nearly left him breathless. They were alive, and Lucas looked well and whole with his face buried in Hannah's neck.

"Lucas," he called out. "Are you okay? Is he okay? Are you okay?"

"We're fine."

"Uncle Tate," Lucas cried out his name and reached out to him. Tate took him into his arms, the feeling of joy indescribable.

"Tate, we're fine, but Viktor—" she broke off.

Tate noticed him then, stretched out on the gurney. Viktor's normally fair complexion looked gray and blood oozed from somewhere because bright red splotches seeped through white bandages on his chest. Tate gently touched his friend's arm.

"Viktor?" he asked but got no response.

He flicked his eyes toward the paramedic across from him. "Is he going to be okay?

"He was shot, but we're taking care of him."

Tate watched helplessly as they loaded the man who was a like a father to him into the ambulance. Hot tears burned his eyes as worry clutched at this chest.

He felt Hannah tug on his sleeve, but it took a few seconds for the motion to register. Her voice sounded sharp in his ear. "Tate, come on—move, we're going to the hospital."

He followed Hannah to her SUV. He deposited Lucas into the backseat where he scrambled into the booster seat Hannah had borrowed from someone weeks ago so Lucas would always be safe in her car.

Safe... How...?

He debated about whether he should talk in front of Lucas and then decided he'd probably seen much of the action anyway. "What happened? Where's Penny?"

"Grandma shot Viktor, Uncle Tate. Why would Grandma make Viktor dead?"

Hannah answered. "He's not dead. Remember, he opened his eyes and smiled at us? The doctors are going to make him better at the hospital." She cut hopeful eyes toward Tate as she confidently maneuvered the vehicle out of the parking lot.

Tate marveled at her composure, sealing his belief that Hannah was the strongest person he'd ever known. She could have died—Lucas could have died. Viktor… A bout of nausea caused him to break out into a cold sweat.

"The police have her."

"Why would Grandma shoot Viktor?" Lucas repeated.

"Grandma is…sick, Lucas."

"She's not very nice, is she?"

"No, buddy, she's not."

"I know. She smelled like whiskey. That's why I called the police."

She glanced at Tate, then into the rearview mirror.

"You what, sweetie?"

"When Grandma came and got me I could smell the whiskey smell. You told me, Hannah, that if I ever smelled that on anyone that I should never ride with them. That it would be an emergency. So I called the police."

"I did say that, Lucas. And you're right, it certainly was an emergency. But how did you…?"

"I told Grandma I needed to go to the bathroom before we went from the community center. When I was in the bathroom, I saw my swim teacher and asked if I could use his phone. He made a weird face but gave me the phone, so I pressed 911 like we practiced, Hannah. I told them it was an emergency and that I was at swimming. Then I gave the phone back and Grandma yelled at me to hurry up and come out."

Hannah used a palm to cover her mouth and Tate could see that she was stifling a sob.

He reached into the backseat and took Lucas's hand. He placed the other on Hannah's knee. Lucas's tiny fingers felt so cold. "Lucas, I'm so proud of you, little man."

"I love you, Uncle Tate. I didn't want to go with Grandma. I want to stay with you."

"And you're going to, buddy—forever. Just like I promised."

Hannah pulled into the parking lot of the hospital. "Me, too, Lucas. So, so proud of you. You did great."

"I love you, Hannah."

"I love you, too, Lucas."

"Thank you for saving me. Hannah stayed on top of me on the ground, Uncle Tate. So I wouldn't get hurt."

Hannah unbuckled her seat belt and scrambled out of the car. She opened the backseat and gathered Lucas into her arms. "Oh, Lucas," she wrapped him in the hugest bear hug and kissed his cheek. "I think you're the one who saved us all."

They hurried into the hospital where Hannah saw one of the nurses, Denise Manson, outside the emergency room doors.

"Denise, there was a man just brought in here."

"Yes, do you know him?"

"He's… Yes."

"His name is Viktor?"

"Yes."

Denise moved around the counter and picked up a clipboard. "What's his last name?"

"Kovalenko," Tate said, stepping up beside her and then spelling it out.

"Are you a family member?" Denise asked.

"Yes. He's like my dad. He was my legal guardian when I was growing up."

Denise nodded and said, "That's family where we come from, isn't that right, Hannah?"

Hannah had never been so glad to be from a small town in her life. Denise took Tate firmly by the elbow and led him through the double doors.

Hannah sat in one of the low, padded chairs

right outside the doors and settled Lucas on her lap. He closed his eyes and rested his head against her shoulder, and she was absolutely certain she couldn't love this child any more even if he was her own.

Not for the first time, she wished she could have said yes to Tate.

TATE STARED DOWN at Viktor where he lay in his hospital bed, a gut-wrenching mix of worry and anger churning within him. The doctor said he'd been really lucky. He'd lost some blood, but the bullet had gone into his shoulder without inflicting significant damage. Right now he was sedated for the pain because they'd had to remove a few bullet fragments.

According to the police officer who'd talked to him after the doctor, Penny had wildly fired several shots up into the air. She'd screamed at the officers to back off but wouldn't lower her weapon. Officer Berkeley had been about to shoot her when Viktor had appeared in the parking lot.

Officer Berkeley said Viktor hadn't even hesitated when he'd spotted Penny, but instead had charged in her direction. She'd turned the gun on him and fired, whereupon the officer had taken the opportunity to tackle her.

"Where is she now?"

"She's incarcerated in one of our jail cells, Mr. Addison."

"Good. Don't let her go."

"No, sir, we won't. I don't think she'll be getting free for a very long while."

Tate nodded but couldn't help wondering if he would ever really be free of Penny or the damage she continued to inflict.

"I hate to ask you this, but we're going to need you to come down to the station and answer a few questions."

HANNAH WAITED AT Tate's house. Viktor was staying the night in the hospital, but the doctor felt confident he would be released within the next day or two. She'd slipped a movie in the DVD player and Lucas had fallen asleep on the sofa next to her with Cuddles held firmly in his arms. He hadn't even stirred when she had put them both to bed.

After kissing him on the forehead, she flipped on the walkie-talkie and headed downstairs to wait for Tate. It wasn't long before she heard him come through the door leading from the garage. The grim look on his face filled her with concern.

Without saying a word he walked in and

lowered himself onto the sofa. Worry seemed to have exaggerated his beautiful features; his mouth was tight and tiny lines stood out around his eyes, even the light crease that was always evident between his brows had formed into a deep furrow.

"Tate—"

"My mother tried to kidnap her own grandson." His voice was rough with emotion.

It was just as she'd expected, yet Hannah still felt ill. She dropped onto the sofa and placed an arm around Tate's shoulder.

"Talk to me," she said. "Tell me."

"There was a letter."

"What kind of letter?"

"A letter demanding a ransom for Lucas's safe return."

"Tate—"

"There's more."

His voice held an edge and so much… coldness. Tingling began at the nape of her neck as he continued to relay details in the same icy tone.

"They also found a formula—a recipe."

"A recipe?" she repeated the word with a whisper, but somehow she knew what he was going to say.

"Yes. The correct dosage of sleeping pills

needed to put a forty-pound, six-year-old child out for days. Or forever. Just mash it up and add it to a glass of milk."

Her stomach roiled as this information sank in.

"So either way—ransom paid or not…it seems my *mother*," he spat the word, "planned to drug her own grandson."

TATE KNEW OF course that Penny had issues, but he realized now that he'd always believed somewhere deep inside that she was redeemable. That was what had compelled him to keep trying to help her, save her, even protect her at times when in reality he'd been enabling her.

As he had gradually risen to the top of his sport, he'd tried to take care of Lexie as much as possible—sending money, gifts, cards and letters. And money for Penny. Always money. He admitted now that's all she'd ever really wanted from him, and that fact hurt. Which was crazy, because he'd known it. Or he thought he had.

Still, after all these years, after all the disappointment, he'd held on to a kernel of hope that someday she would get better. He'd blamed her addiction and her own sorry past for so much of her behavior.

But this… This was his fault. Hannah could have been killed, Lucas could have been killed, Viktor…

He was surprised at how much it hurt to finally, truly let her go, and with that realization came another. His worst fear had materialized. He would never truly be free.

"I'm so sorry. Is there anything I can do?"

TATE STARED BACK at her, but Hannah could tell he didn't really see.

"No," he said.

Dread, thick and menacing, overtook her as she watched Tate mentally check out on her.

"Tate—"

"We're leaving."

"What do you mean you're leaving?"

"As soon as Viktor is well enough—he and I and Lucas… I'm so glad you said no to me, Hannah, because eventually I would have ruined your life, too. It was stupid of me to believe that I could ever have a normal life. That we could be a normal family. That I could ever have… We've got to get away from Rankins."

He stood up. "Thank you so much for staying with Lucas and for all of your help. I'll, uh, I'll let you know our plans as soon as I've finalized them."

He turned and left the room, and Hannah knew that with this one painful, critical decision he had proved her suspicions once and for all; when the going got rough, Tate bolted.

CHAPTER TWENTY-ONE

THE FBI HAD been called in because Penny and an accomplice had been charged with attempted child abduction, which was a federal offense. Added to a slew of other federal charges, it looked as if Penny would be serving some substantial prison time.

Hannah had gone into work early again so she could hang out with Lucas that afternoon while Tate and Viktor had a meeting with two FBI agents. She and Tate agreed it would be best for them to carry on as if things were fine until he was ready to leave town. Which it turned out wouldn't be quite as soon as he had anticipated.

As usual, Lucas opened the door for her as soon as she stepped up on the porch.

"Hi, Hannah."

"Hey, Lucas. Wanna go feed the koi with me before we get started on those paper airplanes?"

"Yes." His face transformed with a wide

grin. "We have grapefruit." Remarkable how much he looked like his uncle when he smiled, although she hadn't seen much smiling from Tate lately.

This situation with Penny, while horrible, seemed to be eating away at him excessively. Of course he was upset, but she knew he didn't have much of a relationship with his mother, so she couldn't quite wrap her brain around the extent of his despair.

"Okay, but make sure you ask Viktor first, so we don't feed the last of his grapefruit to the fish if he has plans for it."

He trotted off toward the kitchen as she bent down to remove her boots. When she rose she was startled to find Tate standing before her.

"Jeez, you scared me. You should have been a spy or something instead of a snowboarder."

One side of his mouth nudged upward and she decided an attempt at a smile was better than nothing.

"Sorry, I didn't mean to."

It filled her with despair to see that the sadness, the solemnity she'd first encountered in him had returned—in excess.

"I know," she said, feeling certain there was a touch of melancholy in the smile she returned. "How are you?"

"I'm fine," he returned tightly. "Can I talk to you for a minute?"

"Sure." What else could possibly be wrong she wondered, feeling a stab of pain in her ankle as she took a step forward, reminding her that her appointment was only a few days away. If it wasn't for her leg, she would make Tate come to his senses.

He motioned for her to follow. She trailed him into his office where he walked around the desk and took a seat. She lowered herself into a chair on the opposite side of the desk. He handed her a piece of paper.

"What is this?" She stared down at the words and columns of numbers, obviously something to do with Snowy Sky.

"The changes I've made to the proposal for the resort."

"You're changing your proposal?"

"Yes, I am. I'm going to be honest with you. When I made that proposal my motivation was in large part for Lucas's sake. I wanted to teach him to snowboard. So you were partially right when you said I wanted Snowy Sky for my own playground. But I wouldn't have made the recommendation if I didn't believe it would work, but now that we're not going to be here it also works for you to continue with your original plan. It's a great plan, Hannah."

An interesting combination of surprise, happiness and irritation brought her up short. She'd been right when she'd assumed Tate had wanted Snowy Sky for himself, so why didn't she feel a sense of validation about that? Because she now knew he had been doing it for Lucas. And even if he'd been a little misguided, that motivation made it okay. It made it better than okay, actually.

She should be pleased he was trying to make things right where she was concerned. Instead she just felt sad because he was taking Lucas away. And because he'd already taken himself. Sad and frustrated. Why couldn't he see that leaving wasn't the answer?

"I still believe you should consider putting in a half-pipe in a few years, and my recommendation will include that. But you can do it on your time and include it in your marketing package. I'll be available for you to consult with anytime. No charge. I wanted you to know that I'm going to try to make things right for you—easy and convenient. And I'm…"

Hannah stared blankly, hearing maybe half of what he said, as her emotions waged a war within her. She needed to tell him. He needed to see once and for all how shortsighted he could be. And why shouldn't she? What did she have to lose? It's not like they were a couple.

"That's very generous of you. Thank you." It was generous and she did appreciate the gesture.

He smiled and she could tell he was relieved. "I'm glad you feel that way. Because I—"

Unfortunately for him, the reprieve was going to be short-lived. She interrupted, "But maybe I don't want what's 'easy and convenient.' Maybe I don't want you to make things convenient for me. You've already made them extremely difficult.

"I love Lucas. I love Viktor. And you know what? I love you, too. And I realize you've made *your* mind up and I appreciate that you're trying to clean up the mess you created. But the part you don't seem to get is that you've done it without even consulting me. Maybe Adele was right when she said that I should cry and scream and stomp my feet once in a while so people will know what I'm feeling. I don't do that. It's not my style, but it doesn't mean I don't have feelings. You've turned into a bulldozer again and I thought we agreed you weren't going to be that guy anymore."

"Hannah—"

"I'm not through. You think you have problems, Tate? It's true—you do. And I know you believe I have it so much easier because I have the support of my family and what you call a 'normal' upbringing. But here's some news for you—we all have problems. Everyone has issues and obstacles to overcome. I don't even get what this *normal* means that you keep referring to."

He looked dubious and then he said, "But it *is* different for you. You're so…lucky. You really can't understand adversity like this—like Lucas and I have experienced. You have your family and—"

She literally wanted to strangle him for not being able to see beyond his own situation. The words seemed to fly out of her mouth before she could stop them.

"Lucky? Yeah, I know," she continued sarcastically. "I'm excited for my doctor's appointment on Wednesday where I find out whether or not I get to keep my leg or if they have to amputate it. So, yeah, yay, lucky me, right? All the family support in the world isn't going to help me with that, Tate. The freaking royal family couldn't help me with that."

"Your… What?"

She would have laughed at the look on his face if she wasn't so incensed.

"My leg," she tapped on her left knee, "might have to be amputated. Remember how I told you I have to go to Anchorage on Wednesday? Well, it's not to go shopping. I hate shopping. I'm going to see my doctor because I've developed this pain in my leg and... They told me after the accident that it might be a possibility someday."

She stood as Lucas came into the room holding a plastic bag. He lifted it proudly. "Got 'em. Viktor even helped me cut them up."

"Awesome. Let's go feed some fish, kiddo. I could use some koi time right about now."

TATE SAT BACK hard in his chair. Amputate her leg?

Cricket had said that Hannah's recovery had been difficult, but he hadn't mentioned this. How had he missed this? Thoughts flashed from one clue to the next; the sledding episode, the occasional limp, she'd even mentioned it bothering her that night at Big G.

He'd missed every one. Hannah was right; he had been so focused on his own problems that he hadn't stopped to consider that someone else might have them, too. That they might be even worse than his. And Hannah's had been much worse than he could have imagined.

He stared absently at the computer screen where he'd pulled up some of the data he and Park had been using to formulate their proposal, letting guilt and regret mingle uncomfortably within himself. The feeling was no less than he deserved.

He thought love was supposed to make life easier, not complicate it like this. Could he ever get it right where Hannah was concerned? She definitely should be with someone who could get it right, who had the right answers, said the right things, someone who wasn't afraid. But he wasn't afraid of her losing her leg. He wanted to be there for her if that happened.

And that's when it hit him.

Hannah was afraid, too, yet she wanted to take that chance with him. Tate hadn't wanted to subject Hannah to the craziness that was his life—that's what he was afraid of. That he couldn't give her the life she should have. And in doing so, in trying to protect her, he'd distanced himself.

That's why she hadn't told him about her leg. She'd been scared of how he would react, scared that he wouldn't be able to handle it. But she was wrong about that. He would be there for her.

Just like she'd always been for him.

She'd said she loved him. How could he prove that he loved her, too?

The answer to a completely different question hit him right then, jumped out at him actually from the monitor. The reason Park was so wound up about the development of Snowy Sky.

He had assumed Park didn't want Hannah to get the best of him again. But if his guess was correct, Park had a whole lot more to lose than a battle of wills with Hannah. He studied the figures again, pulled up some more documents, and finally picked up the phone and made a call.

By the time he'd finished confirming his theory, Hannah was gone.

"ARE YOU SURE that entire sleeping bag is going to fit into that tiny sleeve thing?" Adele pointed at the down bundle as Hannah began to shove it into its cover.

"Positive." Hannah had it tucked inside in a matter of minutes. "What else is on the list?"

"Flashlight, batteries, matches."

Peeking into a pocket of her pack Hannah confirmed with the words, "check, check, check."

"Are you sure you want to do this?"

"Positive. Are you sure you don't want to come along? We've been snowshoeing enough now that I know you could make it."

Adele leveled a flat look at her. "Positive. A few hours is different than an all-day-long trek up the mountain where the prize is an overnight campout in a freezing cabin."

Hannah's phone buzzed on the table beside her. Tate had been calling and texting, but she wasn't ready to talk to him. She picked it up, intending to silence the call. She scowled as she looked at the display.

Curiosity got the better of her. She tapped on the screen and said, "Hello?"

"Hannah, hi, how are you?" Park asked her from the other side of the line.

"Busy, Park, so you might want to quit inquiring about my health, which I know you don't care anything about, and get to the point."

He let out an irritable sigh. "Actually, I was hoping we could put some of this…hostility behind us. Could we get together sometime soon and talk?"

"Not possible," she said, knowing she had

a snap in her tone. She didn't care. Revealing her circumstances to Tate had left her with a burning desire to use her leg one more time before she found out if she was going to lose it. And yes, she was also afraid he would come around feeling sorry for her, and she couldn't abide the idea of his pity.

"I'm leaving for the night."

"This is important. There's something I'd like to discuss with you. A, uh, a possible solution to our, um, differences. Could we meet before you leave? It'll only take a few minutes."

"Fine, if you want to meet me at the Moose Gulch trailhead in an hour, I'll give you five minutes."

TATE WAS TRYING to figure out how to proceed when his phone alerted him to Cricket's call. Maybe Cricket would want to meet him at the Caribou for dinner and help him sort this out. Maybe he'd contact Jonah, too, since he could use some legal advice.

"Hey," he said into the phone.

"Did you know Hannah was going snowshoeing?"

"No, but Hannah snowshoes a lot. I'm sure her lungs look like a marathon runner's."

"No, Adele called. It seems she's taking off

by herself into the backcountry because she's upset. Do you know anything about that?"

"Maybe. She just told me about her leg and—"

"Okay, you can tell me all about it on our way to Moose Gulch."

"Moose Gulch? The trail?"

"Yes, that's where she's taking off from, headed to one of Bering's cabins. Get your coat and boots. I have extra snowshoes if we need them. Adele and I are pulling up in your driveway right now. Hannah is meeting Park over there so—"

"Park?" Tate interrupted sharply.

"Yes, Adele said he called and told Hannah he wanted to speak to her. Adele doesn't trust Park and she's worried—"

"I'll be right there."

Tate shut off his phone, grabbed the stack of papers he'd printed, and took off through the house. He gathered his coat and boots even as he wondered what to do with Lucas. Maybe Janie could watch him? Did he have time to drop him off before he could get to Hannah? Or should he take him along? He had no idea what Park would do when he confronted him with this information.

He was getting ready to call for Lucas when Adele charged through the door.

"Go." She pointed. "I'm staying with Lucas."

Lucas had obviously heard Adele come in because he jogged into the entryway and seemed excited to see her. Tate explained that Adele was going to hang out with him for a while, then hugged him goodbye and ran to Cricket's pickup. Cricket began pulling away before Tate could even get buckled.

"I'd like to get there before she takes off," Cricket muttered and shook his head. "So unlike her to not check the weather."

"What do you mean?" Tate asked. He hadn't checked the weather either, although he wasn't going anywhere.

"Storm coming. I texted her, but Moose Gulch is notorious for its lack of cell service."

Tate's bloodstream seemed to hum with the added surge of adrenaline. "That's not the only reason we need to hurry."

"What are *you* talking about?"

"It seems Adele's distrust of Park may be completely valid." Tate went on to explain what he'd discovered, the crime he suspected Park had committed.

When he finished, Cricket shot a quick, sharp look at him. His eyes latched back on to the road where snow had begun to fall fast and hard. "People have killed for less than that, Tate."

"Now, what is so important that you felt you needed to interrupt my leisure time?"

Small, dry snowflakes pelted Hannah and Park where they stood beside the Moose Gulch sign. Theirs were the only cars to be seen. Park looked around, obviously puzzled by their meeting place.

"Snowshoeing," she explained. "Up to one of my cousin Bering's cabins."

He gazed longingly at the mountain. "I've never been snowshoeing before."

She couldn't imagine. "Really?"

"I bet it's beautiful up there, huh?"

She was leery about Park's sudden chumminess, yet she sensed something about him that seemed almost pitiful. She didn't have the heart to blast him like she normally would. "It is. I highly recommend it. Bering rents his cabins out. They're very cheap in the winter, too."

"I was raised in the city. Lucky for me it was Seattle where good snowboarding is only a short car ride up into the mountains, but it doesn't actually snow much in the city. My mom didn't move here to Rankins until after

I graduated from college. She's from Alaska and always wanted to come home. But, um, anyway, Hannah—let me get to the point..."

TATE HAD NEVER seen anyone drive so fast on snow-covered roads, and yet Cricket seemed to be in complete control. Even then it seemed to him as if the ride took about three days. That was one thing about Alaska—one important place could be so far away from another.

Finally Hannah's SUV came into sight at the trailhead. Park's crossover was next to it and he felt a wave of relief when he saw them standing under the covered Forest Service sign that marked the start of the trail.

Cricket parked and they both jumped out, Hannah and Park both looking on in surprise.

Hannah asked, "What are you guys doing here?"

"We came to find you." Cricket explained about the weather.

"Oh, yeah, I know it's supposed to snow."

"Not just snow, Banana—storm."

Tate jumped in, "That's not the entire reason we're here either."

He didn't see any reason to hold off on confronting Park, although a piece of him wondered if he should have alerted the police first.

After the experience with Penny, he had come to realize just how capable people really were of horrible actions.

"I was concerned about your safety."

She appeared bemused. "I'm very experienced, Tate."

"No, not about this," he said, gesturing at the mountain.

He looked at Park. "I know what you've been doing. I figured it out and I have the proof."

Park looked utterly confused. He said, "I don't know what you're talking about."

"The legal definition is graft."

"Graft? Like the tree thing?"

Cricket let out a chuckle, while Tate stared at Park. He was doing a fine job of playing dumb.

"You contacted Nordic Verse about construction of the half-pipe."

"Yeah, so what? I was just explaining this very thing to Hannah. Hoping I could convince her to get on board. I offered her the share I was planning on giving you. And her ex-boyfriend wants a piece of the action, too."

Park focused on her and added, "I think he wants you back, Hannah. He seemed a lot more interested in you than the business deal."

Was it possible he really didn't understand? "Park, what you've done is against the law."

His face went slack. "What do you mean?"

"It's called fraud—financial fraud. You can't take money from Nordic Verse and guarantee them a half-pipe and terrain park construction contract. I've already called Jonah Cedar and we're going to have to notify the authorities."

"The authorities? You mean like the police?"

"More serious than that."

"More serious? But that's not… I didn't…" Park's voice petered out as his face transformed with a look of sheer terror.

And then they all watched transfixed as he burst into tears. One gloved hand came up toward his chin as a plaintive sob surged out along with the words, "No, no… I…I didn't know. Please, I was only trying to figure out a way to pay my mom back. I owe her so much money. I will never hear the end of it. She is going to kill me."

With a gentle voice Cricket asked, "Park, have you received any money? Has Nordic Verse paid even one dime?"

Park's mumbled response was incoherent through his sob.

If Tate hadn't already been in love with Hannah, he would have fallen hard at that moment. Because she reached out, wrapped her arms around Park and gathered him close for a hug.

"Hey, Park. Buddy, don't cry. It'll be fine. We'll figure it out. Let's head back to town, okay?"

CHAPTER TWENTY-TWO

TATE STARED AT his mother sitting across from him in an orange jumpsuit. They were transporting her to Anchorage today where she'd eventually stand trial for some very serious charges including child abduction, unlawful possession of a firearm and attempted murder. There would be a host of lesser charges, as well.

Tate hadn't seen her since she'd been taken into custody, had debated about whether he wanted to at all.

"I wasn't going to kill him, Tate—he's my grandson. It was just in case I needed to keep him quiet while we were traveling. If the police would show you the paper you would see there's a chart outlining how much to give a person per pound just to put them asleep for a while."

"Can you not hear yourself? Do you know how dangerous that is? You were going to drug

him. He's six years old. What if you would
have given him too much?"

She swallowed, her eyes flicking away and
then back to him. She waved an arm dismis-
sively. "This whole thing, Tate… I did it because I wanted to get your attention. I was
afraid this time. I was afraid that you meant
it when you said you wanted me out of your
life for good."

"Well, you've pretty much taken care of that
on your own, haven't you?"

"I love you, Tate, and I love Lucas, too."
Tears trickled down her cheeks.

Even after everything she'd put them
through, he wanted to believe her. What was
wrong with him?

He stood up and walked from the room before he caved.

She called to his retreating back. "Tate!
Wait, Tate. I'm sorry. Come back, please! I
want to explain."

He kept walking. Hannah met him outside.
She put her arms around him and held him
tight for a long moment.

She stepped back and took his hand. "Let's
walk." She started across the parking lot toward the bay. They continued for a few blocks,

stopping when they'd reached the park overlooking the water.

"How are you feeling?" she asked him.

"I'm glad."

"What are you glad about?"

"I'm glad that I'm finally not the one to have to make a decision about her—about Penny. I'm glad I don't have to take care of her or try to make her better because I don't think I can. Maybe someone else can, but not me."

She nodded, swallowing the lump that was trying to clog her throat. "You're right about that, Tate. You can't fix her. The only people we can really fix in this life are ourselves— and only when we want to be fixed."

ARTHRITIS?

Hannah stared blankly at the doctor as the word sunk in. *Arthritis*, she repeated silently, not *amputation*.

Big difference.

Huge.

Like the difference between leg and no leg. She let out a giggle and slapped a hand over her mouth.

"I'm sorry, Dr. Grant. I'm just so…"

He smiled kindly and patted her hand. "You

have a great attitude, Hannah. But then again, you always have."

She'd always *tried* to have a good attitude, and even when she didn't, no one knew. Okay, Tate had started to figure it out, and Adele was getting pretty good at reading her.

"Not always. Believe me, I've had my moments."

"You wouldn't be human if you didn't."

She couldn't seem to stop smiling. She thought about Dr. Voss's "act happy, be happy" strategy. Adele wasn't sure the approach was 100 percent the right one for her, but in all honesty, it had helped to a large degree.

She could see how she may have taken this approach to the extreme, but for Hannah, the alternative would have been so dark and depressing. She was by nature a happy person and that was never going to change, although in light of her experiences with Tate she was going to try to communicate her true feelings a little better.

"You're bound to have more of these painful episodes, too, I'm afraid. This type of arthritis is no picnic. It can be a debilitating condition, and you're very young to have started developing symptoms already. But on the other hand, you're also young and strong.

"I want you to understand, though, that you don't have to worry anymore about losing the leg. It's healed very well under the circumstances, better than I'd hoped. I can understand why you had the fear, but amputation was only a concern early on."

Dr. Grant went on to say that it wasn't uncommon for someone with her injury to eventually have to deal with the pain of arthritis.

Hannah could handle pain.

She'd been handling pain nearly all of her life. First as a professional athlete, then as a former professional athlete who had been the victim of a drunk driver.

He also said that she'd endure bouts where the arthritis inflammation was worse than other times. There were factors believed to irritate the condition...

Hannah listened and tried to absorb as much as she could, but she couldn't wait to share the news with Tate. What did this mean for her and Tate? She wasn't in perfect physical condition, but she wasn't losing her leg either. She had refused to discuss their future before she knew what was going to happen with her leg, but now she desperately wanted to believe they might have a future.

Cricket stood as she stepped into the waiting room. He'd flown her to Anchorage for the appointment. She'd sworn him to secrecy. She hadn't wanted to worry her family unnecessarily. Only he, Adele and Tate knew.

She stopped, stared up at him and let out another burst of delighted laughter.

Cricket swooped her up into his arms. "It's okay?"

She laughed and he lowered her gently to her feet. "It's pretty much okay," she repeated. "Arthritis."

He let out a whoop and then his face evolved into a look of horror. "Jeez, Hannah, I'm sorry. Arthritis, that's still not good."

"Oh, Cricket, trust me—I had the same reaction. It wasn't quite as loud, though." She looked up at him. "And no, it won't be fun, but I can deal with it."

He looped an arm around her neck and planted a kiss on the top of her head. "Banana, I'm beginning to believe there's nothing in this world you couldn't deal with."

Tears sprang to her eyes. "Thanks, Cricket."

"Can I call Adele? She's texted me like ten times."

"Of course—please do." She took out her own phone to call Tate. She couldn't wait to give him the news. But he didn't pick up. That was okay; she needed some time to think about what this might mean for them.

Checking the time, she called him again. No answer, but maybe his meeting with Park had stretched on a little longer than he'd anticipated. Turned out, Park hadn't accepted any money from Nordic Verse yet because his contact had wanted to be assured the contract was theirs. He would escape prosecution, and since she, Tate, Cricket, Adele and Jonah were the only ones who knew what he'd attempted to do, they were hoping they could keep it from his mother, as well.

Strange how life worked out. Who would have ever thought she and Park would end up being friendly? Who would have thought she'd ever fall in love with another snowboarder?

She sent Tate a text. He didn't respond.

She tried him once more before they got to the airport, and again after they boarded Cricket's plane. She felt a swirl of concern mingle with her happiness. Why wouldn't he be picking up? Once or twice she could understand— cell service could be spotty in Rankins and if he was driving or in certain locations... But it had been an hour since she'd gotten out of the doctor's office. He knew what time her appointment was.

Then, just as they were about to take off a text came in: Hannah, can't talk now. I'll meet you at the airport. Can't wait to see you.

She felt better just knowing he was okay.

Cricket glanced at her. "Everything, all right?"

She smiled. "Yep." She buckled in for the flight, which suddenly seemed as though it would take forever.

She dozed off. She hadn't slept well the night before, in spite of her efforts to not worry. She awoke to the sound of Cricket's voice in her headphones.

"Hey, we're going to take a quick detour on the way home."

She tried not to let her disappointment show. "Okay, where to?"

"Actually, we're going to fly over Snowy Sky. Tate asked me to show you one of the slopes from the air."

"What? Why?"

"Almost there," he answered. "You can decide for yourself."

She was baffled. Why in the world? She loved Snowy Sky, but she didn't want to look at it right now. Besides, she'd seen it from the air many times.

Or maybe she did, she realized as she absorbed the scene while Cricket dipped the plane low over the hillside. Giant purple letters spelled out in the snow under chairlift two, "HANNAH, WILL YOU MARRY ME?" Tate and Lucas were waving. She couldn't help it, she waved back even though she knew they couldn't see her. She turned toward Cricket, who gave her a big smile and a wink.

Tate and Lucas met them at the airport. Lucas flew toward her and launched himself into her arms. Scooping him up, she hugged him tight. Tate slipped an arm around each of them.

"Before you say anything, I have something to say."

Hannah set Lucas on his feet. "Don't you want to know what the doctor said?"

"No," he said. "I mean, yes, of course. But first I want you to answer our question. I wanted to ask you before I knew, so that you would know that it doesn't matter to me. And I couldn't figure out how to do that without you thinking that I either felt sorry for you or I was asking because you weren't going to lose your leg."

"Tate, that's amazing. That is so sweet. I just wanted to know what we were facing first before we made any decisions about our future."

"But that's just the thing. That's what you've taught me. There are no guarantees when it comes to the future. All you can control is how you deal with whatever life hands you. And I've never met anyone who does that better than you. With you by my side, I don't think there's anything I couldn't handle.

"More than that, I know with every fiber of my being that there's nothing we can't handle together. And I *can* fight, Hannah. And I will always fight for you, for Lucas, for us.

"That's a promise." He squeezed her shoulder. "I might need a little push into the ring now and then, and I'm counting on you to do that for me."

Hannah felt tears well in her eyes as she stared at him. This man who needed her, but she needed him, too. Did he know that? She made a vow right then and there to make sure he always did.

"I need you, too, Tate."

He grinned. "I know."

Then she felt Lucas tug gently on her jacket. She looked down into his scrunched face. "Have you answered the question yet? Are you going to marry us? This is a lot of talking and I'm kind of confused."

"Yes, Lucas, it sure is."

"Yes, you've answered. Or yes is your answer?"

"I don't know. But the answer is yes—yes, I'm going to marry you and your uncle."

Tate smiled as Lucas let out a shout of joy.

Hannah couldn't believe she was facing a lifetime of making this man smile, and she smiled, too, knowing how much easier it was for him now than when they'd first met. Did she deserve this kind of happiness? She wasn't sure, but she was going to embrace every bit of this good stuff life was finally handing her— just as she always had the bad.

* * * * *

YES! Please send me **The Montana Mavericks Collection** in Larger Print. This collection begins with 3 FREE books and 2 FREE gifts (gifts valued at approx. $20.00 retail) in the first shipment, along with the other first 4 books from the collection! If I do not cancel, I will receive 8 monthly shipments until I have the entire 51-book Montana Mavericks collection. I will receive 2 or 3 FREE books in each shipment and I will pay just $4.99 US/ $5.89 CDN for each of the other four books in each shipment, plus $2.99 for shipping and handling per shipment.*If I decide to keep the entire collection, I'll have paid for only 32 books, because 19 books are FREE! I understand that accepting the 3 free books and gifts places me under no obligation to buy anything. I can always return a shipment and cancel at any time. My free books and gifts are mine to keep no matter what I decide.

263 HCN 2404   463 HCN 2404

Name	(PLEASE PRINT)	
Address		Apt. #
City	State/Prov.	Zip/Postal Code
Signature (if under 18, a parent or guardian must sign)		

Mail to the **Reader Service:**

IN U.S.A.: P.O. Box 1867, Buffalo, NY 14240-1867
IN CANADA: P.O. Box 609, Fort Erie, Ontario L2A 5X3

* Terms and prices subject to change without notice. Prices do not include applicable taxes. Sales tax applicable in N.Y. Canadian residents will be charged applicable taxes. This offer is limited to one order per household. All orders subject to approval. Credit or debit balances in a customer's account(s) may be offset by any other outstanding balance owed by or to the customer. Please allow 4 to 6 weeks for delivery. Offer available while quantities last. Offer not available to Quebec residents.

Your Privacy—The Reader Service is committed to protecting your privacy. Our Privacy Policy is available online at www.ReaderService.com or upon request from the Reader Service.

We make a portion of our mailing list available to reputable third parties that offer products we believe may interest you. If you prefer that we not exchange your name with third parties, or if you wish to clarify or modify your communication preferences, please visit us at www.ReaderService.com/consumerschoice or write to us at Reader Service Preference Service, P.O. Box 9062, Buffalo, NY 14269. Include your complete name and address.

MMLPBPA15

LARGER-PRINT BOOKS!
GET 2 FREE LARGER-PRINT NOVELS PLUS
2 FREE GIFTS!

♦HARLEQUIN®

super romance®

More Story...More Romance

READERSERVICE.COM

Manage your account online!

- Review your order history
- Manage your payments
- Update your address

---

*We've designed the
Reader Service website
just for you.*

Enjoy all the features!

- Discover new series available to you, and read excerpts from any series.
- Respond to mailings and special monthly offers.
- Connect with favorite authors at the blog.
- Browse the Bonus Bucks catalog and online-only exculsives.
- Share your feedback.

Visit us at:
ReaderService.com